Additional Praise for *Mrs. March*

"A brilliantly tense psychological study from a writer who keeps pace with the grandees she invokes—Du Maurier, for one. . . . [*Mrs. March* is] also a fine addition to the current wave of feminist-inflected horror. . . . [Virginia Feito] has done that most horrible, wonderful and truly novelistic of things: she has seen right through Mrs March and into the shameful, petty, maggoty secrets that everybody carries."

—Sarah Ditum, *Guardian*

"[Virginia Feito] manages to capture this world entirely, while simultaneously ratcheting up the tension caused by Mrs. March's increasingly fractured psyche, in a way that recalls novels by Patricia Highsmith and Margaret Millar. . . . [T]he final pages are shocking . . . readers may find themselves tempted to return to the beginning in order to understand just what Feito has so convincingly managed to achieve within her accomplished debut."

—Christine Mangan, *New York Times Book Review*

"*Mrs. March* is just the Madame Bovary–meets–Patricia Highsmith feminist psychoanalytic comedy-of-manners thriller that I didn't know I so desperately needed. I almost destroyed my life by staying up so late reading. I am lucky my house is still standing."

—Elif Batuman, author of *The Idiot*

"This is an elegant, claustrophobic psychological thriller that bears the influence of a handful of brilliant writers, from Shirley Jackson to Daphne du Maurier to Patricia Highsmith, but feels incredibly original. . . . Mrs March is the most beguiling protagonist I've encountered in a long time; I can't remember when I was last so excited about a new voice in fiction."   —Jessie Thompson, *Evening Standard*

"*Mrs. March* straddles the line between psychological thriller and social satire—think HBO's *The Undoing* or *The Talented Mr. Ripley*. . . . Indeed, for all its gleeful nastiness, *Mrs. March* is very much a comedy of manners—one where every Vicuna scarf and monogrammed napkin signifies something greater than itself."   —Harrison Hill, *Vogue*

"A little bit Hitchcock, a little bit Patricia Highsmith, a little bit *The Yellow Wallpaper*. . . . [T]here's a relentless build to this book, a gnawing dread that sets in early and never quite lets up. And between Feito's silver-polish sentences and her eerie psychological acumen, you don't want it to." —Constance Grady, *Vox*

"In a horror-laced psychological drama, the wife of a bestselling New York novelist learns his latest protagonist is modeled on her. . . . Feito is Spanish and lives in Madrid, but somehow she is the love child of Patricia Highsmith and Shirley Jackson. On her way to the screen played by Elisabeth Moss, Mrs. March is absolutely right—everyone is talking about her." —*Kirkus Reviews*, starred review

"*Mrs. March* is window-dressed to perfection as a psychological thriller-cum-cosmopolitan grotesque. . . . [Mrs. March] could be describing Feito's novel when she refers to the life of the prostitute in George's book as 'something so ugly described so beautifully.'" —*Shelf Awareness*

"I delighted in every page of this clever, twisted debut. . . . Feito's fiendish narrator presents Mrs. March to readers like a fine wine, uncorked, zooming in and out of Mrs. March's paranoia as her psyche unravels. This book is an intoxicating experience."
—Carole E. Barrowman, *Milwaukee Journal Sentinel*

"This crisp, delicious portrait of a woman coming apart is a brutal, darkly funny, sharp blade of a book. I loved it."
—Amber Sparks, author of *And I Do Not Forgive You*

"By initially setting up *Mrs. March* as a domestic thriller that comments on the relegation of women to the home and the elevation of men's careers and creative pursuits, the perfect foundation is laid for Mrs. March to escape all of that and fantasize—and materialize—that she's in her own crime novel, taking the dead girl muse trope into her own hands." —Scarlett Harris, *Observer*

"Like Mrs. March herself, I spent most of Virginia Feito's trippy novel wondering, What the devil is going on? When she figured it out, I was haunted for days." —Helen Ellis, author of *American Housewife*

Mrs. March

A Novel

Virginia Feito

LIVERIGHT PUBLISHING CORPORATION

A Division of W. W. Norton & Company

Independent Publishers Since 1923

For information about permission to reproduce selections from this book, write to Permissions, Liveright Publishing Corporation, a division of W. W. Norton & Company, Inc., 500 Fifth Avenue, New York, NY 10110

For information about special discounts for bulk purchases, please contact W. W. Norton Special Sales at specialsales@wwnorton.com or 800-233-4830

Manufacturing by Lakeside Book Company
Book design by Lovedog Studio
Production manager: Julia Druskin

Library of Congress Cataloging-in-Publication Data

Names: Feito, Virginia, author.
Title: Mrs. March : a novel / Virginia Feito.
Description: First edition. | New York : Liveright Publishing Corporation, a division of W. W. Norton & Company, [2021]
Identifiers: LCCN 2021001035 | ISBN 9781631498619 (hardcover) | ISBN 9781631498626 (epub)
Subjects: GSAFD: Suspense fiction. | Humorous fiction.
Classification: LCC PR9155.9.F45 M77 2021 | DDC 823/.92—dc23
LC record available at https://lccn.loc.gov/2021001035

ISBN 978-1-324-09196-7 pbk.

Liveright Publishing Corporation, 500 Fifth Avenue, New York, N.Y. 10110
www.wwnorton.com

W. W. Norton & Company Ltd., 15 Carlisle Street, London W1D 3BS

1 2 3 4 5 6 7 8 9 0

For my parents,
Mr. and Mrs. Feito

The gossipers have lowered their voices,
Willing words to make the rumours certain

—Dylan Thomas, "The Gossipers"

Mrs. March

1

George March had written another book.

It was a large tome, the cover featuring an old Dutch oil painting of a young handmaiden touching her neck modestly. Mrs. March passed a rather impressive pyramid of hardcovers in the window of one of their neighborhood bookstores. Soon to be heralded as George March's magnum opus, the book was—unbeknownst to her—already creeping its way onto all the bestseller and book club lists, selling out in even the less transited bookshops, and inspiring enthusiastic recommendations among friends. "Have you read George March's new book?" was now the latest cocktail-party conversation starter.

She was on her way to her favorite patisserie—a lovely little place with a red awning and a whitewashed bench in front. The day was chilly, but not unbearably so, and Mrs. March took her time, admiring the now-barren trees lining the streets, the velvet poinsettias bookending storefronts, the lives on display through the townhouse windows.

When she reached the pastry shop, she glanced at her reflection in the glass door before pushing it open and stepping inside, the bell overhead tinkling to announce her arrival. She was immediately flushed by the hot breaths and clammy bodies within, mingled with the heat of the ovens in the kitchen. A generous queue had formed at the counter, snaking around the few scattered tables occupied by couples and convivial businessmen, all having coffee or breakfast, indifferent to their own loudness.

Mrs. March's pulse quickened with the telltale excitement and wariness that always manifested right before she interacted with others. She joined the line, smiling at the strangers around her, and pulled off her kidskin gloves. A Christmas gift from George two years earlier, they were a very distinct color for gloves: a sort of mint green. She would never have picked that color out, not once believing she could pull such a thing off, but she thrilled at the fantasy that strangers, when they saw her wearing them, would assume her to be the kind of carefree, confident woman who would have selected such a bold color for herself.

George had purchased the gloves at Bloomingdale's, which never ceased to impress her. She'd pictured George at the glove counter, bantering with fawning saleswomen, not in the least embarrassed to be shopping in the women's department. She had once attempted to buy some lingerie at Bloomingdale's. That particular summer day had been sweltering, her shirt sticking to her back and her sandals to the pavement. Sweat seemed to ooze from the very sidewalks.

In the middle of a workday, Bloomingdale's mostly attracted well-to-do housewives—women who approached the clothing racks languidly, pastel pink smiles smeared over frowning lips, looking as if they didn't really want to be there but oh, there was just no way around it, what could one do, really, but try on some clothes and perhaps buy a few. This type of energy proved more intimidating for Mrs. March than the one that pervaded the store in the evenings, when working women threw themselves at the racks with absolutely no grace or dignity, flipping swiftly through the hangers and not caring to pick up the clothes that slid to the floor.

That morning at Bloomingdale's, Mrs. March had been ushered into a large fitting room swathed in pink. A heavy velvet settee sat in a corner next to a private telephone from which she could call the saleswomen, whom she pictured giggling and whispering just outside the door. Everything in the room, including the carpet, was a sappy, sticky pink, like the bubblegum breath of a fifteen-year-old girl. The bra they had selected for her, dangling provocatively on a silk-padded hanger on the fitting room door, was soft and light and sweet-smelling, like whipped cream. She pressed a lacy piece of string to her face and sniffed it, touched her blouse tentatively, but could not bring herself to undress and try the delicate thing on.

She ended up purchasing her lingerie at a small store downtown owned by a limping, mole-ridden woman who correctly guessed her bra size after one quick look at her fully clothed form. Mrs. March liked the way the woman had pandered to her, complimenting her figure and, better yet, maligning other clients' figures between disappointed *oy veys*. The women in this store gazed at her expensive clothes with perceptible yearning. She never returned to Bloomingdale's.

Now, standing in line at the pastry shop, she looked down at the gloves in her hands, then at her nails, and was dismayed to see that they were dry and cracked. She pulled the kidskin gloves back on and, as she looked up, discovered that somebody had cut right in front of her. Thinking it an obvious mistake, she attempted to determine if the woman was simply greeting someone already in the queue, but no, the woman stood in front of her in silence. Uneasily, Mrs. March debated whether or not to confront the woman. It was rather rude to cut the queue, if that was indeed the woman's intention, but what if she was mistaken? So she said nothing and instead chewed the inside lining of her mouth—a compulsive habit inherited from her mother—until the woman paid and left, and it was Mrs. March's turn.

She smiled over the counter at Patricia, the big-haired, red-cheeked woman who managed the shop. She liked Patricia, whom she saw as a sort of plump, foulmouthed yet kindly inn-keeper; the type of character who would protect a gaggle of lowly orphans in a Dickens novel.

"Ah, and here's the most elegant woman in the room!" Patricia said as Mrs. March approached, and Mrs. March beamed and turned to see whether anyone had heard. "The usual, honey?"

"Yes, black olive bread and—well, yes," she said. "And this time I'd like two boxes of macarons, please? The big ones."

Patricia scuffled behind the counter, flinging her massive frizz of hair from one shoulder to the other as she gathered the order. Mrs. March took out her pocketbook, still smiling dreamily at Patricia's compliment, stroking the raised bumps on the ostrich leather with her fingertips.

"I've been reading your husband's book," said Patricia, temporarily out of sight as she crouched behind the counter. "I bought it two days ago and I'm almost finished. Can't put it down. It's great! Truly great."

Mrs. March moved closer, pressing against the glass case of assorted muffins and cheesecakes, in an effort to hear over the din. "Oh," she said, unprepared for this exchange. "Well, that's nice to know. I'm sure George will think it's nice to know."

"I was just saying to my sister last night, I know the writer's wife, and boy must she be proud."

"Oh, well, yes, although he's written many books before—"

"But isn't this the first time he's based a character on you?"

Mrs. March, still fingering her pocketbook, experienced a sudden numbness. Her face hardened just as her insides seemed to liquefy, so that she feared they might leak out. Patricia, oblivious, set her order on the countertop and tallied up the bill.

"I . . ." said Mrs. March, struck by a sliver of pain in her chest. "What do you mean?"

"I mean . . . the main character." Patricia smiled.

Mrs. March blinked, her mouth agape, unable to answer, her thoughts sticking to her skull despite her pulling at them, as if they were trapped in tar.

Patricia frowned at the silence. "I could be wrong, of course, but . . . you're both so alike, I just thought—well, I picture you when I read it, I don't know—"

"But . . . the main character, it—isn't she . . ." Mrs. March leaned in and in almost a whisper said, "a *whore*?"

Patricia let out a loud, good-natured laugh at this.

"A whore no one wants to sleep with?" Mrs. March added.

"Well, sure, but that's part of her charm." Patricia's smile faltered when she saw the expression on Mrs. March's face. "But anyway," she continued, "it's not that, it's more . . . the way she says things, her mannerisms, even, or the way she dresses?"

Mrs. March glanced down at her long fur coat, her stockinged ankles and polished tasseled loafers, then back up at Patricia. "But she's a horrible woman," she said. "She's ugly and stupid and everything I would never want to be."

The denial came out a little more visceral than she had intended, and Patricia's doughy face kneaded itself into a look of surprise. "Oh, well . . . I just thought . . ." She frowned and shook her head, and Mrs. March despised her for her imbecilic expression of puzzlement. "I'm sure I'm wrong then. Don't listen to me, I almost never read anyway, what the hell do I know." She smiled brightly as if that settled it. "Will that be all, honey?"

Mrs. March swallowed, nauseated, and looked down at the brown paper bags on the counter, which held her olive bread and her breakfast muffins and the macarons she had ordered for the party she was hosting tomorrow evening—an intimate, tasteful affair to celebrate George's recent publication in the company of their closest friends (or at least their most important ones). She sidled away from the counter, looking down at the gloves clutched in her ugly hands, surprised to discover that she'd taken them off again. "I'm—you know, I think I forgot something," she said, stepping backward. What was once safe, heavy background noise seemed to have dissipated into conspiratorial whispers. She turned to identify the culprits. At one of the tables, a woman, smiling, caught her eye.

"I'm sorry, I have to see if I—"

Abandoning her bags on the counter, Mrs. March made her way to the exit through the winding line, their murmurs ringing in her ears, their butter-scented breath hot against her skin, their bodies almost pressing against her. With desperate effort she pushed herself out through the door and onto the sidewalk, where the biting air sheeted her lungs and she was unable to breathe. She clutched a nearby tree. As the bell on the patisserie door jingled behind her, Mrs. March hurried to the other side of the street, not wanting to turn in case it was Patricia behind her. Not wanting to turn in case it wasn't.

Mrs. March walked briskly down the street, with no identifiable purpose, not following her usual route, and anyway nothing was usual without her daily olive bread and breakfast muffins. The macarons could be replaced, she supposed; there was still time before the party. Or else she could send Martha to get them later. Patricia and Martha had never met, after all, although Patricia might suspect if Martha commissioned the very same items. "Can't send Martha there, too risky," she said aloud, and a man passing next to her gave a little jump.

She found it strange—never seeing Patricia again. Patricia, who had been a regular presence in her life for years. She had certainly not imagined, as she had pulled on her pantyhose that morning, and selected the maroon skirt to pair with her ruffled ivory blouse, that this would be the last day she would see Patricia. If someone had told her so, she would have laughed. Patricia would eventually work out that this had been the last day they had seen each other, and perhaps she would also dissect the minutiae of their last encounter—what she was wearing and doing and saying, and she too would wonder at the sheer impossibility of it all.

Maybe it wasn't really so dramatic, that Patricia should have acted so thoughtlessly. An unfortunate thing, yes, but really, Patricia had been the only person to venture any parallel between her and that woman. That *character*, she corrected herself. She's not even real. Quite possibly *based* on a living model . . . but George would never . . . would he?

She turned frantically into a busier street swarming with pedestrians and trumpeting with car horns. A woman smiled at her knowingly from a billboard, eyebrows raised at her like that woman in the patisserie. SHE HAD NO IDEA, the ad copy read, and Mrs. March stopped so suddenly that a man crashed into her. After a series of profuse apologies, she decided she needed to sit down and went into the nearest establishment, a poky little café.

It was drab inside, and not at all cozy. The paint on the ceiling peeling off in spots, the tables marked with swirling streaks where they had been wiped down in haste, the bathroom doorknob scratched as if someone had tried to break in. She counted two customers in total, and not very glamorous ones at that. Mrs. March slouched by the entrance, waiting to be seated, although she knew that wasn't how this kind of place worked. She removed her mint green gloves and, as she looked them over, the recent unpleasant events flashed at her like headlights. Patricia's words. George's book. *Her.*

The shameful truth of the matter was, she had not read the book. Not really. She had barely managed to skim through a draft the previous year. The days when she would read George's early manuscripts, sitting barefoot on a wicker chair while sucking on orange wedges in his old apartment, were long gone, unrecognizable in her gray, polluted present. She had a general sense of the book, of course—knew what it was about, knew about the fat, pathetic prostitute—but she had not stopped to consider it further. She had been, she now decided, too repulsed by the main character and the graphic, distastefully accurate story, to allow herself to continue. "Mannerisms," she muttered under her breath. She inspected her nails again. She wondered whether that was one of them.

"Morning, ma'am, you're alone?"

She looked at the server, clad in a black apron, which she found a tad lugubrious for a café—"I, no, not alone—"

"Table for two then?"

"Well, I'm not sure, the person I'm waiting for might not make it. Yes, let's say for two, for now. That one?" She pointed to a table against the wall nearest the bathroom.

"No problem. Would you like to wait for this other person or shall I go ahead and take your order?"

Mrs. March could almost detect the trace of a bluff-calling smirk on the server's face. "That's fine," she said. "I'll order for both of us."

"Yes, ma'am."

Mrs. March remembered the first time she had been called "ma'am," or, more precisely, "madame"—she'd been unprepared, it had stunned and hurt her like a slap. Just shy of her thirtieth birthday, she had traveled to Paris for one of George's book tours. Alone in their suite that morning, with George out signing books, she ordered herself a decadent breakfast: croissants and hot chocolate and crêpes with butter and sugar. When the waiter rolled in the cart, she received him in an oversized bathrobe, her hair still wet from the shower, her makeup streaked. She worried that she must look almost too provocative, too sensual, her lips a little swollen from rubbing them with a terrycloth towel to eliminate traces of last night's wine. However, when she thanked the waiter (a lanky young man, barely out of his teens, neck ringed with sunburn) and tipped him, he said, "Thank you, madame," and left the room. Just like that. He had not found her desirable in the least. In fact, he would likely consider the very notion of her naked body repulsive, and even though she wasn't old enough to be his mother, he probably saw her as such anyway.

Now, the black-aproned waiter hovered at a slight distance, scratching absentmindedly at a scab on his wrist. "What can I get for you, ma'am?"

Once she had ordered two coffees—an espresso for her and a latte for her imaginary potential plus-one—she inhaled deeply and returned to the topic at hand. *Johanna*—that was the name of the protagonist, she recalled. Johanna. She whispered it to herself. She hadn't given much thought to the name before, had never questioned why George had selected that particular name for that particular character. She didn't know a single Johanna, nor had she ever. She wondered if George had. She hoped so, as that would indicate with almost complete certainty that this monstrous caricature was based on someone else entirely.

Nursing her espresso, she recalled—feeling sad for herself—how she had supported George at the beginning of his career by listening to him, by nodding at whatever he said, by not complaining. Even though she'd known there was no money in writing. George had said such a thing often, apologetically, as had her father (less apologetically). In those days George would take her out to his favorite cheap little Italian joint, where the waiters rattled off the menu—always different, always fresh—each night from memory. There, seated at a table sans tablecloth, a candle in a wine bottle flickering between them, he'd tell her about his latest story, his newest idea, as if he too had a fresh menu every night. She'd marveled at the genuine interest this respectable college professor appeared to have in her opinions. Not wanting to jinx it with her personality, she smiled at him and nodded and flattered him. All for him, for her George.

What could have merited this humiliation? Now the whole world would look at her differently. George knew her so well, maybe he had assumed she would never read it. A risky maneuver. But no, she concluded with scorn, he didn't really know her that well at all. Johanna—she imagined her vividly now, sitting beside her in the cramped café, sweaty and black-toothed, she of spotted bosom and paltry existence—was nothing like her. She considered storming into every bookstore, buying every copy, destroying them somehow—a huge bonfire lit on a cold December night—but that was mad, of course.

She drummed her fingers on the table, checked her wristwatch blindly, and, unable to bear the anxiety any longer, resolved to return home and read the book. George had several copies of it in his study, and he was away until evening.

She paid for the coffees, apologizing for her absent friend, Johanna, whose untouched latte cooled, foamless, on the table. The black-aproned waiter paid no heed as she stepped out, pantyhose wrinkling around her ankles like furrowed brows, as if in reaction to the cold.

Walking home, Mrs. March passed a clothing store where two saleswomen were undressing a mannequin in the window. The women pulled at the dummy's clothes viciously, one taking off her hat and stole and the other tugging at her dress, exposing one glossy, nipple-less breast. The mannequin looked on with such vivid, black-lashed blue eyes, and such a painful, wretched expression, that it compelled Mrs. March to look away.

III

Mr. and Mrs. March lived in a rather agreeable apartment on the Upper East Side, with a dark green entrance canopy displaying the address—*Ten Forty-Nine*—in cursive script, each word capitalized, as in the title of a book or a movie.

The building, its small, box-shaped windows stacked with small, box-shaped air-conditioning units, was presently guarded by the day doorman, rigid in his uniform, who saluted Mrs. March courteously as she entered the lobby. Courteous but contemptuous, Mrs. March thought. She always assumed he must despise her—and most likely everyone else in the building. How could he not, when he was there to serve them and adjust to the patterns of their lives while they lived in luxury and never once bothered to glean anything about *him*? Although, she now considered woefully, maybe the others *had* made an effort to know him. Maybe the fact that she never asked him anything about himself, that she'd never after all these years noticed if he wore a wedding band or if he displayed any children's drawings by his desk, accounted for the starch in his manner toward her. How inadequate and unworthy he must find her, especially when compared to the other women in the building—retired ballerinas and former models and heiresses to great fortunes, some of them.

She crossed the lobby, which had been decorated for the holiday season as it was every year. A Christmas tree stood in the corner nearest the entrance, adorned with secular stars and candy canes (no choir of angels or rustic Nativity), and wreaths of artificial fir hung over the lobby mirror. She looked at her reflection in passing and, as usual, found it substandard, and tried to plump out her hair.

She was careful, when entering the elevator—a grand, ornate contraption—to check behind her in case anyone else intended to enter. It was often taxing, interacting with neighbors, and the ensuing expectation to comment on the nation's state of affairs, or the building's state of affairs, or, horror of horrors, the *weather*—she was simply not up to it today, of all days.

The mirror paneling inside the elevator revealed several Mrs. Marches, all looking at her, alarmed. She turned away from them to focus on the numbered buttons lighting up in sequence as the elevator arrived at the sixth floor. She closed her eyes and sighed in an effort to center herself.

Her nerves dissolved when she reached door number 606. Such a beautiful, round number, she had always thought. She would have felt worse after this bad day if she had come home to a 123, or some such discomfiting number.

She opened the door to a rush of fresh air—Martha must be airing out the living room—and hurried through the hallway, wishing to avoid her housekeeper at all costs. She ducked into her bedroom, where she could hear through the wall the fast-paced jazz playing at the neighbors'. The walls were shamefully thin for such a luxurious apartment, and Mrs. March wondered, not for the first time, why they hadn't addressed the issue when they first renovated. She may not have even noticed it back then.

She shed her coat and gloves as if removing a suit of armor, then stepped out of her shoes and walked into the hallway, treading lightly on the creaking wooden flooring that was so fond of betraying her presence. She stood still for some seconds, illuminated only by the lazy sunlight drifting into the hallway through the open door of her bedroom. The other doors along the corridor were closed, including the one to George's study. She tiptoed toward it. A voice, likely Martha's, called out from the living room as she slid inside and closed the door softly behind her.

Half expecting to be greeted by an audience applauding her pitiful stupidity, she was received instead by dark red toile wallpaper depicting Chinese scenes and brimming bookcases and lofty abstract paintings. Mrs. March was secretly convinced that George was just as baffled by modern art as she was, even though they were both self-proclaimed enthusiasts. Against one wall sat a huge leather chesterfield sofa, fitted with paisley sheets, speckled with crumbs, and marked by burn holes from his cigars. George occasionally slept here when under one of his writing spells.

The windows faced a rather bleak brick wall. George couldn't deal with distractions while writing, and he must deem even this uninspiring view too diverting, for his desk was turned away from it to face the door.

Mrs. March approached the desk almost apologetically. She had never wielded the confidence to enter this room unattended, much less to do what she was about to do. The word for it, in her mother's vocabulary, was *snoop*.

She moved her fingers over the table like a blind person, rattling the monogrammed pens, lifting the lid off a porcelain jar to finger its contents (cigars and matchboxes). Her eyes fell on the corner of a newspaper clipping protruding from a notebook. She pulled it out with a gentle tug. A beautiful young woman smiled up at Mrs. March from a black-and-white yearbook photograph. She had long dark hair and dimpled cheeks, and the easy smile of someone not deliberately posing. SYLVIA GIBBLER STILL MISSING, PRESUMED DEAD, the headline read. Odd, thought Mrs. March, for George to have saved a clipping of such a grisly event. It made her insides churn. Sylvia Gibbler, she recalled vaguely, had been all over the news after disappearing from her hometown in Maine. She had been missing for weeks. Research for a book, she told herself, tucking the article back into the notebook.

As last she spotted her quarry—her eyes registered the rich, baroque colors of the cover before her mind could process them—on the edge of the table. On the floor to the left of the desk lay a whole box of them.

She picked up the novel. It sat heavy in her hands, her fingertips leaving oily prints on the glossy dust jacket. The texture of it unnerved her. It was strangely smooth, like the skin of a snake she had once been forced to pet in science class. She opened the book nervously, slowly, at first, looking for the dedication. She flipped from the title page to the first chapter, then back to the title page. She could find no dedication. This in itself was strange, for George included one in all of his novels. She had been the recipient of one herself, years ago. Once the novel was published she had asked George to sign that particular page when gifting friends, so that it wouldn't go unnoticed.

She turned a few more pages and accepted, with frustration, that there was no dedication. She opened the book at random, the spine crackling. She read quickly, superficially, but still managed to absorb the words, so beautiful and soft they melted off the pages like butter.

The whore from Nantes. A weak, plain, detestable, pathetic, unloved, unlovable wretch. Johanna's physical description could safely match her own, but then her appearance was so unremarkable she couldn't say for sure whether it was intentional. Always coated in fur, her coarse hands protected by gloves (Mrs. March flipped through the pages for any reference to the color—if it was mint green she would die), her petticoats regularly steamed and perfumed—although they were rarely seen, for her clients, who paid her out of pity, would not touch her. And finally, an inevitable fate, one of pauperism and squalor, a death worthy of an Italian opera, open wounds seeping into the mink . . .

Something so ugly described so beautifully. To trap you, surely, to trap you into reading and slowly seduce you into agreeing with this deplorable portrait. And the whole world would know or, worse still, would *assume*. They would see inside her, wickedest of all violations.

On a frightening hunch, she leafed through the bloated book to the acknowledgments page, scanning the names—editor, agent, professors of French history, mother, father (*always in our thoughts and prayers*)—until reaching the very last line: "lastly and most importantly, to my wife, a constant source of inspiration."

Mrs. March clutched her breast, breathing hard, faintly aware that tears were falling amidst convulsive gasps. Then she shook the book, smashed it against the desk, opened it to the author photograph on the jacket flap, clawed out George's eyes, scratched out the threaded spine, and pulled out fistfuls of pages—which flew around the room like feathers.

Only when the last airborne page fluttered to the floor did Mrs. March register what she had done. She gasped. "Oh no," she said aloud. "Oh no, oh no, oh no . . ." She clasped her hands, wringing them as she often did when she was nervous. Something, she had now irreversibly learned, Johanna did too.

She replaced the book with one from the box on the floor, laying it on the desk with care to compensate for the one she had maimed, then hiked up her skirt and yanked down her pantyhose. Bending over—her hair in her face, her nose runny—she stepped out of them, shifting her weight precariously from one foot to the other. She knelt on the floor and stuffed everything into the tights—whole pages, bits of paper, and the remnants of the hardcover—wrapping and tying the glossy fabric around the mess until it was a secure, albeit swollen package. It was the only way, she told herself, to safely transport the evidence to the kitchen trash can (where George would never look).

She gave one last glance at the study before she slipped out, as quietly as she had snuck in.

She leaned on the hallway wall, a little shaky, as she made her way past the living room—flinching at the sound of a scraping chair—and into the kitchen. Cold, tiled heaven.

The trash container was hidden behind the kitchen sink skirt. Mrs. March pulled it out with some effort and lodged the stockinged ball under a greasy cake box. She emerged from the waste in triumph, right as Martha appeared through the kitchen door.

"Oh," said Martha, surprised to see her there. They had long ago forged a silent agreement in which Mrs. March had ceded her the kitchen, and whenever they both occupied the apartment, they engaged in the complicated dance of avoidance. They'd tiptoe around each other, rotating through the rooms as if they were playing an elaborate game of musical chairs, never quite meeting in the same place. Or at least, Mrs. March did.

"Everything all right, Mrs. March?"

"Oh yes," said Mrs. March, short-winded. "I was just thinking of making some pasta for dinner tonight. The dish George likes, with sausage."

"Well, we don't have many of the ingredients. And pasta for dinner—I would advise against it, Mrs. March. Especially after last night's chicken pot pie."

Martha was about fifty, broad-shouldered, with hair forever tied into a small, painfully tight bun, with slightly freckled skin free of makeup, and pink-rimmed blue eyes that seemed to suffer eternal patience. In truth, Mrs. March was rather afraid of her. Specifically, she was afraid Martha wished—or rather *knew*—that *she* was the boss, and that Mrs. March should be the one cleaning the apartment.

"I would recommend the swordfish for tonight," said Martha.

"Well, maybe," Mrs. March said, "but George does like that pasta—"

Martha took a step toward her. The enormity of her! "I really would leave the pasta for next week, Mrs. March."

Mrs. March swallowed, then nodded. Martha smiled gravely, almost consolingly, and Mrs. March backed out of the kitchen, hoping Martha hadn't noticed her bare calves.

IV

Mrs. March observed George that night as they convened for dinner. He entered the room looking at his shoes and scratching his chin, distracted. She stiffened, smile in place for his first glance at her. When he failed to look up as he gripped the back of his chair and sat down, her smile drooped.

They ate in the small dining room, which was connected to the living room by sliding French doors. Chopin's nocturnes played in the background. The table was lavishly set, a habit instilled in Mrs. March by her mother, who told her daughter, numerous times, that a healthy marriage is built from the outside in, not the other way around. A husband, upon returning home from work, should always be received by a wife looking her best, and by a house so thoroughly kempt as to maintain his pride in it. Everything else would spring from that. Her mother emphasized that if she couldn't be a good homemaker, she would have to hire someone who was. Martha had been trained to set the table, every day and every evening, with the silver candlesticks, the monogrammed napkins, the black olive bread in the silver breadbasket, and the wide carafe for the wine. All of it was laid out atop the embroidered linen tablecloth that used to belong to Mrs. March's grandmother (and part of a trousseau her mother was very disinclined to give her, seeing as how she was marrying a divorced man, and in a civil ceremony no less).

This was the default display even if it was just Mrs. March having dinner, which happened often. When George was immersed in his book-writing, he barely ate, except for a few sandwiches brought to his study by Martha. Otherwise he was away on book tours or at conferences or meeting for gourmet dinners and long lunches with his agent or editor. On those days, Mrs. March still played Chopin, and still used the silver platters and fine china, and sipped from her nut-molded wineglass under the watchful eyes of the Victorian oil portraits lining the dining room.

Mr. and Mrs. March sat mostly in silence. George seemed to find silence soothing. She glanced sideways at him, his belly protruding from his sensible gray cardigan, his beard growing out unevenly in irregular tufts along his jaw. He chewed his food audibly, even through a closed mouth. She could hear the snapping of the asparagus between his teeth, the way he rinsed the wine slightly before swallowing it, the saliva at the corner of his mouth when he parted his lips. It made her cringe, not to mention the way he would occasionally give one loud, startling sniff. He caught her looking, smiled. She smiled back. He asked, "Everything ready for the party tomorrow?"

"Hmm, I think so." She added a hint of uncertainty to her answer, as if she weren't completely sure the preparations were under control. As if she wouldn't have a total and irreparable breakdown if they weren't. Then, casually, serving herself more of Martha's swordfish from the platter: "How is the novel doing? Any news?"

George swallowed as he patted his mouth with his napkin, which Mrs. March took for a tell. "Good, good," he said. "You know, I think it might be my best one yet. Or at least my most successful one. That's what Zelda says, anyway."

Zelda was George's agent. Chain-smoking, raspy-voiced, partial to square hairstyles and brownish lipsticks. A woman whose idea of a smile was baring her teeth. Mrs. March doubted that Zelda, who was always flanked by a flock of hardworking assistants, had ever actually read one of George's novels. Certainly not from beginning to end.

"That's wonderful, dear," she said to George. "Would you . . ."—carefully—"would you like me to read it?" She could hear Martha having her own dinner in the kitchen, the clink of utensils against her plate echoing down the hallway and into the dining room.

George shrugged. "You know I always love your feedback. In this case, though, there's not much I can change now that it's out."

"You're right, of course. I won't read it. What would be the point after all."

"Now, that's not what I said."

"No, I know," said Mrs. March, softening, "I mean, I'll read it eventually. When I finish the one I'm on. You know I hate to read two books at once. Can't concentrate fully on either one, and everything just begins to blur—"

She felt something on her hand and looked down. George had placed his hand on hers, reassuringly. "You'll read it when you read it," he said kindly.

She relaxed a bit but, unwilling to give up, knowing it would gnaw at her later, said, "I did read a bit of it, you know."

"I know."

"It was very . . . graphic."

"Yes. That's what it was like in those days. I did a lot of research. As you know."

She did know: the trips to Nantes, the meetings with the

historians at the Bibliothèque Universitaire, the books delivered to their apartment from helpful experts worldwide—she had been witness to a full year of research. And yet she had not paid attention, had never suspected the possibility of such a betrayal. She pursed her lips in preparation for one last prod. "Did you research the—the whores?"

"Of course," he nodded. "Everything."

He went on eating, unconcerned, and Mrs. March breathed in deeply. Perhaps Patricia had made a mistake. Perhaps the whore from Nantes, the wretched Johanna, wasn't based on her at all. Perhaps, she considered with sudden relish, she was based on George's *mother*! Mrs. March stifled a happy chortle.

After dinner they bade good night to Martha, who was waiting by the door, out of her uniform, square olive purse hanging from her wrist. They locked the front door after her, and as George slipped into his study, Mrs. March retired to the bedroom, to the freshly turned sheets and her white flannel nightgown and the hardcover copy of *Rebecca* on the nightstand.

She sank into her pillow, sighing with a relief she mistook for contentment. She held the novel with cautious fingertips so as to avoid staining it with hand cream, but as she tried to turn a page, her thumb slid across the paper, blurring the word *cowardice* to illegibility. She looked over morosely at the books piled high on George's nightstand. She had always been jealous of George's intimate relationship with books: how he touched them, scribbled on them, bent and folded them, their pages impossibly ruffled. How he seemed to know them so thoroughly, finding in them something she couldn't, as much as she tried.

She turned back to her book, determined. After a few moments she found she was having trouble concentrating—thoughts of intimidating party guests and potential catering fiascos inter-rupting every phrase on the page, overflowing in every inden-tation—so she took some pills she had bought over the counter a couple of weeks ago. The pills were very light, the pharmacist had assured her; purely herbal, but they did the trick, and soon she was swimming into a deep sleep, not even noticing when George finally came to bed—or whether he ever did.

Having failed to secure a chef from the fusion place in the West Village that was all the rage and now boasted a two-month wait (Mrs. March had never been), the Marches hired caterers instead. Mrs. March called once, twice, three times to confirm. They were to be supervised by Martha, who knew the kitchen far better.

The morning of the party, Mrs. March busied about the living room, checking the stereo system and room temperature. She placed a row of chairs along one wall in case George or his agent wanted to give a speech to a sitting audience. She wheeled the television set out of the living room and into her bedroom. She replaced the bulb inside the picture light over the original Hopper, and eased the Christmas tree into a corner, mindful of its ribbons and trembling baubles. They had acquired it, following Rockefeller Center's lead, right after Thanksgiving. Or rather, George had, dragging it home with the help of his editor. "After all these years he still delights in boyish things like lugging around a Christmas tree," Mrs. March murmured to herself. She was prone to rehearsing potential snippets of conversation; she liked feeling prepared.

As she positioned the tree against one of the windows, where it was sure to be avoided, a large framed photograph on one of the bookshelves caught her eye. She waited until the workers had retired to the kitchen before inspecting it.

It was an old picture of George's daughter from his previous marriage. Paula. Or, as her parents called her, much to Mrs. March's disgust: Paulette.

Mrs. March began dating George in secret during her senior year, when she was twenty-one. George, thirty-two at the time, was a promising author who taught English literature and creative writing at the university. She had never attended any of his classes. They met for the first time at the cafeteria, where they happened to be in line together when George added a carton of yogurt to his tray and offhandedly commented, "Subdue your appetite, my dears . . ." in her general direction. Although Mrs. March was unaware he was quoting Dickens, she responded by laughing delightedly—repeating the quote while smiling and shaking her head, mock-admonishing George for his cheekiness.

The words *George March is the most attractive man on campus*, uttered by her roommate their freshmen year, had resonated with Mrs. March long before she'd even seen George in person, and she had found motivation in them from their very first encounter. Words she summoned, to this day, with triumph, cherishing them like priceless family heirlooms.

George had courted her slowly, subtly—so subtly that she oftentimes wondered whether he was courting her at all. He would show up randomly wherever she was, but it always felt coincidental, spontaneous. They dated for six years, which saw his rise to polite fame and subsequent stardom, and then he proposed, adorably, over yogurt.

She had longed for a traditional church wedding, but George had wed his first wife in one, so Mrs. March settled for a civil ceremony, at which her mother scoffed to this very day between spells of dementia.

Marrying George in front of all the people who had attended his first wedding had been predictably grotesque. They had beheld his promise to love this other woman in sickness and in health until his dying day. And only a few years later—vows severed, photographic tributes retired from frames and mantels . . . it was inevitable that the value of this second marriage would diminish in their eyes. When George and Mrs. March were exchanging vows, she was sure she heard one of George's guests murmur, "Let's hope the food is better at this one."

Along with a new, shared apartment and a joint checking account came his eight-year-old daughter Paula. In the months leading to the wedding, Mrs. March had been dreading meeting George's ex-wife, bracing herself for a jealous confrontation or at least barely concealed hostility, but she was pleased to discover that they got on quite civilly. The former Mrs. March had invited the soon-to-be Mrs. March over for coffee, and the two spent close to two hours superficially discussing the benefits of an education abroad, as each courteously took turns to look sideways at the clock until the meeting ended.

The problem, Mrs. March had been disappointed to discover, was the daughter. She had been expecting a compliant, smaller version of herself; one she could dress in eyelet pinafore dresses and mold to her liking. Instead, Paula was cocky. Opinionated. Too pretty. She asked impertinent questions ("Why are your hands so dry?"; "Why does Daddy work but you don't?"). She made a habit of vying for her father's attention; "Daddy, oh *Daddy*," she'd cry—pathetically, thought Mrs. March—whenever there was a storm or a scraped knee (her voice suspiciously strong for someone supposedly in so much pain). Mrs. March couldn't stomach the way George boasted about Paula to friends. She would invariably chime

in—parroting that the child was indeed special and gifted—
while on the inside she screamed.

She dreaded the weekends when Paula came to visit, and
after the child had departed, traces of her always remained.
A pink frilly shirt, folded by Martha among Mrs. March's
own things in the closet. Sticky chocolate fingerprints on Mrs.
March's favorite camel-hair blanket. Smudged glasses of unfinished water left on every counter.

Even in her absence the air still carried Paula's scent: that milky,
flowery, entitled smell that resisted the bergamot room spray
spritzed frantically by Mrs. March throughout the apartment.

As a way to prove to everyone she could rear an infinitely
more gracious and sensitive child, and also as a sort of punishment to Paula, Mrs. March herself had a child. She was glad it
was a boy, glad she hadn't been sentenced to witness her youth
reflected, pure and unwithered, in a girl.

Jonathan, now eight, occupied the bedroom Paula used to
sleep in on her visits. A room Mrs. March had flayed and redec-
orated beyond recognition. She papered the walls with plaid
fabric from Ralph Lauren, which gave off a coziness in the
winter but turned stifling in the hot months, when the room
would develop its own microclimate. She threw away all of
Paula's branded toys, the Mickeys and the Disney princesses, in
favor of plain, old-fashioned ones, like a wooden rocking horse
and an antique sled. The shelves she furnished with absurdly
expensive first editions of old children's books (*Huckleberry
Finn*, *Little Lord Fauntleroy*). On one wall she'd hung a row of
framed *National Geographic* covers. Jonathan had never read a
single issue—nor would Mrs. March ever allow it, for him to
come across photographs of topless tribeswomen, their collar-
bones adorned with thick beaded necklaces, their flat breasts

pointing at their belly buttons. But she proudly claimed those framed issues were his favorites, when encountered by guests. The room was ready to be photographed for a magazine, if need be, at any given time.

Jonathan was a messy and occasionally pouty child, but he was quiet and thoughtful and smelled modestly of fresh laundry and soccer-field grass. He was currently away on a school trip to the Fitzwilliam Chess and Fencing Retreat in upstate New York, and would be returning in a couple of days. Mrs. March was proud of herself for occasionally wondering what he was doing, which she had decided was a symptom of missing him.

Paula, now twenty-three, enjoyed a fabulous lifestyle, as she probably assumed was her birthright, and lived in London no less, where Mrs. March herself had long fantasized about living—steak at the Wolseley and drinks at the Savoy, a play in the West End on Saturdays. Paula called often to catch up with George. She never failed to ask after Mrs. March, which Mrs. March regarded as prying.

Mrs. March studied the framed photograph in which a ten-year-old Paula posed, her eyes liquid caramel under arched eyebrows, her plump lips pursed—Mrs. March thought with scorn—ever so seductively. Ten-year-old Paula had insisted George place the photograph there, surely because it was at eye level, ensuring that everyone would see it upon entering the living room. Mrs. March now moved it to a higher shelf, face-down, and resumed her preparations for the party.

She arranged the cushions on the couch, bringing to the forefront the chintz one, covered in a pattern of thrushes eating fruit. She tossed the cashmere throw on the back of the couch, then repeated the action again and again until it achieved an artfully careless look suggesting that Mrs. March had been reading and lost track of time, so at ease that she had forgotten about the party she was hosting, and only after a polite reminder from Martha (a meeker, subservient version of Martha), she had flung the throw to one side and had gone about her work.

That morning Mrs. March had gone to the florist—the pricey one on Madison Avenue, which boasted its own little greenhouse—where she bought several large bouquets: red roses nestled in eucalyptus and winterberry branches; and hairy, drooping pine boughs that resembled the drum brushes she'd seen the jazz musicians brandish at the Carlyle. She placed a couple in the living room, and one in the guest bathroom, where she also set down a magnolia candle, an impressive display of foreign soaps, and a gilded glass bottle of hand lotion she usually hid in her nightstand. This was out of concern that Martha might mistake it for soap. The lotion was French, and Mrs. March suspected Martha couldn't possibly know that *lait pour mains* meant "hand cream."

She straightened the painting that hung over the toilet—a flirty, playful piece depicting several young ladies bathing in a stream. Rays of light shone through the trees on the bank, illuminating the women's waxen hair and bodies. They smiled modestly, eyes lowered, all of them facing the viewer. It was an invaluable piece, acquired for a song after it was unearthed in an old art gallery on the brink of bankruptcy. Mrs. March stood admiring it for some time, satisfied at the idea that she was a woman who could appreciate suggestive art, despite not knowing the name of the artist or feeling remotely comfortable with nudity, before exiting the bathroom, which now smelled overwhelmingly of pine.

She moved to the kitchen, finding it so pleasurably dark and peaceful with the gentle snoring of the fridge she almost felt guilty about the imminent invasion of the caterers. In the end she had decided against the macarons for dessert, settling instead for raspberry cheesecake tartlets from a tiny bakery on the other side of the park (a zip code away from Patricia's) and good old-fashioned strawberries and cream. The strawberries, stacked on the kitchen floor in wooden crates, were really something to look at. They shone bright and scarlet, like poppies. The cream, whipped with Madagascar bourbon vanilla and confectioners' sugar, could have floated out of the crystal serving bowl like a cloud. She envisioned her guests' faces, flushed with joy and admiration—tinged with envy, too—and could almost feed off the image itself.

She admired her handiwork spread out across her kitchen. This was surely going to be the most enviable of parties, she concluded, certainly the most impressive one that *she* had ever been to, and the literary world was going to remember it for a long, long time.

VI

Not that she hadn't been to sophisticated parties. A fair number of them, in fact.

When she was young, her parents often threw ostentatious dinner parties in their apartment. Black-tie affairs with private chefs and jazz quartets. On these evenings, Mrs. March and her sister Lisa would be given an early dinner in the kitchen—usually a selection of leftovers they'd consume sulkily while the pink, glossy canapés that would be served at the party taunted them from the counter, warranting a surreptitious spit or two.

Their parents would then lock them in their rooms, which were connected by a bathroom. They would mostly spend the evening in Lisa's room, since she was the eldest and that was the room with the television, and would watch horror movies and the occasional European art film, giggling at the nudity at increasingly breathless intervals.

Sometimes they would be startled by a shrill outburst erupting from the living room or animalistic snorts in the hallway. One evening the bedroom doorknob turned slowly, then more violently, shaking the whole doorframe, under the rapt gaze of the girls, who sat together, motionless, until the rattling ceased.

The cat, along with its litter box and food and water, would be locked in with them so that the guests wouldn't be disturbed by it meowing or shedding on their coats or—God forbid—pouncing on the table. It would scratch at the door, yowling incessantly to escape. Upset by its suffering, Mrs. March would paw at the door in a pretend attempt to open it, then would feign vexation so that the cat would understand that she, too, was trapped inside.

The mornings after these parties the house would smell different, like sandalwood perfume and cigars and—confusingly, because her parents owned none—scented candles.

When Mrs. March turned seventeen, she was finally asked to attend one. It was her father who mentioned it offhandedly to her one Saturday morning from behind his newspaper.

Feeling very mature or very nervous or a combination of both, she stole a bottle of sherry from the liquor cabinet and drank from it in her bedroom, shyly and haltingly at first, then in great consecutive gulps.

That night, she debated somewhat too animatedly with her parents' friends about theater and art. She laughed mindlessly at jokes she was not sure she understood. She interrupted a profound, intellectual discussion of the nature versus nurture debate, quoting Mary Shelley, whose work she'd been studying in class. She ate every single course the chef had prepared—a heavy, decadent Tudor-era feast—including roast venison and meat pie—and continued to drink until she realized all the guests had left and she was standing alone holding a glass of port she didn't remember pouring.

She hugged the toilet bowl through the night, kneeling on the cold tiled floor of the bathroom she used to share with her sister, and was sick well into the morning, purging her body of the thick, meaty meal, which came out of her in stringy pieces.

She hid in her bedroom until well past lunchtime the next day. When she eventually emerged, the furniture placement in the living room seemed to be ever so subtly off by an inch, her father's books looked to be out of order, and the blue china vase on the piano depicted a dragon when she was sure it had always been a bird.

Her parents sat at opposite ends of the sofa, each reading a copy of the same book, seemingly oblivious to the stench of liquor-dampened velvet. They didn't look up as she walked in. Neither made mention of the party at all, which Mrs. March took as their grim tacit acceptance of her flaws—but her mother did insist on washing her hair. It was something she had always done for her daughter and continued to do until Mrs. March left for college.

On this day, the day after her parents' party, Mrs. March knelt on the bathroom floor as her mother sat on the rim of the tub and lathered. They did not speak but her mother did tug especially hard on her hair, and Mrs. March fought to curb her nausea, which was particularly challenging with one's head upside down. She considered this to be her punishment for her behavior the previous night. As her mother roughly rubbed her scalp, she vowed not to drink another drop of alcohol until she had graduated college.

She kept her word, attending university parties more as a spectator than as a reveler. Like a ghost, she would weave through the dorms and fraternities, observing the drunken Ping-Pong matches and the couples kissing ravenously in dark corners.

She met her first serious boyfriend, Darren Turp, at one of these early campus parties. Mrs. March had imposed upon herself another steadfast rule: she would lose her virginity to the first boy to ever tell her that he loved her. And so she did, a year and a half later, on an unseasonably hot spring day, sweating on Darren's dorm mattress (his father, good friends with the dean, had secured for him a single room). Afterwards, they fell asleep, and when Mrs. March awoke that evening, she struggled to recall anything other than sunlight on closed eyelids and sheets tangled tight around her ankles like clutching hands. She eased out of the bed as quietly as she could and inspected the sheets using Darren's Eagle Scout flashlight, but there was nothing—not even a rusty, menstrual-like smudge. Her hymen, that so-called sacred piece of her, must have broken a long time ago.

She continued to date sweet, unassuming Darren until her senior year, when she met and became infatuated with George (*George March is the most attractive man on campus*). She told Darren she was leaving him without so much as an explanation. He beseeched her to stay, or to at least sleep on it, and when she pointedly refused, he pestered her to call his mother and break the news to her personally. "My mother at least deserves an explanation," he said hotly, "after everything she's done for you." Mrs. March had spent several Thanksgivings at the Turps' home in Boston, where she and Darren slept in adjacent rooms so as to please the proudly traditional Mrs. Turp. Each morning, at the crack of dawn, Darren's mother would creep into her room—at first Mrs. March assumed it was to ensure the couple had not spent the night together, but it turned out Mrs. Turp was grabbing her guest's towels to warm them in the dryer for her before her morning shower.

And so Mrs. March dialed Mrs. Turp from a pay phone outside the cafeteria minutes after breaking up with her son. It was raining considerably, the sky lighting up and rumbling at three-second intervals. The women could barely hear each other over the thunder.

"I have seen it fit to propose that Darren and I part ways—"

"What?"

"Darren and I have agreed that it would be best—"

"Can't hear ya!"

"I'm leaving Darren!" Mrs. March screamed into the receiver pressed against her left ear, her finger plugging the right. This outburst was met by silence, followed by Mrs. Turp's cold, clipped voice: "All right then. Thank you. Good luck with everything." With that, the line went dead, and Mrs. March left the phone booth without another word to Darren, who had been pacing outside the entire time, drenched. She allowed herself sixteen minutes to weep for their relationship, which was the exact duration of her walk back to her dorm.

Once married to George, she lifted the self-imposed drinking ban and began to enjoy wine and kir royales at the growing number of events to which her ascendant husband was invited. One function, an exclusive event at the Met that took place after operating hours, involved a private tour of an upcoming exhibit, followed by a cocktail party in the members-only dining room. The partygoers drifted from table to table, clinging to them as if to lifeboats.

It was at this party where Mrs. March saw Darren again. Eight or nine years had passed since their breakup, but Darren had the same blotched cheeks, the same curly hair, the same style of striped linen shirt (though her heart sank when she realized this particular shirt was unfamiliar to her—as if she somehow retained the right to know his entire wardrobe forever).

George was lost in animated conversation, which gave her an opportunity to approach Darren, who was in a corner sipping at something pink. She tapped him on the shoulder, and when he turned, his face fell. "Oh," he said, "it's you."

Entirely because there were people watching, Mrs. March belted out a honking laugh, pretending he had made a joke.

"I saw you earlier," continued Darren, "with Professor March. Are you two actually dating?" His eyes darted toward George, who was still chatting away.

"Yes—well, we're married," said Mrs. March with unconcealed pride, her hand rising to flash the sizable ring on her finger. "He's not a professor anymore," she added, hoping Darren would inquire about George's recent success.

He huffed. "I should have known," he said.

"Known what?"

"That you cheated on me with a professor."

Mrs. March swallowed. "I did no such thing."

"Of course you did! Someone told me they saw you two together the day after you dumped me. Couldn't even wait forty-eight hours, could you?"

Mrs. March was left speechless. It seemed silly, albeit somewhat flattering, that someone would go to such lengths—would consider her important enough to spy on.

"And of course you went for the professor," said Darren. "Everything you do is just for show."

"Don't be silly."

"Did you even care about me? Or did you zero in on me because my family had money?"

Mrs. March was about to point out that her own family had much more money than his, but she shushed him instead, saying, "People are staring."

"Well, I'll have you know I'm doing quite well now. I've been hired at *The New Yorker*. They pay rather well, as you might know."

This news stung a little, for George had recently submitted a story to *The New Yorker*, where it had been firmly rejected.

"Congratulations," said Mrs. March meekly. She longed to throw her drink on him, to spit in his face—no, what she really wanted was to know who had told him about her and George and if anyone else knew about it, this small tarnish on her reputation. Dizzy from the alcohol and the music, she walked away from Darren, her small, stupid "congratulations" now tormenting her. She managed, with effort, to appear chipper and carefree the rest of the soirée, all the while avoiding the curly-haired figure bobbing menacingly among the crowd.

Later, she eventually unearthed, through gentle prodding of friends in common, that he had lied to her. He was merely a copy boy—and a poorly paid one at that. As George continued to soar, Darren, as far as Mrs. March could tell, failed to arrive in the literary world (or any world for that matter). She had won. What she desperately hoped for now was that Darren would never lay eyes on George's new book. It would give him so much satisfaction.

VII

The day of George's book party lurched forward at a frustrating pace. The subject itself seemed to hang in the air, like a disruptive fog. It hovered over every one of Mrs. March's conversations, waiting for her in every pause. The apartment seemed to agree with her—every room now primped and oddly spaced with new furniture arrangements, enduring the anticipation with something like reproach.

She was too agitated to eat anything but asked Martha to prepare her something light, "so as to avoid bloating." She didn't want Martha to know how anxious the party made her, how it took up all the space in her thoughts and relegated all other priorities to the background.

She picked at her vegetables languidly, swallowing bits with great gulps of water and breathing through her mouth, the way she had done as a little girl when forced to eat something she didn't like. The grandfather clock tutted disapprovingly in the foyer, like some sort of wigged Victorian judge clicking his tongue and—when the clock struck the hour—tolling his bell on the court steps in proclamation of her guilt.

The cook and waiters, having organized everything, had left to change into their uniforms. Mrs. March considered suddenly, outrageously, that they had all come back already or had never even left and were hiding in the hallway, waiting to startle her. She pushed her plate of vegetables away and arranged her napkin on top of her plate in an attempt to mask how little she'd eaten.

She scampered off to her bedroom as Martha cleared the table. At this time of day, strips of direct sunlight perforated their suite like stabs. Mrs. March drew the drapes, afraid of a headache. She removed her shoes and lay on the bed, straightening her skirt and looking up at the ceiling, her hands resting on her stomach. She tried to nap, but her pulse, thudding in her ears, was too loud to ignore, as was the constant, hounding certainty that she had made some irredeemable mistake with the catering. Were her guests currently in a similar state of expectation? Did her party paralyze their every thought, dominate their every activity? Probably not. She swallowed, her throat scratchy and dry. She looked at her wristwatch, at the ticking, trembling hands, until they marked quarter to four, the earliest hour at which she had allowed herself to dress for the party.

She jumped up and opened the doors to the built-in closet. She had long been haunted by the suspicion that although her wardrobe was tasteful and of good quality, the way she arranged or styled her clothes made them come across as cheap and tacky. She suspected this of her furniture, indeed of all her belongings, but especially of her clothes. Clothing didn't seem to suit her the way it suited other women; everything was either too tight or too short or it hung off her, shapeless and billowy— she always appeared to be wearing somebody else's clothes.

She stood motionless in front of the closet, her eyes scanning the fabrics and patterns of her dresses, skirts, and pantsuits. How strange, she thought, that one day she would select the last ensemble she would ever wear. The last blouse that would heave as she breathed, the last skirt that would press against her gut when she ate. She might not die in them necessarily (flashes of hospital gowns came to mind), or be buried in them (her sister, a slave to protocol, would probably pick her most drab, least flattering outfit), but they would still be the last clothes she had ever chosen to wear. Would she die tonight, before she had a chance to host the party? As long as she actively imagined the scenario, it would not come to pass. This was a little game she often played with herself. If she wondered whether an outfit would be her last, it wouldn't be. If she pictured herself dying today, she wouldn't. It was a silly superstition, but really, what were the odds that something terrible would happen when you expected it to? Very low indeed. Nobody ever said, "My wife died today, as expected," or "I was in a terrible accident, as I predicted."

She made her way through the hangers, looking for the dress she'd had in mind for the party ever since it had been decided there was to be a party. It was a bottle green dress with long sleeves. Her upper arms had turned flabby with age, and she took care to conceal them.

She found the dress hiding between two houndstooth pantsuits and yanked it out. She recalled wearing it only once before, to a dinner months ago with George and his cousin Jared. Although she had pored over the invitation list for tonight, a nagging fear now surfaced as to whether Jared would be in attendance. Mrs. March had only met Jared twice, and she couldn't possibly be seen wearing the same dress two out of three times. He would greet her warmly enough, surely expecting the wife of his illustrious cousin to impress him, but upon realizing she was wearing the same dress, jewelry, and hairstyle, his attention would no doubt flit to the more stylish women in the room.

Her eyes fell on a royal blue off-the-shoulder number hidden at the deep end of the closet. She had never worn it. In fact, the tag was still on. What a strong yet elegant color, she thought, and one unlikely to be worn by the other guests. Sadly, however, the dress was sleeveless. She pulled it out of the closet and inspected both dresses in each of her hands. The blue was certainly pretty, but she simply couldn't take the risk of somebody with a camera capturing her bare arms. She thrust it right back into the closet.

Slipping the bottle green dress off its hanger, she carried it to the bed carefully, as if it were a sleeping child, and spread it out over the coverlet. Beside the dress, she placed a golden brooch and round gold earrings.

Next she started on her hair, wrapping locks tightly around rollers, strand by strand.

She filed and polished her nails, something she always did herself to avoid professional manicurists, lest they judge the state of her nails (which they often had in the past, asking her, "Why are your nails so yellow? Do you leave the polish on for too long?" in front of the other clients).

Waiting for her nails to dry, she looked steadily at her watch ticking the seconds away. Then she removed the hot rollers from her hair. As she unrolled a ringlet, the roller, still hot, grazed her skin, burning the back of an earlobe. She breathed in sharply and patted her stinging ear with a wet piece of toilet paper.

She undressed, taking care to avoid the sight of her naked body in the mirror. The skin on her stomach was dented, having never quite recovered from Jonathan. Her gut was scratched with stretch marks that branched out toward the thick dark patch of hair between her legs. She managed, with some difficulty, to scoop her sagging belly into the tight, flesh-colored girdle, before shimmying into the bottle green dress. When she finally allowed a good look at herself in the bathroom mirror, she smiled—unnaturally, as if posing for a photograph. Swaying, pretending to hold a glass in her hand, she mimed laughter. "Thank you for coming," she said to the mirror. "Thank *you*, for coming."

She tried on different lipsticks—all of them unused, hard and gleaming like candle wax—only to rub each one off angrily, staining her whole jaw, chafing her chin with paper towels and at one point furiously, purposefully, drawing a gash across her neck in vermilion—before returning, defeated, to the sensible cream-colored lipstick she always wore.

In a fit of indecision, she wiggled out of the bottle green dress, went back to the closet, and tried on the royal blue. In the mirror she winced at the protruding curve of her midriff; at her arms, somehow simultaneously tight and saggy. She tore the dress off with a stifled cry. She threw on a silk blouse— the one she usually wore with her mother's old rhinestone cufflinks—and black skirt, only to end up back in the bottle green dress.

✦

GEORGE ARRIVED HOME at twilight, just as Mrs. March was experimenting with the ceiling and floor lamps to determine which combination would inspire a cozy yet vibrant atmosphere. As she hummed softly to herself in a way only a calm and collected woman could, her performance went unnoticed by the waiters, who politely ignored her as she fiddled with the lights.

She glanced fretfully at her wristwatch. Some of the guests were probably already on their way: the married couples bickering in elevators and the backseats of cabs, the women so tightly coiffed they looked like they'd just undergone cosmetic surgery, the men pretending they still fit into ten-year-old Armani suits.

She was making one last halfhearted attempt to change her dress while George knotted his tie in the bathroom, when out of nowhere he said, "You know, Paulette called to congratulate me."

"Oh?" she said.

"Now, now, don't start."

"Don't start what? I was merely saying 'oh.'"

"Well, it was very sweet of her to phone, especially as she's so busy now with all her shoots—"

"Well, she's very *talented*," she said.

"Yes, she's doing very well for herself."

Mrs. March's stomach dropped picturing George's pride in Paula spilling over into the party. She had worked too hard and had fabricated hopes that were now too high (daydreams of George directing a loving speech at her, guests congratulating her impeccable taste, among others) to share George's admiration this evening.

"So well, in fact," continued George, now fastening a cufflink, "that she's put in an offer on a townhouse in Kensington."

"How lovely."

"Yes. It's beautiful apparently—and a landmark to boot. She says that we're welcome to stay whenever we visit."

To be a guest of Paula's, to be *thankful* to her for anything, was so alien, such an anathema, that one of Mrs. March's eyelids twitched. She steadied herself by focusing on George's fingers as they worked on another cufflink. Had she seen these cufflinks before?

"She's really done quite well for herself," he repeated, distracted, under his breath.

She definitely hadn't seen these cufflinks before, which troubled her. She was familiar with each and every one of George's cufflinks and ties and pocket squares, as most of them were gifts from her over the years. Where were those cufflinks from? She took a step forward, opening her mouth to speak, when the doorbell rang.

The first guests arrived in a group of five, as if they all had conspired to meet up somewhere beforehand. "Oh God, who would want to be alone in that apartment, talking to *her*?" she envisioned one of them saying to the others. In any case, the prospect of making small talk with one or two early arrivals was enough to make the backs of her knees sweat. Relieved, she left them in the living room while she made a show of attending to a task, which in this instance involved hiding in her en suite bathroom, perched carefully on the lowered toilet lid so as to avoid rumpling her dress.

Soon, the apartment was thrumming with guests, the music—a livelier, jazzier version of *The Nutcracker* she considered a perfect choice for a winter cocktail party—in harmony with the throbbing bass of voices and occasional percussion of tinny laughter.

A few guests—old friends of George's—gifted him with a framed black-and-white photograph of his grandfather, who posed gravely by his freckled English setter, one hand holding his rifle, the other dangling a dead duck by its feet. Mrs. March hated it immediately. The solemnity of it, the august expression on the man's face—and on the dog's—was absurd. That anyone believed the thing merited framing made it even more so.

She made a mental note to hide it behind her hatboxes in the closet as soon as the guests left.

As the party progressed, the living room fattening with each new arrival, Mrs. March tasked Martha with attending to the guest bathroom regularly, to fold the towels and freshen the toilet seat and floor with a light ammonia solution. The sharp antiseptic vapors merged with the sticky, sappy scent of pine, creating a smell so distinct that guests would, on future visits to hospitals or upon passing a storekeeper emptying a bucket of mop water onto the street, instantly recall that last party at the Marches'.

VIII

Mrs. March observed the women. Her attention was particularly drawn to one in her mid- to late twenties, easily making her the youngest guest at the party. Mrs. March took in her glossy golden mane, her wine-colored dress—stunning in its simplicity and exquisitely draped over her thin frame. Mrs. March shrank inside, feeling gauche and exposed; she looked like she was trying too hard, "mutton dressed as lamb" as her mother would say. And her hair, so limp and so plain she didn't even know what color it was. She had been sweating and her curls were beginning to wilt, thin wet tendrils falling flat across her forehead.

The waiters, bearing trays of smoked salmon canapés and onion and brie tartlets, weaved among the guests, as the stereo played a dreamy piece sung by Anna Maria Alberghetti. Mrs. March fixed her gaze once more on the woman, who was conversing with a pair of awed men, and, seeing her casually tuck a loose strand of golden hair behind her ear, Mrs. March instinctively mirrored the gesture. Her fingers brushed against her burned earlobe, angering her raw, peeling skin. Wincing softly through clenched teeth, she approached the group furtively, as if she had committed a crime. "Everything all right over here?" she asked them, wringing her hands. They turned their heads to look at her. The woman was smoking a fancy cigarette, thin and long and ivory, like her neck. The bracelets on her bony wrist jangled when she brought the cigarette to her lips.

"Mrs. March, lovely to see you," said one of the men, whom Mrs. March remembered dimly as George's private banker. She couldn't recall his name, but she did know that he and George occasionally played tennis together.

"I hope you're having a good time," Mrs. March said, more to the young woman.

"Good turnout," said the private banker.

"Oh, yes," said Mrs. March. "We have quite the crowd, I barely know anyone." The young woman was looking elsewhere, tilting her head back as she smoked, as if drinking from a ridiculously long champagne flute.

"Well, I can start by introducing you to Tom here," said the banker, "and to Ms. Gabriella Lynne, whom I'm sure you recognize from last month's *Artforum*."

Mrs. March beamed a touch too aggressively at the gazelle-like Ms. Lynne, who—exhaling a plume of smoke—said nothing.

"Ms. Lynne happens to be the most sought-after book jacket designer of the moment," Tom piped up.

Gabriella shook her head, blowing out another wreath of smoke, her exhalation morphing into a quiet laugh. "I fear these two are impressed by just about anything," she said to Mrs. March, at which Mrs. March giggled, happy to be included in this aside. "This is an absolutely wonderful party, by the way, thank you so much for inviting me," Gabriella added in a listless monotone. Her accent, seductive and untraceable, had been acquired, Mrs. March would later learn, through an itinerant European childhood.

"Oh, of course, it's my pleasure," replied Mrs. March. "And

any friend of George's is a friend of mine. Have you designed any of his books?"

"Oh, I wish." Gabriella twisted her cigarette into the remains of her caviar and crème fraîche blini, which a waiter promptly removed. Mrs. March couldn't decide whether to feel offended at Gabriella's behavior. The blini, unfinished, was destined for the trash anyway, but desecrating it in such a manner could be conceived as an insult to her hospitality. A sudden desire to cry invaded her, and the mere possibility of this terrified her.

"Actually, I had been asked to come up with the cover for his new novel," Gabriella continued, "but sadly I had another commitment. Everything worked out, though—the designer they used instead chose that iconic painting. It's just so perfect, and it suits the spirit of the novel more than anything I could have come up with."

Mrs. March nodded blankly, wondering what Gabriella's body looked like underneath her thin satin dress: what color her nipples were, whether she had any freckles or moles— perhaps one Gabriella considered unsightly but which all men agreed was impossibly sexy.

"I assume you read the book?" Gabriella asked, looking straight into her eyes and cocking her head to one side, her lips parted slightly in a show of playful curiosity.

"Oh, I, of course, I read *all* of George's books," Mrs. March said, her voice wavering. Before the conversation could veer into the dreaded direction of the book's main character, another man—recently arrived, by the looks of it, as he was still wearing his coat, raindrops glistening on the shoulders—swooped in to greet Gabriella with a kiss on both cheeks. Mrs. March felt Gabriella's attention yanked from her almost physically, wrenched from her body like a still-beating organ. She glanced down at the coffee table. In the ashtray lay three white cigarette butts stained with lipstick. Next to it sat Gabriella's silver cigarette case, engraved with her initials. Pushed by an unfamiliar impulse, Mrs. March snatched the case and slipped it into her bra, where it lodged uncomfortably against her left breast.

She walked away unnoticed, slightly dizzy from the rush of her misdeed but making an effort to smile—partly to avoid suspicion, but mostly to mask her own guilt over what she had just done. Unfortunately, or perhaps thankfully, she was at that moment accosted by George's agent.

"How are you, darling, the party is simply spectacular," Zelda said, all in one breath, then inhaled sharply. A committed chain smoker, Zelda struggled to get out long phrases; her lungs seemed to collapse every time she tried. Her voice was growing huskier by the second, and Mrs. March imagined by the end of the night her statements might be reduced to mere whistles.

"Thank you, Zelda." Her eyes fell on Zelda's teeth, stained with russet lipstick and yellowed by decades of nicotine. "Do try the foie gras," she added as a waiter approached bearing a log surrounded by caramelized onion and strawberry compote. "It's from a little farm on the outskirts of Paris. My sister gave it to us. Her husband made it himself. On that very farm while on holiday."

"How spectacularly *rustic*!" Zelda said, stretching out her arms and looking up at the ceiling dramatically.

"Isn't that made by brutally force-feeding the goose?"

Mrs. March turned toward this new voice, which belonged to the long, emaciated figure of Edgar, George's editor. His hands behind his back, his head bowed, he was always curved, like a question mark.

"Surely not!" protested Zelda, although her face expressed no such disbelief as she turned to Mrs. March, her body shaking with a laughter her lungs weren't strong enough to produce.

"It's a process called *gavage*," Edgar said, in an irritating French overpronunciation, his little mouth filled with saliva, "which is the term for force-feeding the animal with a tube to the stomach."

"Ooh!" Zelda said, pulling a face but still laughing, her painful titter now intermittently audible, like the whine of a dog.

"That's why the liver has that distinctive flavor," said Edgar.

As if on cue, the waiter reappeared with the foie gras, which was sweating viscous rivers of yellow grease.

Edgar pulled up his cuffs, took the small blunt knife next to the foie gras, cut himself a piece as the waiter held the trembling tray, and lathered a piece of toast. His eyes fixed intently on Mrs. March, a small smirk playing on his lips as he popped the toast into his mouth. She returned his gaze, fixating on his thick, clear-colored eyeglasses and thin, milky, wispy hair, like a baby's. The color of his skin was a nauseating white tinged with pink—the pink of his knuckles, of his raised moles, of the spider veins streaking his nose.

The sound of a spoon clinking repeatedly against a glass interrupted her momentary odium, and she and Edgar both turned away from each other, toward the source of the noise. It was George, God bless him, standing awkwardly in front of the fireplace, thanking everybody for coming. Zelda had sidled up to him at some point, without Mrs. March and Edgar even realizing she had left.

"I want to thank everybody here," George began, "because if you're here, then it means you had something—big or small— to do with this book. Be it editing, promoting, dealing with my writerly whims these past few months, or simply inspiring this latest story." His eyes fell on Mrs. March, whose buttocks immediately clenched.

Zelda interrupted to say something about how the industry's winter fiction lists had looked especially crowded, and what a feat it was that George's book had yet to meet its match.

"Well, the fans are loyal—" George said, looking down as he clutched the stem of his champagne glass.

"Nonsense, nonsense, don't be modest," interrupted Zelda again as she turned to the partygoers: "He's being modest!" She laughed, and it wheezed out in a barely audible grate.

Mrs. March brought her fingers to her burned earlobe, stroking the crackling scab with her thumb. She was reminded, fleetingly, of a pork rind, and without realizing she was doing it, licked her thumb.

"The truth is," Zelda continued, "this is a game-changing book, one that appeals not only to his fans, but to *everyone*, no, hold on"—she wagged a finger at George, who had begun to protest—"and, I'm compelled to say, is *my* favorite book of the past *decade*! And I *hate* to read!"

Raucous laughter erupted. Mrs. March eyed the slightly crooked vase on the mantelpiece behind Zelda, forgetting to join in.

"So without further ado, let's raise a glass—to the charming, talented George! Edgar?"

Mrs. March's gaze turned to Edgar as Zelda pulled him out of the crowd. He raised a hand in a modest gesture as the audience cheered, urging him to speak. "Well . . . you know what?" he said, adjusting his dotted silk scarf. "Let's not toast to this book, because—let's be honest—it doesn't need it. Let's toast instead to George's next book, because *that* one is screwed."

"Hear, hear!" As people searched for others to clink glasses together, some turned toward Mrs. March, whose face stretched into an exaggerated, almost maniacal smile, her eyes wide and gleaming—before she thrust her champagne glass toward her mouth and the now-warm, bubbly liquid burned its way down her throat.

IX

Mrs. March took advantage of the toast and the ensuing merriment to slip out of the living room and into the kitchen, where Martha bent over the island, swaddling the leftovers tightly in plastic wrap. The cook had left already, the waiters had moved on to serve digestifs, and it was now time for dessert.

The strawberries sat in the colander in the kitchen sink, washed and ready. Mrs. March placed them, one by one, on a porcelain platter, marveling at their freshness, their dewy porosity. She asked Martha to prepare the cream and moved to take the strawberries into the living room, in the hopes that they would be admired beforehand.

Just as she was about to cross the threshold to the hallway, a clear, impassive female voice made its way to her from the living room:

"Do you think she knows? About Johanna?"

Mrs. March stopped, one heel in the kitchen, the other in the hallway. There was laughter, in the midst of which Mrs. March was certain she could discern George's hearty guffaw, followed by shushing and scattered giggling.

Dread rippled through Mrs. March. Her ears rang, then seemed to clog. Her arms sagged, and the platter she was clutching drooped. The strawberries tumbled in a scarlet hail all over the floor, rolling into corners and under furniture (some would not be found until weeks later).

She stood there blinking, until Martha made a little noise behind her and her thick, blotchy hands appeared to pry the platter from Mrs. March.

"Oh, dear, I—what a mess. I'll get cleaned up," said Mrs. March in a strangely drowsy sort of voice, as Martha kneeled to pick the strawberries off the floor.

Mrs. March stumbled past the living room and into her bedroom, pacing in circles before entering the adjoining bathroom, where she closed and locked the door. She sat on the edge of the bathtub and fumbled the silver cigarette case out from her bra, stopping to caress the engraved initials before unlatching it with a little click. She took out a cigarette and, hands shaking, lit it with a match from a matchbox in one of the bathroom drawers. She smoked one, then two, then three cigarettes, sucking in the foul air greedily. She tipped the ash into the bathtub and left the cigarette butts in the drain. As she finished what she promised herself would be her final cigarette, a black blur scuttled across the floor. Her eyes followed the sudden movement and she identified—a dark veil of horror settling over her—a cockroach running across the tiles. Mrs. March yelped and ran out of the bathroom, slamming the door behind her. She pressed a hand to her mouth to keep from screaming, and another to the wound behind her ear. Then she snatched the pillows from the bed and placed them to block the gap between the floor and the door.

Drained, she sat on the bedroom floor, resting her back against the bed. She considered briefly the prospect of not returning to the party, but custom dictated she make her way back. Perhaps she could feign a terrible illness? But people would talk. They would see her absence as confirmation that Johanna was based on her, and more pitifully: that she cared.

"Did you hear about Mrs. March?" she pictured George's private banker saying to his wife. "The poor woman. She now spends her days locked up in their apartment. Terrible shame."

She then imagined his wife (whom she hadn't met, and who may in fact not even exist) pitying her, this pathetic ugly stranger (the banker would have rushed to describe her as plain) whose husband despised her so much that he based this dreadful character on her. "What character, exactly?" the wife would ask as she dried her delicate hands on a kitchen towel.

A smile would play on the banker's lips, and he would describe Johanna, the whore, and how no one wanted to sleep with her, even her regulars. "The book's really rather good," he would say. "There's talk the clever bastard will win the Pulitzer for insulting his wife."

They would chuckle somewhat guiltily about it, and the wife would remark what a pity the whole thing was, as she had thought the Marches were a happy couple. "Well, I guess now we know the truth."

Mrs. March wondered how other women would suffer this humiliation if they were to find themselves in her position; surely Patricia, the simple-minded baker, with her frizzy hair and stupid, dumpling face, would find it hilarious that her husband had based a sad whore on her. She wouldn't give a damn about anybody else's opinion. But was this the type of woman Mrs. March wanted to be? The type of woman who couldn't care less about her image, about how the world might see her? She attempted to picture how Gabriella would take it. But this would never happen to Gabriella, she concluded miserably.

Gabriella, without a doubt, would be portrayed as an attractive, vulnerable yet resilient goddess, someone the male characters would duel and die for. A less profound character, most likely, less "realistic" (what was it about realism anyway, that people praised it so?) but much more likable. Of course, Mrs. March's problem wasn't so much that Johanna herself was unlikable. It was that there seemed to be no doubt in people's minds that she was, too.

Had the guests even noticed she was gone? Or were they relieved? She considered changing her stupid dress, wearing something simpler, sexier, but everyone would notice, would judge her, would write her off for caring too much. She yearned for some sort of revenge, and although stealing Gabriella's ciga-rette case—which she had returned to her bra—had somewhat soothed this itch, they deserved worse. She should poison them, she mused—with arsenic. In Victorian days, George once told her, every household was equipped with poison. Arsenic was sold, unregulated, to anyone, and used in pigments in wallpa-pers and dresses. She could bring out another dessert—poison them all with a dish of toasted cheese and opium. She pictured them falling all over her living room, then the silence, an odd peace after such a boisterous party, and herself stepping over the bodies in a stunned daze.

She was jolted out of this fantasy by the realization that the party had gone silent. What if the guests had left, urged by a still-giggling George, because they had upset his oversensi-tive wife, you know how she is, fragile, can't bear this sort of embarrassment, you've read the book?

She stood up from the floor, went to the bedroom door, and opened it a crack. The party—its music and noise and laughter still alive—trickled down the hallway. She took a deep breath before stepping out and walked, with hesitation, to the living room, holding on to the walls with her hands as she ricocheted in slow motion from one side to another. Something crunched underneath her feet. She glanced down at a winterberry twig, as several little red berries rolled across the floor.

How silly, she told herself, to assume that anything would stop on her account. The party continued on with the clinking of glasses, the record spinning on its turntable, the grandfather clock ticking in the foyer, its red-cheeked moon face smiling down at her. Everything was as she had left it.

On a side table the last of the strawberries lay scattered on the platter, some splotched with cream, some drowning in it, others bleeding red. Mrs. March contemplated them with a small sadness before sinking back into the party, as if she were submerging in water and looking up at the other bathers' limbs from the depths.

She approached a group engaged in conversation. "The book," they were saying, and "talent" and "his generation." She smiled and nodded at them, but they did not acknowledge her presence so she turned away, her smile frozen in place as she wiped a drop of sweat from her temple. It was then that she saw Gabriella standing next to George in the middle of the room, the two glowing under their own self-made spotlight, leaving everything—and everyone—else dimmed. Gabriella was pressing one hand on his arm while she covered her mouth with the other, as if laughing were a social faux pas, like a yawn or a burp. Mrs. March watched them, drinking from a random glass of room-temperature champagne she had picked up near the strawberries. George stood beaming—that irritating smile of his, detestable in its false humility—until a friend of his approached to introduce himself to Gabriella.

Cheery under the influence of the alcohol (and the attention, no doubt), George spotted Mrs. March and steered her by the elbow to introduce her to two women, a blonde and a brunette, who, George explained with pride, had been among the last of his students before he turned to writing full time. Mrs. March hadn't invited either woman—presumably George had invited them himself without telling her, although it was unclear how he had resumed the relationship after all this time.

"Professor March—"

"Oh, please, you're not my students anymore. Call me George."

"Okay . . . George," said the brunette, giggling.

Mrs. March stared at the women, unsmiling. They couldn't be much older than thirty, she guessed, but she wasn't sure if that made sense. When exactly had George stopped teaching? She tried to recall the year.

"Aren't you just so proud, Mrs. March?" said the blonde with yearning, as if she longed to be asked the same question someday.

"Oh, my wife is quite tired of me, I think," said George, smiling at Mrs. March. "It's a lot, putting up with a writer."

The pair giggled again, then sighed, as if the giggling had drained them. Meanwhile a small commotion had broken out across the room. Gabriella was in search of her missing cigarette case, aided by willing volunteers—all of them male and on all fours—who were peering under furniture and between cushions. Mrs. March could feel the case pressing against her breast as she made a show of looking for it on the shelves.

The party didn't last much longer, as the walls were thin and the neighbors were known to complain. By the time the last of the guests stumbled merrily out the front door,

Martha had already left, boxy little purse in hand, as had the caterers—coats buttoned over soiled uniforms—leaving everything as neat as possible.

In the master bedroom, Mr. and Mrs. March undressed in silence.

Standing near the bathroom, he sniffed at the air. "Have people been smoking in here?"

Mrs. March swallowed, then pinched herself. "George," she said, hoping he'd mistake her unsteady voice for drunkenness, "did you base that woman on me?"

He blinked. "What?"

"Johanna. Did you base her on me?"

"She's not based on anyone, she just . . ." He gestured with his hands, looking for the right word, which turned out to be a disappointing "*is.*"

"Why did you laugh, then, when that woman said so?"

George frowned, peering at her over his glasses. "What woman?"

"That woman! The woman at the party! She said, she *implied*, that Johanna was based on me!"

George seemed to consider this. "Well, it hadn't even occurred to me. Honestly, I hadn't thought of it like that when I was writing. I suppose you may have certain things in common—"

Mrs. March scoffed. "Oh, really, oh like what, George, tell me. Which lovely part of myself do I share with the whore?" Even through her rage, she spoke at a controlled volume, fretful the neighbors might hear.

George sighed. "Now, I think you're taking this the wrong way. Johanna isn't based on any one woman, although I suppose she *is* a mixture of qualities from many different women that I've known over the years. I no doubt could list traits she shares with several women who have influenced me, and yes, you would be among them. That's what fiction writers do."

"Do it, then."

"What?"

"Sit down and make a list. A list of traits."

"Are you serious?"

"Yes!" she said. "I want to know all these women who have inspired you. I want to know where I stand with Johanna."

"Where you *stand* . . . ? She's a fictional character!"

"Then why does it feel like she exists and I don't?"

This last question, posed at a volume that could only be considered by one of Mrs. March's measures as yelling, echoed limply in the now-silent room. She didn't really know where it had come from, wasn't sure what sentiment she had been trying to convey, but it was solid enough to leave a bitter taste on her tongue once uttered.

George frowned. "I don't want to get into this. I think you're—well. You're tired, we're both tired. Let's try and get some sleep. We can talk about this in the morning."

"I won't sleep now. Not if you're here," said Mrs. March, hugging her waist.

George sighed. "I'll sleep in the study." He picked up a wool throw from an armchair in the corner. "Good night," he said, not even glancing her way as he walked past her and out the door, which he closed behind him.

When he'd left, Mrs. March stared blankly at the white paneled door. She locked it, then slowly backed away as if bracing for someone to smash it in with an ax. Swaying on her feet, she walked to her side of the bed, the one nearest the window, and sank into the cold linen face-first.

A pair of raucous pigeons perched on the sill outside Mrs. March's window. They cooed in crescendo, one especially shrill, sounding increasingly, embarrassingly like a woman on the brink of orgasm, so that Mrs. March was relieved to wake up alone in the bedroom. Light sliced in through the window around the gaps in the curtains, and she shielded her eyes and moaned, rolling to the other side of the mattress to call Martha on the kitchen extension. She asked for breakfast in bed: only a fruit salad and soft-boiled egg, please. And an aspirin.

Some minutes later the doorknob shook a little and, after a pause, there was a knock on the door. Mrs. March jumped out of bed and turned the lock, and with a sheepish look, welcomed Martha in.

"We really must air out this room," said Martha, setting the breakfast tray on the bed. "There's an unpleasant odor."

Mrs. March sniffed at the air, but it was impossible to detect anything but the invigorating scent of coffee Martha left in her wake. "Really?" she asked. "Like what?"

"Like a room that hasn't been aired out in a long time."

"Well, I'm feeling unwell, so you can open the windows later. The cold air will do me no good now."

"Certainly. Is there anything else you need, Mrs. March?" Martha stood staring in the direction of the bathroom, arms hanging at her sides. Mrs. March followed her gaze to the haphazard pillow fortress she had built last night at the foot of the bathroom door.

"No, nothing for now," she said, a slight sharpness in her tone. "Thank you, Martha."

She locked the door behind the housekeeper. Those little addenda of hers—"nothing *for now*," "not *really*," "yes, *I suppose*"—most likely tormented Martha, a woman who regarded indecisiveness as weak and wasteful, the clearest mark of a spoiled upbringing.

Mrs. March turned her attention to her breakfast, ornately displayed on the rustic flower-patterned china she had bought at a market on the outskirts of Paris. The aspirin rested on its own hand-painted saucer. Martha had also, unasked, fried a few thick strips of oily bacon. Mrs. March surprised herself by tearing into them with her hands, salivating wildly as the grease ran down her wrists.

She dissolved the aspirin in a glass of water with a spoon. As she drained the glass, she heard a whisper of sorts behind her and turned to see an envelope being slipped under the bedroom door. From George, she supposed. She tiptoed over in case he was still on the other side, and immediately recognized the eggshell stationery, the burgundy initials: G.M. (he didn't have a middle name). She had helped him pick it out at Dempsey & Carroll thirteen years ago, after his first big book advance. He hadn't changed the design since.

The envelope sat there, untouched, on the carpet, for what seemed like forever, until she made up her mind to snatch it up and tear it open. Inside, an invitation: "Truce? Tartt's at six." She crumpled it up and threw it into the unlit fireplace.

◆

THAT MORNING, she kept to her bedroom, reading, clipping her fingernails, and avoiding George. Whenever she entered the bathroom, she slapped on the light in one violent motion, in an attempt to catch the roaches by surprise. She scanned the floor and the space under the sink but saw none.

By lunch hour, she had given up on hiding. Martha called out, announcing that lunch was served, and Mrs. March heard the door to George's study—directly across from their bedroom—creak open. She pressed herself against her door and listened to his steps disappear down the hallway. She inspected herself in the bathroom mirror, tucked loose strands of hair behind her still-raw, slightly puckered ear, and made her way to the dining room.

The hardwood floors had been mopped, and the Christmas tree and sofas pushed back to their original positions. George was already sitting in his usual place at the table and pouring himself a glass of water when she entered through the French doors. She took her chair in silence, looking down at her leather loafers and at the embroidered napkin in her lap to avoid making eye contact with her husband. She thought she could make out from the periphery of her vision a blurry George, baring his teeth at her oddly. She cleared her throat as she reached for a piece of olive bread from the breadbasket. She had resorted to buying her favorite bread from the same bakery where she had bought the desserts for the party. It was a pocket-sized place below street level, cramped between a laundromat and a cheap nail salon—nothing like Patricia's homely, tasteful, downright magical patisserie, but it was a small price to pay to never see Patricia again.

"Gabriella called earlier," began George, breaking the silence so abruptly that Mrs. March jumped in her seat. "She still hasn't found her cigarette case."

Mrs. March didn't answer. She had stashed the silver case in one of her underwear drawers, wrapped with care in an organza shawl. How irresponsible of Gabriella to prance about with such an heirloom, taking it to parties and forgetting it on strangers' tables. Served her right.

"So . . ." continued George, likely realizing that this deflection was not getting him anywhere. "Will you accept my dinner invitation?"

Mrs. March shrugged, buttering a piece of bread. "Don't feel like you *have* to take me out—"

"I feel nothing of the sort. I want to take you out. It would be my absolute pleasure."

"Well, it seems to me that you're taking me out to indulge me, to shut me up, like I'm one of your children."

"All right, all right," said George, showing her his palms in a gesture of surrender. "How about this? We're going out to dinner to celebrate the incredible party my wife threw me."

"So . . . we're celebrating a celebration?"

She had meant to make George feel stupid, but his face lit up at the notion. "Celebration of a celebration!" he said. "I love it. It sounds like us, doesn't it?" He took her fingers to his mouth and kissed them.

To Mrs. March it didn't sound like them in the slightest, although she wasn't sure what would. Rather than unsettle her, the question quite intrigued her: Who were they? They used to laugh and fight and stay up late talking. She would squeal when he kissed the nape of her neck, and she would click her tongue in mock displeasure when he slapped her rear as they climbed out of the subway. Wouldn't she? Or were these scenes she'd picked up from movies and books? She looked sideways at George, who was chomping heartily on his sautéed mushrooms. Who was he?

XI

They took a cab to the restaurant. The place could be reached on foot, but tonight the sidewalks were wet, the air humid and chilly, and Mrs. March was in heels.

They rode most of the way in silence.

"The Monkey Bar is getting to be so drab," said George as the cab trundled along 54th Street.

"Mmm," she said.

The loud cartoon murals of the Monkey Bar had hosted their romantic dinners for years. Over time George started taking his friends and business associates there too. As he did with almost everything, he reveled in it in excess, only to grow bored of the place once the novelty wore off. And so, they exchanged the red leather booths and mirrored columns of the Monkey Bar for the quiet, wallpapered rooms of Tartt's.

The cab stopped at the curb with a splash. George paid the driver as a uniformed valet hurried over with an umbrella. They entered the restaurant at precisely six o'clock, where the maître d', a pasty man with slicked hair and a perky nose, asked them under what name their reservation had been made. Mrs. March scanned the man's face for a hint of recognition as George stated his full name, but he remained unreadable as he checked them off in his book and escorted them to their table.

"Why aren't we in a private room?" she asked, once they were seated and the maître d' was out of earshot. Their usual table was in a small space separated from the main dining area by thick curtains lined with pom-pom trim. It made her feel royal and safe.

"Well, I made the reservation this morning," said George, "and it was a challenge to get a table at all."

"But wouldn't they have given you a better table if you told them who you were?"

"Come on now, dear, this table is perfect. Plus, I wouldn't want to look like an asshole."

"No, I suppose you're right," said Mrs. March, supposing nothing of the sort. She craned her neck to survey the space. It was tasteful, and dimly lit. Quite a few people were seated already as more arrived, all of them impeccably dressed and coiffed. No one seemed to notice them or recognize George, the latter of which would have annoyed Mrs. March in the past, but which today provided her with relief. She lowered her eyes toward her menu. *Wood sorrel*, *Marsala sabayon*, *kabocha squash* . . . George's tortoiseshell glasses hung on his chest from a cord, slapping occasionally against his shirt buttons. Mrs. March peered over her menu at him and cleared her throat, but George remained oblivious. When he finally slipped on his glasses to read the wine list, Mrs. March sat back and returned her gaze to the unintelligible entrées. "It all sounds so yummy, dear," she said, "I just can't decide. Why don't you order for me?"

"I will," said George, without once looking up, "and I'm also going to order us some lovely wine."

The waiter appeared, hunched, hands clasped in front as if he were asking for forgiveness, and with a practiced caution ("Do we know what we want? Any questions?") took their order. As George rattled off their requests, Mrs. March's attention wavered and her vision dimmed, the chatter and tinkling of utensils temporarily quieted. From far away, the waiter asked George if they had any desire for baked Alaska, because apparently it took an inordinate amount of time to prepare. As if emerging from water, she surfaced to see George reply in the affirmative. She had not been consulted, but it was for the best, as she always either regretted not ordering dessert or regretted ordering it. Better for George to make the decision for her. Mrs. March had given up on dieting years ago, never able to sustain it. When Martha wasn't around to keep her in check, she'd invariably give in to the peculiar cravings she'd harbored since she was a little girl (cookies with rice, tomato sauce in yogurt).

She looked down to see a plate of pearly razorfish, tonight's special. She hadn't noticed it being served to her. Had they eaten their appetizers already? She couldn't recall whether George had ordered any. The razorfish looked cartoonish with its colorful stripes and bright yellow irises. She pushed it around her plate, reluctant to eat it, watching George while he slurped at his. The fish's eye stared at her, the pupil circled by one colorful ring after another. Suddenly it blinked. Mrs. March thrust her chair back and excused herself to go to the bathroom.

The ladies' room at Tartt's was surprisingly masculine—oak-paneled and dimly lit, smelling of cinnamon and citrus. In a corner stood a wooden bookcase with wire mesh doors, and along the furthest wall there was a very long porcelain sink—with faucets curved like swans' necks—where a woman stood retouching her makeup in the mirror. Mrs. March attempted a greeting, but the woman didn't register her presence. Mrs. March rapped politely on the door to the toilet and, hearing no response, pushed it open. The stall she selected was almost fancier than the entire bathroom, with its own sink, golden fixtures, and walls papered in Chinese silk. From a sound system emerged a man's voice, reading an audiobook in a soothing British accent. She caught snippets as she undressed, hoisting up her tight skirt and rolling down her pantyhose, careful not to rip them.

The scent of the woman who had used the toilet before her lingered. The smell of her insides, like raw meat. Mrs. March swallowed to suppress a gag and crouched over the toilet, careful to avoid touching the seat with her bare flesh, as her mother had taught her. She hovered, waiting for her bladder to empty as she swayed over the toilet. To maintain her equilibrium she focused on the audiobook narrator's words.

"She removed the scrimshawed busk, which was pressed against her bosom, yellowed with sweat between pimpled breasts. The initials 'B.M.' were carved into the whalebone. It did not belong to her, for her name was Johanna."

Mrs. March gasped, and the stream of her urine diverted to the floor. It couldn't be; had the audiobook even been released? She managed a clumsy dab of toilet paper before pulling up her pantyhose, ripping them in the process—*"She had stolen it, a pathetic figure in the dark of night, from another prostitute a few years back"*—a drop of urine streaked down her leg as she operated the golden faucet—*"a sailor had carved it for B.M., expressing a tenderness Johanna had never experienced from anyone, not even one of her tricks"*—she splashed her hands clumsily, reaching for a paper towel, the voice erupting from the speakers louder, threatening—"We know you're in there, *Johanna*"—she yelped, throwing herself at the door, fumbling with the gilded handle.

When she burst from the stall, she found the bathroom

deserted, one of the taps open. She tossed her crumpled paper towel into the trash and fled the restroom.

The restaurant seemed to have gone quiet. No sounds of knives and forks on porcelain, of clinking glasses, no buzzing of conversation or rustle of the sommelier's stiff trousers. Silence. She walked through the dim dining room as diners on either side watched her, their heads turning to follow her, expressions serious and judgmental. Even the waiters were staring, one of them leering at her over the roast beef on the carving trolley. Only one couple in a far corner wasn't looking at her, but laughing, instead, between themselves. Then the woman turned her head to look at her, a smile still playing on her face, her lips purple from the wine. Mrs. March rushed to her table, where George continued to eat without a care.

A waiter appeared out of nowhere, brandishing tongs. He thrust the tongs straight at her, locking eyes, and she quailed, squeezing her eyes shut. When she opened them she saw that he had used the tongs to place a fresh napkin over her lap. Afraid to turn to face the diners again, she looked instead into the reflection on the inside of her silver spoon. The dining room sprawled, upside down and concave, around her own deformed reflection, and she was unable to make out the faces of her jury.

The baked Alaska was wheeled in ceremoniously from across the dining room. The waiter placed it atop a cake stand between the Marches, and with a flourish set the dessert on fire. Mrs. March watched it burn under a psychedelic blue flame, its creamy meringue spirals like white roses withering in a drought.

She drank deeply from her wineglass. She hated George for lying to her, hated herself for always being so quick to believe that he had good intentions. From now on, she vowed, she would give *herself* the benefit of the doubt. She drank again, tipping the glass as she looked up at the ornate crown molding on the ceiling. She deserved to take herself more seriously, to value herself. After all, when had *she* ever betrayed herself? As she refilled her glass, not waiting for her server, a warm gush of tenderness for herself erupted within her. Her poor beautiful self, always fighting to make everything work. From now on, she pledged with an air of triumph, her attitude was going to change.

XII

All her resolutions faded in the cold, pragmatic light of morning. She was especially disheartened by the sight of another cockroach. In the middle of the night, unable to hold it in any longer after all the wine she'd downed at dinner, a reluctant Mrs. March slipped into the bathroom. As soon as she turned on the light, her eyes darted toward a black spot in the middle of the white floor. Antennae swaying, a fat little body crawled forward. She screamed, calling for George, who wasn't in bed, and smashed her slipper down again and again upon the insect, leaving a black jelly-like stain on the marble. She used toilet tissue to scoop its remains into the toilet bowl and spent more time than probably necessary scrubbing the sole of her slipper and the tile. "Out, damned spot," she said out loud. A fluttering laugh escaped her lips, surprising her.

The next morning she pounced into the bathroom, brandishing a slipper. She caught her wild-eyed, disheveled reflection in the mirror and felt sorry for herself. The idea of a uniformed exterminator walking through the lobby and eliciting questions from the doorman terrified her. She weighed her options at breakfast with George. Both sat in silence, George reading the newspaper, Mrs. March stirring her tea. She stared at the centerpiece as George's teeth crunched into his toast, crumbs dropping on the paper like loud raindrops. Meanwhile, the grandfather clock ticked, ever faithful, in the foyer.

Amidst the ticking, George's chewing, and the crumbs scattering, it dawned on Mrs. March, in a flurry of inspiration, that she would head to the museum today. She had studied art history (a degree her father had deemed "absolutely pointless"—probably picturing his daughter sketching her classmates' braided hair all day and filing her nails as she awaited a potential husband), in a New England college so bucolic, so engulfed by red and mustard-colored foliage and detached from the outside world, that she had felt she was in a painting herself. She had luxuriated in the concept of art— the idea of it, yes—but was intimidated by how it seemed to encompass everything, from medieval iconography to Kandinsky's paintings to avant-garde operas and books and baroque architecture. She even shared a cinema course her senior year with the bohemian students from the drama department, who smoked in class and walked out with an air of casual indifference when told to put their cigarettes out. She had been studious and quiet, an obedient student who received satisfactory but never stellar grades. She was most comfortable as an observer, an awed witness to the spirited debates about what constituted art, about its true value.

"Art is intention," her favorite professor had said once. "Art has to move you. In any way—positive or negative. Appreciating art is really just about understanding what the piece set out to do. You don't necessarily want to hang it in your living room."

Over the years Mrs. March repeated these words as if they were her own at various charity dinners, publication parties, and awards ceremonies. She never stopped to interpret the professor's message, and would never admit, even to herself, that she couldn't. Still, she liked the idea of possessing this knowledge, this small intellectual advantage over others. And she quite enjoyed visiting museums. She tingled with the possibility as she prowled the cold, quiet halls that someone she knew might find her there, appreciating it all.

She was going to go today, she decided, and all her troubles would disappear. Smiling, she sipped her tea.

◆

IT WAS COLD but the sun was shining brighter than it had in a long time, and in a bout of optimism she decided to walk, leaving behind her umbrella, which she often carried with her as a precaution. If it began to snow, she could flag a cab, although it always made her nervous to hail one for such a short trip.

The morning air was chilled, rouging cheeks and running noses. Mrs. March experienced New York as if for the first time. Making her way up the street, she smiled at a discarded sofa—cotton frothing from the upholstery—sitting on the curb next to an overflowing trash can. She sauntered past a row of fragrant Christmas trees stacked against some scaffolding, and waved at the sellers huddled against them as they warmed their hands with their breath. On the other side of the street, a hot dog vendor, his face threaded with engorged veins like a horse's, manned a cart under a striped parasol, while others offered stacked pretzels kept warm under heat lamps. Mrs. March exchanged the last of her cash for a scoop of roasted chestnuts in a brown paper cone. She stuffed them into her purse, with no intention of eating them—she just liked the smell.

She passed an elderly woman in a plush fur coat pushing a toddler in a stroller. The woman had spiky white hair—short like a boy's—which impressed Mrs. March. She would never be so brazen as to reveal her age like that. Short hair only ever looked good on women with thin frames, anyway, and at the rate she was going, Mrs. March very much doubted she would be a skinny grandmother.

Her heart swelled with undeserved pride as she approached the majestic building with its grand Beaux-Arts façade. Red banners hung between Greek columns in official pronouncement, which gave her a sense of importance but also a feeling of fraudulence, of attempting to belong where she didn't.

At this time of day, the museum was almost empty, except for a few tourists and chaperoned groups of schoolchildren. A larger party walked past her toward the exit, and among their clothing Mrs. March caught the blurry glimpse of a familiar tennis racket print. Alarm spurted in the dark recesses of her mind as a memory resurfaced—like the whiff of a rotting fruit forgotten in the back of the fridge—but when she turned to look back at him it wasn't him at all, it was a lady in a strawberry-patterned raincoat.

The click of her heels echoed as she made her way toward the galleries upstairs.

Here, they all needed her, these people in their portraits. Their eyes seemed to find hers no matter what corner of the gallery she was in, some craning their necks to watch her. Look at me, they all seemed to be saying. Mrs. March made her way through the endless labyrinth of corridors, each gallery crowded with eyes and hands and frowns. She passed by an oil painting of Jesus in which his spent body was being lowered from the cross onto a pile of luxurious fabrics in hues of red and blue. Such images were familiar to her, evocative of all those Sunday mornings spent in church. Her parents had always favored St. Patrick's, right down the street from their apartment. The sermons had bored her. Once, she leaned over to her mother and asked in a whisper why women couldn't be priests. "Women get pregnant," her mother whispered back.

She looked now upon the Crucifixion scene, in which Christ was looking to the heavens, eyebrows raised, lips slightly parted. The suffering painted on his features was so dramatic, so enduring—so very female, now that she thought about it.

She continued to the end of the room and turned right, stepping into the gallery that she knew displayed, in its baroque gilded frame, Vermeer's less popular counterpart to *Girl with a Pearl Earring*. Cocking her head to one side, Mrs. March took in the portrait. The girl, wrapped in a shimmering, silky shawl, was so ugly, her facial anatomy so odd—ample forehead, wide-spaced eyes, barely-there eyebrows—that if she weren't smiling, she would be terrifying. There was something unsettling about that grin, too. Like she knew some gruesome fate awaited you, and was enjoying the vision.

"Hello, Kiki," Mrs. March said.

She had first encountered the girl on a visit with her parents when she was nearing puberty. Upon first glance, she had assumed the girl was slow, or, as shouted by cruel children in the schoolyard, retarded. The eyes did not align properly, and there was something dim-witted about her vacant expression. Mrs. March had hidden behind her father when she'd first seen the painting; when she peeked out from the folds of his jacket, she swore the girl was smirking at her.

Mrs. March saw the similarities between the two of them immediately: their pale complexions, plain looks, and yes, that stupid little half-smile. There were enough unflattering photographs of her at home to reinforce the connection.

That night, in the dark of her bedroom, she awoke to the

sounds of thick, phlegmy breathing. It was the girl from the portrait; somehow they had brought her home with them. Panic seized her at first, but after a few evenings, the familiarity of the breathing almost comforted her, and she found herself talking to the girl.

Soon, Mrs. March was interacting with her on a daily basis: playing with her and taking baths with her and dreaming about her too. The girl's face merged irrevocably with her own, and the girl was no longer the girl from the portrait, but her twin, whom she named Kiki. Her parents, to whom Mrs. March had introduced Kiki over an awkward dinner, brushed it off as a phase, until Kiki began showing up at every meal. A psychologist friend, consulted in passing so as not to arouse suspicion, theorized that Kiki was an elaborate tool for Mrs. March to convey her feelings. Kiki, like Mrs. March, didn't like pumpkin pie, for example, so Mrs. March would request them not to serve it. Kiki didn't like the cold, so the maid was asked to be quick in airing out the rooms.

Mrs. March took Kiki with her everywhere. Kiki whispered the answers in her ear during a math test. Kiki amused her while her mother looked at curtain samples at the department store. She would call her school friends on the telephone and tell them her cousin Kiki was visiting and would put her on the phone, speaking in a kind of infantile lisp. Once she wrote a praising letter to herself—with her left hand, so her handwriting couldn't be traced—and displayed it proudly to her friends, alleging it was from Kiki. Not long after that, one of her classmates told her she wasn't welcome in their friend group anymore because they didn't like liars. "I wasn't lying," Mrs. March replied indignantly. She knew she had been lying, of course, but she couldn't face the humiliation of confessing, and she wouldn't be able to explain why she had done such an absurd thing anyway. Mrs. March's shame upon revisiting these memories was palpable. To this day she had confided in no one about the lengths she had gone to with her fictitious friend.

She took one last, searching look at the girl, at her Kiki, who looked back at her, tight-lipped, her eyes tired, almost disappointed.

XIII

Mrs. March spent the following day busying herself about the apartment in preparation for her son's return from his school trip. She stocked the fridge with chocolate milk, string cheese, and wieners, and the pantry with toffee and nougat cookies. She arranged his stuffed animals—from tallest to shortest—on the shelf. There were no signs of cockroaches, and the back of her ear was soft again, the scab having sloughed off. One could describe her current mood as, for lack of a more exciting word, content.

As she fluffed up the pillows on Jonathan's bed, she began to sing, "I'm nesting, nesting, nesting," quietly to herself. She hadn't done that since she had been pregnant with Jonathan, and making the connection untethered a succession of unpleasant memories. Memories of the baby shower, for which she had decorated her living room with paper storks and blue streamers. She had invited Mary Anne, her college roommate, hoping she might feel envious of Mrs. March for landing George (*George March is the most attractive man on campus*), and Jill, a dull acquaintance who had followed Mrs. March around in high school until it was just assumed that they were friends. Two of George's cousins were also present, as was a former student of his, who seemed almost bitter to be there. Nobody from Mrs. March's own family could make it.

In a particularly nasty bout of nausea, Mrs. March had

retired to the guest bathroom, and between fits of retching, she overheard one of the women say to the rest, "You all know that she's not ready for a baby. She can barely take care of herself." Another said, "And with someone who's already *had* one with somebody *else*? I could *never*. He's not going to care about this pregnancy, *or* about this baby—he's already gone through it all before! I mean why bother." As Mrs. Marsh flushed the toilet, she swore she could hear laughter.

Wiping her mouth, she returned to the living room wearing a big smile, her voice quavering with overstated euphoria as she announced, "I'm back!" She played a few demeaning games— including "Guess the Mother's Measurements," at the gleeful request of her guests, who gripped the yarn and scissors with such relish that their knuckles paled—then she excused herself, claiming further nausea, and sent everybody home. Alone, she stood in silence in the baby's room, staring up at the hook nailed to the ceiling for the mobile, which she had never gotten around to hanging. Later she gathered up the leftover food and decorations, as well as the baby gifts, in a big black trash bag, and threw everything out.

Then came the birth, a ghastly affair. Despite her attempts to block it out, she could still recall the doctor prying apart her sweaty legs, which she fought, sloppily, to clamp shut in her epidural haze in an effort to hide her vagina from the glaring spotlight. When a nurse folded and cleared away an absorbent pad from underneath her—a telltale sign of defecation—she dissolved into tearless sobs. The medical team assumed it was a hormonal reaction, but the abject humiliation of being prodded and exposed for hours on end was agonizing. All they wanted was the baby, she realized. Nobody cared what happened to her.

In the drugged lethargy the doctors called "recovery," she woke up alone in her hospital bed to find her father sitting at her bedside reading the newspaper, which was rather unexpected seeing as how he had been dead for two years at that point. "Papa," she had called to him, over and over again. Not once did he look up.

After the birth, her hair fell out in clumps. Her body secreted a thick discharge tinged with blood. Sanitary napkins were no match for the meaty threads, and the adult diapers from the box she hid behind the guest towels crinkled noisily whenever she moved. Her stitches were slow to heal, causing her discomfort long after the stipulated four weeks of recovery. But that wasn't the worst part. The very act of being pregnant had been special. People—friends, family, strangers on the street in stores and in restaurants—had smiled at her, had loved her, had seen her. Once the baby arrived and her bump receded, saleswomen no longer approached her excitedly with questions about her due date, nobody volunteered to help her carry groceries home, nobody offered her their cab.

At first people would drop by for visits with the baby, or neighbors would ask after him in the elevator, but by the time her son was walking, their interest faded, and a silent mist of indifference settled over her once again. She blamed her child for this, for their sudden lack of attentiveness, for the wretched changes in her body, for the rapid, mutual loss of interest between her and George. She was angry at her offspring, but her guilt made her simultaneously afraid for him, for his veined, milky fragility. Out of compulsion she would check to ensure that he was breathing, up to thirty or forty times a day, once rushing back to the apartment in the middle of a performance of *Swan Lake*, humming the score as she ran through a dark Central Park, alarming the vagrants—and the nanny when she burst into the nursery, chest heaving.

She would hover over the crib, sometimes well into the night—in her unwashed nightgown, her hair hanging in long greasy threads—unmoving, observing the rise and fall of Jonathan's belly, each time convincing herself she'd imagined it, and waiting to see if it would move again. It was after a few unsettling late-night encounters with this unresponsive, ghost-like Mrs. March that George stepped in and hired the baby nurse full time. Mrs. March still felt compelled to check on the baby, but the urge was less strong now that he was under the care of a woman much more qualified than her.

It struck her, now, as she refolded a blanket on Jonathan's bed, how long it had been since she had checked in on him like that. He had never been a needy boy; he slept well through the night, had few nightmares, harbored no fear of monsters under the bed or in the closet—and she supposed she had adjusted to his self-reliance. A sharp sliver of self-reproach accompanied this observation: What if she hadn't cared enough for him? Shouldn't she be picking him up from his school trip herself, rather than having him ride with Mr. and Mrs. Miller, the parents of a classmate who lived just a few floors up from the Marches? But how could she manage that? Mrs. March didn't know how to drive, and George was at a book signing in midtown.

The Millers were fine people, she supposed, although she didn't like the way Sheila Miller sometimes regarded her with a sort of pitying smile, or how Sheila had cut her hair so short, exposing the naked nape of her neck, or how the Millers were always expressing physical affection with each other, hold-ing hands or massaging the other's shoulders, as if they just couldn't restrain themselves. Perhaps they were pretending at passion, Mrs. March had fantasized. Or, she theorized, an electric thrill running up her spine, he is hiding his homosexuality and she cries every night, wishing he would touch her in the privacy of their bedroom like he does in public.

As it turned out, Sheila Miller arrived without her husband when she knocked on apartment 606. In tailored jeans tucked into shiny, colorful snow boots—both items age inappropriate in Mrs. March's eyes—Sheila seemed to be trying too hard to be a cool, modern mom. What rankled Mrs. March most was the ire-inspiring truth that Sheila managed to pull it off with ease. Indeed Sheila was the kind of mother her son would brag about because she could unpeel an orange in a single coil. The kind of mother who was also a friend. Mrs. March's own mother had often reminded her as a child, "I'm not your friend, nor do I care to be. I am your *mother*." Mrs. March knew never to come to her mother with any issue that could be more appropriately relayed to a friend instead.

When Mrs. March opened her door to let her in, Sheila beamed, locking eyes as she always did, prompting Mrs. March to look at the floor. Behind Sheila, in walked Jonathan. Jonathan—with his upturned nose and eyes shadowed by dark circles, giving the boy a melancholy appearance and leading George, in a pretentious fit of literary whimsy, to nickname him "Poe." Jonathan was quiet, unusually so, for a boy his age, but he did manage to exhibit a base rowdiness in the company of a friend. With a partner in tow he tended to make sounds he never made otherwise—chortling and whooping and braying—noises that echoed through the apartment like the hauntings of rabid ghosts.

Mrs. March bent down to hug him, smiling so widely that

her face felt like it would split apart, and began speaking to him in a singsongy voice, one she did not use with him in private. Jonathan's hair smelled of the cold outside and slightly of smoke, like a bonfire. He remained quiet, nodding at her high-pitched questioning ("Did you have a good time? Was it lovely there? Was it all snowy?"), while fidgeting with a Rubik's cube that, Sheila explained, her son had gifted to Jonathan. Meanwhile, said son, Alec, hovered in the hallway outside the door, shaking his head when Mrs. March offered him some chocolate milk.

"I think they're still full from all the sweets and French fries they've been eating for the past few days," Sheila said, her tone mock-chiding. She winked at Mrs. March, who wasn't sure how she was expected to react.

"Well, thank you so very much for bringing him, Sheila," said Mrs. March. "Would you care for anything? Tea? Water?"

"No, thank you. We'll just get out of your hair so you can spend the rest of the day with your boy."

"Very well," said Mrs. March, relieved she wouldn't have to make further conversation. "If you need anything at all, let me know."

"Okay then, bye! Say bye-bye, Alec."

But Alec was already walking toward the elevator. Sheila shrugged at Mrs. March—*boys!*—and walked after him. Mrs. March closed the door. When she turned around, Jonathan had disappeared. She assumed he had run off to his room, eager to greet his familiar surroundings and favorite toys, but when she made her way through the hallway she realized he was in the kitchen, talking to Martha in excited whispers. "I ate the worm," he was saying. "They dared me and I ate it."

Embarrassed to interrupt them, Mrs. March walked on.

Throughout her life, Mrs. March, née Kirby, had lived in a staffed home. The parade of maids, cooks, and nannies that had trudged through her childhood had been long and mostly unmemorable—except for one.

Alma was their last live-in maid. Specifically, she lived in a cramped, windowless room off the kitchen. Initially meant as the laundry, Mrs. Kirby had renovated it to fit a narrow shower and a wall-mounted sink.

Alma was pudgy and olive-skinned. She had long black hair, braided and thick as a ship rope, which she always kept tucked out of sight, because Mrs. March's mother found splendorous loose manes a personal affront. She talked in a sweet, gushing voice, seemingly in singsong, her diction scattered with Mexican terms. Mrs. March, who was about ten at the time, had never met such a humble, nothing-to-look-at woman so willing to laugh, unabashed, at her own faults—nay, to embrace them. "You really eat a lot," she had told Alma once, watching her gulp down samosas on the kitchen high table.

"Ay, I know! That's why I'm so roly-poly!" Alma had replied, squeezing a roll of tummy fat between her fingers. The almost sensual, shameless way she would indulge in food—like it was a carnal part of her, of her body—had made an impression on young Mrs. March, who had grown up surrounded by women on permanent hunger strikes. Her older sister Lisa, who had always been a chubby child, came back from college having shed half her body, accustomed to a diet of boiled potatoes and obsessed with jogging. Mrs. March had witnessed all of her mother's girlfriends waning throughout the years as they offered excuses for refusing a meal ("I had such a big breakfast"; "I'm just never hungry at this hour, but you should see me at dinner"; "I've eaten so much over the holidays!"). Their diets weighed heavily on them, like eternal penances. Her own mother merely pecked at her food, as if afraid it might fight back. She had been so malnourished when pregnant with Mrs. March that she had given birth prematurely. Loose among the pages of the family photo album, there was a photograph of Mrs. March inside the incubator: a tiny pink ball, the plastic hospital tag around her wrist comically huge. She did not recognize herself in that shriveled body, in those bulging, swollen eyes. She had often wondered whether that baby was her parents' real daughter, who had died inside that incubator. Whether she herself had never been related to them at all, but was actually the substitute baby her parents had been compelled to acquire.

There were earlier photographs in the album of her pregnant mother, looking skinny and wan, cigarette to her thin lips, her baby bump barely discernible under her summer dress; and some of her afterwards, holding her newborn daughter, her elbow jutting out of her arm like a twig protruding from a tree.

All of Alma was round and fat, except for her spindly, brown-jointed fingers, which ended in slender, purple-hued nails. Mrs. March would follow her around the house, talking to her as Alma cleaned the apartment. She would often rush through her own dinner in the dining room so she could join Alma as she had hers in the kitchen. Alma would tell her stories: memories from her childhood and old Mexican folktales. She taught Mrs. March how to peel the rim off the mortadella before eating it, and how to place the knives blade-down in the dishwasher for safety.

Alma proved good company during breakfast, when Mrs. March would otherwise eat by herself at the massive dining room table, because her sister was away at college, her father had left for work, and her mother took her cottage cheese and grapefruit in bed. Alma would ask her questions (how was school, did she have many friends, who was her favorite teacher, were any of the other girls ever mean to her), and seemed genuinely interested in the answers.

Mrs. March was not at all interested in any part of Alma's life that excluded her, like the children she had left behind in Mexico, who received the majority of her wages. Alma had a photograph of them pinned to the wall above her bed. Mrs. March had studied it many times, unable to discern the children's genders because of their bowl-shaped haircuts and oversized T-shirts. Even though Alma always told her she was "my special *chica*," Mrs. March could not bear the prospect of sharing her. One day she ripped up the photograph of the children, who grinned up at her, toothless, as she shredded them apart.

When Alma walked in on Mrs. March, the remains of the photograph at her feet, she had wept, passionately and with her face in her hands, rocking back and forth. Mrs. March tiptoed toward the door, embarrassed by such an extravagant display of emotion—unlike any behavior she had ever seen at home— and left the room without a word.

The following morning at breakfast, Alma was quiet and withdrawn. Mrs. March asked her several times why she wasn't talking, softly at first, then almost violently, yelling at Alma over her cereal. Alma just smiled weakly.

Eventually, the weeks passed, and all seemed forgotten. Mrs. March went back to sitting on one of the high stools around the kitchen table, listening to Alma talk over the sounds of the radio and the sizzling frying pan. She'd run to Alma at night during thunderstorms and fall asleep in Alma's damp, mung bean smell. The following morning she would awaken in her own bed, not remembering being carried there, and she would hate that Alma's life had gone on without her as she slept.

It was more or less around this time that young Mrs. March started getting physical with Alma, pinching and scratching and eventually, at the height of it, biting her. Very softly at first, with her gums, then viciously, leaving wet, inflamed teeth marks on Alma's skin. Alma barely ever complained; she would silently brush Mrs. March away or hold her by the shoulders until she settled down.

When Mrs. March's mother saw one of the crescent-shaped dents on Alma's neck, she moved to put an immediate end to it. Mrs. March was taken to a child psychologist—under such secrecy, not even she knew where she was going—who revealed that she was suffering from "a lack of parental attention," and also from "a shortage of emotional tools to constrain her excessive imagination." Her mother listened grimly to these diagnoses. She never took her daughter back to therapy and instead decided to fire Alma. It was just much simpler that way.

Mrs. March had worked hard to forget it all. It was mortifying, to think of herself as such a *needy* child, so spoiled and malicious, that she now wondered whether she had imagined the whole thing. After all, she was such a docile adult.

After Alma was let go, Mrs. March never once asked after

her. She knew better. Her parents' quiet, unsentimental acceptance of her behavior filled her with shame, and she pointedly ignored the rest of the maids from then on. None of them ever lived with the family in the apartment again, and over the years the sad, strange little bedroom off the kitchen turned into a pantry. Over time, Mrs. March learned to appreciate the quiet solitude of her breakfasts.

When Mr. and Mrs. March moved into their Upper East Side apartment, Mrs. March had called Martha at the behest of her sister Lisa, who had employed Martha for many years, and was sorry to part with her upon moving to Maryland to take care of her dying mother-in-law. Lisa now lived on a quaint street in Bethesda, in a red-brick house with dark green shutters. The kind of place where residents found drowned wildlife under their pool tarps, where children stunned ants on the sidewalks until they were called in to dinner at dusk.

Not long after Lisa's mother-in-law died, their own mother, Mrs. Kirby, had started displaying symptoms of senility. She lived alone in their old Manhattan apartment, as their father had died some years earlier. A concerned maid began finding religious cards in the fridge, and a vast collection of subway tokens and loose Russian dolls stockpiled in Mrs. Kirby's underwear drawer. Mrs. Kirby then began refusing the help entry to the apartment, claiming not to know them. Lisa, evidently finding a calling in caring for the elderly, decided to fly her out to Bethesda. Mrs. Kirby was now living out the rest of her days in a residence that boasted a topiary garden and a patio. All expenses were shared by her two daughters. It was a relief for Mrs. March that her sister had taken charge of the situation. Her mother's disease made her uncomfortable. She had been out to see her at the home a few times, and hated the visits. She detested the smell of lemon air freshener, the underlying smell of decay, and the way the old residents clung to her whenever they saw her. Lisa marched through the corridors as if she felt right at home, seemingly oblivious to the attempts at interaction from dementia-riddled strangers who would pull at her cardigan. Mrs. March had resolved, then, not to feel bad about her sister bearing the brunt of their mother's caretaking. She seemed content enough with the situation, and plus, she and her husband traveled a lot (excessively, in Mrs. March's opinion), and so it wasn't like she was seeing their mother all that often either.

Lisa had tried to get Martha to move to Maryland with them; after all, she had reasoned, Martha was unmarried and childless, so what could possibly be rooting her down? But that arrangement was apparently no good for Martha, who wished to stay in New York, for whatever reason they weren't terribly concerned to understand.

When Mrs. March first interviewed Martha, she had been immediately intimidated by her but had concluded that this was the appropriate feeling to have about one's housekeeper; it must mean she was strict and in control and, overall, ferociously good at her job. And Martha entered their home and their lives just like that: firm, straightforward Martha, with her ample shoulders and her gray-streaked bun and her thick, uncut fingernails. Mrs. March was thankful for her; thankful for all the ways in which she was different from Alma, and thankful for everything that had brought Martha here, to her apartment, to her kitchen, where she was now whispering to Jonathan, whispering all sorts of things Mrs. March wasn't privy to.

XV

After waking up to another cockroach contemplating her from the bedroom wall, Mrs. March at last committed to calling the exterminator. She had inquired about the possibility of vermin throughout the building in whispers to the doorman, but he had dismissed the idea, suggesting to Mrs. March a more thorough attempt at regular cleaning. She had responded with a nervous laugh, mortified that he regarded her as unclean, as unworthy of residence in the high-end apartment building. She did not bring up the subject again.

However, upon finding the voyeuristic specimen on her bedroom wall, its shoe-polish black carapace taut over the ridges of its thorax, like an old man's veined, leathery hands, she resolved to put a stop to the problem once and for all. She could not risk anyone catching wind of the infestation—an invasion so foul it was portrayed in films and books as a sure sign of poverty and sloth. Cockroaches thrived in the grimy, decrepit lodgings of junkies, not in tastefully decorated apartments or in the understated but spotless quarters of a working professional. She had never encountered roaches in her parents' apartment, or in George's old place—the one he'd been renting near campus when they first met. Afraid to be judged by her, Mrs. March had avoided telling Martha about the insects—but she shook every time she pictured Martha chancing upon one in the bathroom.

The morning after calling the service, she welcomed the exterminator into her home. He was a kind man of ruddy complexion, dressed in a dark green jumpsuit and heavy boots. He headed straightaway to the Marches' master bath, taking care not to topple anything with his canister of insecticide. He knelt on the floor by the toilet, checked every corner, drain, and crack, and assured her that the roaches did not live in her apartment. "I don't see any . . . and I see no sign of any droppings. Maybe a couple found their way into your bathroom through the pipes?" he said as he examined a tiny crack in the baseboard, "maybe from outside, maybe from another neighbor"—Mrs. March's heart leapt at this particular possibility— "but we're not dealing with a plague here," the exterminator continued, "so here's what we'll do. I'm gonna apply the poison in the bathroom, just a little bit in every corner, and over the next couple of days you might see some dead ones—don't worry about it—and after a few weeks they'll stop appearing altogether." He explained all this while on one knee, gesticulating like a commander explaining a war stratagem to his troops.

The man smeared the poison, a brown, syrupy gel, into every nook, while Mrs. March sipped tea from a mug that said *Today could be a wonderful day!* The mug, old and chipped, was part of a surprise breakfast basket her sister had sent over for her birthday. She would not have bought the mug herself; it seemed too menacingly sanguine for her taste. The basket was a beautiful rattan picnic hamper, filled with juicy, swollen red raspberries and purple grapes, a stoppered glass bottle of freshly squeezed orange juice, sugar-crusted scones, and a small bouquet of daisies. Her sister enjoyed a reputation for her meticulousness with presents. She always managed to gift the most lovely things. It was annoying, really. It almost felt like a competition. Mrs. March probably still had the basket somewhere—probably buried in the linen closet. She could find it, fill it with flowers, maybe put it on a shelf, or on top of the fridge in the kitchen. Why, she could even renovate the entire kitchen accordingly, transforming it into a rustic dream of wicker-backed chairs, red gingham tablecloths, and dried flowers in old tin watering cans or hanging upside down from wooden ceiling beams.

The exterminator looked up from the bathroom floor. "That should kill 'em dead. Mind if I wash this stuff off my hands?"

When Mrs. March saw him off, she strolled, in as casual a manner as she could manage, into the kitchen to toss the tainted hand towel into the trash and ask Martha to bread the chicken cutlets for lunch. She had resolved to tell Martha, only if prodded, that the exterminator's visit was merely preventative as she'd caught wind of an infestation in the building next door, but Martha only nodded her head at the petition for chicken cutlets, and went right on peeling potatoes.

◆

AFTER LUNCH, Mrs. March sat filing her nails in the living room, the television on in the background to keep her company in an otherwise indifferent household—Jonathan was home from school in his bedroom and George was showering. Martha, meanwhile, puttered about George's study, taking advantage of his rare absence to swoop in and tidy up.

"The body of Sylvia Gibbler, missing since November eighteenth, has been found. The cause of death remains unknown, pending an official autopsy."

Mrs. March looked up from her mottled nails to the television screen, which displayed the familiar black-and-white photograph of Sylvia, smiling at her just as brightly as she had done from the news clipping in George's notebook.

"Authorities are questioning friends, neighbors, and the patrons of this quaint gift shop, where Gibbler worked until her disappearance." The camera panned, rather dramatically, Mrs. March thought, across the purple storefront, showcasing a haphazard window display with no apparent color palette, a hodgepodge of old teapots and cookie canisters, gaudy tinsel hanging from the ceiling. Over the purple doorway gold-painted script read *The Hope Chest. "This tight-knit community is in mourning, having lost all hope of ever seeing Sylvia alive again,"* said the news reporter. *"Back to you in the studio, Linda."*

Mrs. March turned off the television, unease wriggling through her belly like a handful of maggots. She headed toward George's study, with the intention of sneaking another look at the newspaper clipping hidden in his notebook while he was in the shower. Instead, she found him pacing from the study to the bedroom as he packed a small leather suitcase laid open on the bed.

"George? What are you doing?"

"I'm packing. For Gentry."

"You're leaving *today?*"

"Yes." He looked at her, somewhat surprised. "Did you forget, honey? We talked about this."

"We did? Are you sure you said today?"

She had indeed forgotten about his hunting trip with his editor. Edgar owned a cabin somewhere near Augusta, Maine, in an unassuming little town called Gentry. She had never been there herself (she'd never been tempted to visit, nor had she ever been invited), but she had some notion of it from photos George had shared with her throughout the years. Mrs. March was almost more attuned to the hunting seasons than to her own menstrual cycle.

She watched George pack. "Must Edgar be there?"

"Well, it would be odd to be there without him. It's his cabin after all."

She looked down at her hands and spied a hangnail. She began to pick at it. "It's just that I feel like he's always picking on me. He makes me . . . uncomfortable sometimes."

"Nonsense! Edgar loves you. In fact, he finds you absolutely adorable. He could eat you up, he's said on more than one occasion."

The memory of a smug Edgar, his yellowed teeth biting into the flesh-colored foie gras, prompted a surge of bile in her throat. "I just don't know why you spend so much time with someone who enjoys killing. It's a cruel sport."

"I know, I know how you feel, and I get it. I do. It can seem savage and unnecessary—the ultimate superiority complex."

"So why do you do it?"

George peered at her over his glasses as he bent over the suitcase, tartan scarf in hand. "It's exhilarating. There's something primal about it, *instinctual* even, despite it being watered down since the Bronze Age." He smiled. "You're so sweet to care about the animals, honey. But don't doubt for a second that they would do the same to us. Or worse."

Mrs. March fleetingly envisioned a moose on its hind legs holding a rifle, its lifeless human trophy propped up for a photograph. An illustration she'd seen once in one of Jonathan's comic books, perhaps.

"Don't worry yourself," said George as he zipped up the suitcase. "It's all regulated anyway. Too regulated if you ask me. It's probably less of a hassle to hunt humans nowadays." He chuckled and approached Mrs. March. "Hold down the fort for me?"

He kissed her on the forehead and headed for the front door, suitcase in tow. She watched him enter Jonathan's bedroom for a quick, hair-ruffling goodbye, then saw him out. Afterwards she remained standing behind the closed door, like a dog with no capacity for understanding that its master is gone. She placed her fingers delicately on the door, when they were met by a sharp pulse-like knock that made her jump. Expecting an absentminded George returning for a forgotten winter hat, she turned the key, which they always left in the lock (her brother-in-law had once told her it was harder to break into a house from the outside if the key was in the lock), and opened the door to Sheila Miller.

They stared at each other with a shared malaise before Sheila said, "Hey there. We were just wondering if Jonathan could come up for a sleepover?"

Sheila was, for once, avoiding Mrs. March's gaze. She was scratching at her wrist and the skin above her neckline, Mrs. March noticed, was flushed. Aware of the sound of Jonathan's bedroom door opening down the hall, Mrs. March said: "Oh. Well, I don't know—"

"Alec is begging me, and they do seem to have bonded quite a bit during the school trip."

Jonathan appeared in the foyer, head cocked to one side.

"Hey, Jonathan," said Sheila, then, to Mrs. March, "Sorry for barging in on you like this, without even calling first. I'm such a mess!" She rolled her eyes and smiled. "So what do you say? Can Jonathan come up?"

A silent Jonathan walked over to Sheila and stood beside her as he looked up at Mrs. March with his dark, sunken eyes.

"But—it's a school night."

"Oh, I'm sure it'll be all right," said Sheila, putting her hands on Jonathan's shoulders.

"You must have your hands full already," said Mrs. March, uneasily. "Are you sure it's not too much trouble?"

"No trouble at all!" said Sheila.

The speed and volume of her response was such that Mrs. March had no choice but to hand Jonathan over to Sheila, along with his school bag, a toothbrush, a fresh shirt, and clean underwear. As he left, holding Sheila's hand, Mrs. March watched the school badge on his bag as it grew smaller, the school's owl mascot (had it not always been a badger?) staring back at her, in their walk down the hall and into the elevator.

XVI

That evening, Mrs. March was alone in the apartment. Martha had asked to leave early for some kind of appointment— she hadn't been paying much attention, instead luxuriating in the afterglow of her magnanimity in granting Martha her request. "Oh please, don't worry about me," she had said, waving her hand, "I'm dining alone tonight, so just prepare a light meal for me and leave it in the kitchen. I'll warm it up myself and leave the plates in the sink for you."

Mrs. March had taken an early bath, careful to use only small portions of the expensive bath salts, which had crumbled from disuse in their respective stoppered jars since she had bought them in Paris twelve years ago.

All afternoon she experienced a lingering, unpleasant sensation. Something about Sheila's demeanor, the vacant, mechanical way she had put her hands on Jonathan's shoulders, gnawed at Mrs. March, and now in the dark of evening, alone, she was finding it hard to shake off. Tying the belt of her terrycloth bathrobe so tightly her stomach ached, she left her bedroom with apprehension, stepping into the hallway gingerly as if it might, at the touch of her slipper, turn into water that would drown her, turning back into parquet flooring once she sank below the surface so that she might never be found.

She walked the length of the hallway, flicking on the overhead lights as she made her way into the living room. She looked carefully about the space, searching for strange men's shoes poking out from under furniture, under drapes. She spotted a bulge behind one of the curtains. She walked over to it, hand outstretched, wondering whose face awaited her on the other side of the fabric, then slapped away her own wrist. The Christmas tree lights blinked in time to the ticking of the grandfather clock in the foyer, bulbs flicking yellow, dark, yellow. Mrs. March clicked her tongue to the rhythm, then envisioned the sound masking a stranger's approaching steps, and turned quickly to face the room. Something in her chest tightened. She unplugged the lights.

Lowering her body onto the sofa in a huff, she tutted to herself in an attempt to feign indifference should anyone be watching, and turned on the television, flipping the channels at a dizzying rate in an attempt to find something, anything, pleasant being shown to bolster her false calm. Images sped before her—a strawberry-flavored soft drink, a bright yellow cartoon duck, a backfiring police car, a black-and-white scream, a dramatic embrace. She continued changing stations, her thumbnail sinking into the soft rubber button of the remote, until:

"The entire Northeast is grieving the loss of Sylvia Gibbler, whose body was discovered after weeks of frenzied searching by police and civilian volunteers."

Mrs. March blinked, willing herself to move on to a different channel. The reporter on the screen looked out from the television, a grave aspect to her face. She stood in a burgundy tweed overcoat and matching burgundy lipstick against a backdrop of snowy streets, the occasional car moving behind her, and was gripping the microphone so tightly that it seemed like her hand had been carved from it. She continued, *"Her body was found by two unsuspecting hunters, in the backwoods of Gentry, Maine—"*

Mrs. March's throat tightened. Her eyes blurred, black spots like inkblots scattering across her vision. A thousand different voices rang inside her skull. A coincidence, just a coincidence, cried one. But what if it isn't, said another. After all, how many coincidences can one woman overlook? Isn't that how murderers were eventually caught, when one observant soul put all the disparate pieces together?

The reporter explained how the victim, an orphan, had been living with her grandmother for the past few years. But no, Mrs. March told herself, George wouldn't return to the crime scene if he were guilty. His indifference to the swarming nest of police and news reporters surely proved his innocence. Her relief was short-lived as she wondered if he had made the trip to destroy evidence now that the body had been found— a clumsy, amateur mistake that could potentially lead to his arrest. And was Edgar in on it? Unclear. George had his own set of keys to Edgar's cabin. He kept them in a bowl in his study. He could come and go without Edgar even knowing.

"The initial autopsy report confirms she was murdered a little less than a month ago, which coincides with the date she disappeared—"

Hadn't George been on another hunting trip about a month ago? He arrived home, making gobbling noises as he walked in, with a wild turkey for their Thanksgiving dinner. The memory had stayed with her because she'd had no clue what to do with the limp mass of feathers, the hanging red wattle, so Martha had taken it to her brother, a butcher in Brooklyn, to deplume and dress it.

Mrs. March swallowed, her pulse so quick and hard she could almost see it thrusting through her wrists.

"—further tests are needed to determine the cause of death, but coroners believe the victim was strangled," continued the reporter

in a flat tone, as if reporting this tragedy with any sense of urgency was somehow gauche. The only trace of feeling lingered in her eyebrows, which arched when she described the particularly gruesome details. *"The body shows signs of rape"*— she paused ever so slightly—*"and blunt force trauma."*

Mrs. March unspooled memories in a panic, tracing every mundane conversation with neighbors in an attempt to recall which of them were aware of George's hunting trips to Gentry. She pictured Sheila upstairs, watching the news, calling to her husband, who would then call the police.

". . . hands bound behind her with a cord . . . scratches indicate a struggle . . ."

George's nickname as a teacher had been "Beauty and the Beast," a moniker acquired decades prior in his own college days. He was generally loved among the students and staff— leather-bound classics and butter cookies and the occasional engraved fountain pen often bestowed on him by way of his mail slot in the teachers' lounge. He was praised for his sense of theatricality, once famously re-creating the Yorkshire moors by dumping bucketloads of moss and purple heath shrubs onto the lecture hall steps while teaching the Brontës. But his wrath was just as dramatic—his admonishments sometimes interrupting the physics department next door—and he had a penchant for dispensing disproportionate punishments for the most minor of offenses (the story of his suspension of his prize student for an honest failure to cite a source stoked fear in the hearts of each incoming class of freshmen).

". . . body partially hidden by snow, and it was only thanks to a trusty hunting dog . . ."

There were casual anecdotes over the years, featuring moon-eyed coeds' requests for "extra credit" or "one-on-one tutoring," but such tales were played for laughs with George's colleagues. Unlike the other professors, he seemed to have kept his trousers on. At least, there had been no rumors to the effect. And she never had reason to suspect. Nor had she cause to fear him either; in fact, over the years he had turned into a quieter, more sensitive intellectual. He continued to enjoy time with his friends—the long lunches, the occasional tennis match, the hunting trips with Edgar and the Scotch and cigars at his gentlemen's club—none of it signs of a deeper corruption. And whenever she had needed to reach him, whether at the club or a restaurant—she could always find him.

Surely, if he were some sort of deviant predator, there would have been signs or stories. Rumors. Had his ex-wife witnessed his transformation into a monster, she would have spoken up, if not to warn the new Mrs. March, then at least to protect their daughter Paula from his violent, perverted grip.

This is all silly, she told herself. Of course George had nothing to do with the poor girl's murder. She fumbled with the remote and the television switched off with a dull *clink*, the screen dissolving into a small white circle before blacking out and revealing Mrs. March's reflection as she sat, mouth agape, on the couch.

"No," she said simply, "no," and rose from the couch, securing her robe tightly once again, as if doing so might protect her. She went to the kitchen, stopping to wash her hands in the guest bathroom. As she dried them, wrinkling her nose at the ever-present, medicinal smell of pine, she heard the neighbors' television through the wall. Recognizing the reporter's monotone, she hurried out—the webbing between her fingers still sudsy—slamming the door behind her.

She attempted to warm up a small portion of the pan-fried

sole Martha had left under tinfoil on the kitchen counter, battling the microwave, which inexplicably kept switching off. Whatever residual satisfaction remained from Mrs. March's benevolent early dismissal of Martha was now replaced with annoyance.

Martha had set the dining room table as she always did—with the linens and silver and Mrs. March's beloved black olive bread cut into neat slices. Mrs. March lit the candles—the lighting felt off without them—and played Chopin's nocturnes on the turntable, because that was the record they played during dinner and flipping through George's intimidating record collection in search of something new would take forever.

Despite the tinkling piano rippling across the empty apartment—or maybe because of it—the night seemed quieter than usual. Mrs. March brought a forkful of room-temperature fish to her mouth. From the street a young woman's drunken laughter pierced the silence, startling her. Picking up her dropped fork, she scolded herself under her breath for her jumpiness.

The figures in the portraits on the dining room wall glared down at her, as was their custom when she ate alone. One featured a middle-aged woman wearing a bonnet and a velvet choker, the other a bespectacled man in clerical garb. She returned their gaze.

Nobody spoke.

XVII

Mrs. March wondered, as she so often did, whether this might be her last meal. What had Sylvia Gibbler's last meal been? Was it something prepared for her by her captor? Had she enjoyed it? What if she had been on a diet to squeeze into a lovely little dress she had her eye on? But she would never make it to that special party now, would she? How terribly depressing.

Mrs. March blew out the candles on the table and the one she had lit on the sideboard, spraying red wax on the wall behind it. She turned off the lights and, loath to find herself alone in the darkness longer than was necessary, hurried on to the kitchen, where she left the plates in the sink, then thought better of it for fear of further vermin. As she was closing the dishwasher, contemplating whether to steep a soothing cup of chamomile tea, the wall phone in the kitchen rang, a trill so loud and jarring that Mrs. March shut the dishwasher door on her left pinkie.

Was George in trouble? she wondered, sucking on her throbbing finger. She imagined him in Edgar's cabin—hands bloody, Edgar dead on the floor. She picked up the phone with trepidation. "Hello? George?"

"Hello," a polite voice answered. It was male, but it was not George's.

"Hello . . . ?" she said, in a cautious yet cheerful tone, in case it was a close friend or someone important.

"Johanna?" the voice said.

Hot lightning struck her chest and she pressed her hand to the wall to steady herself. She could hear loud breathing, but she wasn't sure if it was her own. "Excuse me?" she said into the receiver, more flat statement than question.

"Is this Johanna?"

"Who is this?" There was fear in her voice now, and on the other end the man seemed to giggle from a distance, as if he had turned away from the phone or covered the mouthpiece to laugh.

"Don't call this number again, do you hear me?" Mrs. March said, trying to muster some semblance of authority into her voice. Before he had a chance to respond, she slammed the phone into the cradle—it made a startled little ringing sound—and pulled the cord from the wall with a violent tug. There were more phones throughout the apartment—the one in their bedroom, for starters, but she would not dare unplug it, in case anything happened to Jonathan, or George, or—

Had Sylvia Gibbler been killed near a phone? She pictured her, this woman she had never met, being strangled in an apartment much like hers, and looking at a nearby telephone, pleading with her eyes for it to help her, willing it to ring even though she couldn't pick it up if it did. "You stop it now," said Mrs. March. Pushing back a lock of hair still limp from the bath, she stared the telephone down, backing her way out of the kitchen.

She locked the front door and tried the knob, then unlocked it and locked it again, pulling at the knob one final time. She drank greedily from her wineglass—she must have been holding it all along, without realizing—and took it with her to the bedroom. The long hallway stretched out before her, black and menacing: had she absentmindedly turned off the overhead lights? She remembered how, as a child, Paula had hated that hallway, refusing to venture into it from her bedroom when she would awaken from a nightmare. Instead, Paula would call for her father, and an irritated Mrs. March would respond from the doorframe of her own bedroom, "Don't be ridiculous!," relishing any opportunity she could to chastise the child.

She walked its length with haste now—wooden floors creaking like the deck of an ancient ship—forbidding herself a glance into any of the passing rooms for fear she might see someone standing there.

When she reached her bedroom, she closed the door—fumbling with the lock—and leaned against it, staring down at her ratty woolen slippers, her heart swollen, painful, in her chest. Had Sylvia, stalked in her house by her murderer, locked herself in her bedroom? Was she pulled from it, screaming, her fingertips spiked with splinters as she clawed at the floor? Once her killer had dumped or buried her—Mrs. March wasn't sure which—she had lain outside for weeks, undetected. Maggots would have sprouted on her body by the time she was found.

Mrs. March went to her bedside table to remove her watch, pondering whether any animals had bitten and clawed at Sylvia's dead flesh, like a coyote or black crows. As a child, she had witnessed her cat snatch a sparrow from an open window. It caught the bird in one smooth swoop of its paw like it was nothing, with that quintessential feline indifference, as if the eleventh-floor apartment were a grassy savannah. It toyed with the sparrow for a while, batting it with its paws, then—right before the young Mrs. March's eyes—started to eat it, tearing through feathers and pulling at its skin with pointed teeth. Mrs.

March saw Sylvia's still, soft face pierced and slit into strips by the jaws of a predator, its hot breath blowing at her eyelashes.

She pressed her nails into the meat of her palms. She contemplated smoking a cigarette to relax, but unwrapping the stolen silver case from her shawl and airing out the room afterwards was too much of a bother, and besides, she didn't know what she needed relaxing *for.* So instead she washed her face—the wine webbing her lips like spider veins—brushed her teeth, slathered on some face cream, and climbed into bed with her book. Soothed by the feeling of cleanliness, of fresh sheets against scrubbed toes, the scent of her face cream something jasmine- or lavender-like, she read for a while, until she was interrupted by the clacking steps of the upstairs neighbor, who was wearing high heels again. She didn't know who owned the apartment right above theirs, but every time she saw a woman in heels in the lobby she would consider approaching her, maybe befriending her so that one day she could mention, in a casual, offhand manner, the surprising benefits of house slippers. In response to this thought, the heels clacked harder through the ceiling.

Mrs. March put down her book—the print was too small, which, with the wine, had given her a headache—and got up to get some aspirin from the bathroom.

When she padded back to bed, something caught her eye in the building opposite. A red light in one of the windows. She tensed, her first thought that it was a fire, but as she looked longer, she realized that it was a lamp draped in a cherry-colored organza, which cast a warm glow. The various other windows in the building were mostly dark, some strobing with the soft pulse of a television screen.

She moved closer to her own window, her nose almost

pressing against the glass. It had begun to snow. The snowflakes floated down, the ones passing by the window illuminated red for a split second, lighting up like embers before continuing their descent, the black night flickering saffron, hellish.

Her eyes went back to the glowing room. It was a bedroom, dark except for the reddish glow. After some seconds she managed to make out a woman, bent over, her back to the window. She was wearing a pink silk slip, her milky thighs on full display. Mrs. March cleared her throat, then looked over her own shoulder, as if someone had caught her spying. She trained her eyes back on the woman. What was she bending over? Mrs. March could see the corner of a mattress or a couch cushion. Leaning further, she bumped her forehead with a thud against the windowpane, and, as if she had heard her, the woman in the pink slip turned around.

From Mrs. March's throat issued an unwilling sound, some tortured garble between a gasp and a scream. There was blood—so much blood—soaking the front of the woman's slip and matting her hair and staining her hands—hands now pressed against the window to form bloody prints. Mrs. March pushed herself away from the window in one jerky movement, falling backward onto the bed, her book crunching underneath her spine. She flailed her arms toward George's bedside table, shaking her hands free of the numbness creeping up to her fingers. She pulled the telephone to her and crept to the window. The cord went taut, halting her movement.

She stood there, the receiver pressed to her ear—the dial tone now a harsh beeping—as she looked out across the courtyard. The red glow was gone. The woman was gone, too.

Mrs. March held the phone to her ear, her eyes fixed on the window, acrid perspiration dripping down her neck, her stomach tangled nettle. She remained like this for some time until her sweat dried and her breath steadied.

The snow had turned into rain and the courtyard was noisy with it, the patter shocking her as it struck something close, something metal, with a loud clang.

She placed the handset back in its cradle, her gaze still locked firmly, unwavering, on the window opposite. The window remained dark, although she could still almost see the red light, throbbing in her line of vision like an apparition, like seeing the sun through closed eyelids after looking straight at it.

Still she held the phone, clutching it to her breast, as she considered making the call to the police. But she wasn't sure now—all that blood, the woman staring at her through the window, her slip drenched in it. Had she really seen it? And then there was the other problem, of course, the real reason she couldn't call the police. She had thought the woman—of course it couldn't be—she had thought the woman had her face. She had thought the woman was her.

XVIII

Mrs. March was jolted from a series of gloomy, melancholy dreams by the neighbors' alarm clock, a thick drilling buzz, followed by the neighbors' dull, heavy footsteps pulsing through the ceiling like a migraine.

She sat up in bed slowly and looked toward the window, lit with somber morning light. Through the gap in the curtains she could see the other building. All still. No movement.

She leaned back into the pillows, her heart beating uncomfortably fast. The thought of last night made her sweat—indeed, she must have been sweating all through the night, because, she now noticed, the mattress was drenched. Peering under the blanket and top sheet, she gasped and bounced out of bed. The stain was flaxen, round, burning into the middle of the fitted sheet, darkening the chaste ivory linen. Urine.

"Oh no," she cried, hugging herself, rocking back and forth. "Oh no, oh no, oh no."

She couldn't remember the last time she had wet the bed. It might have been that first night Kiki showed up in her bedroom, with her unsettling smile and unearthly, browless eyes, drawing breath throughout the night.

Mrs. March swept to the bedside table to check the time—Martha wouldn't be here for another half hour. No way would she ask Martha to change the bedsheets. She supposed she could tell her she'd spilled wine on them, but then she would have to pour wine on the bed, and the mere thought of her in her nightgown sprinkling Cabernet onto her sheets made her simultaneously giggle and cry.

She ripped the sheets off the bed and, with them bunched in her arms, opened the door to the hallway. Funny how the space had seemed so narrow and uninviting just the night before. Now, a gentle light fell onto it from the open rooms, dust motes floating in the rays crisscrossing the floorboards.

She ran to the linen closet at the end of the hallway, where their washing machine sat under the shelves. She had often commented to George how fortunate they were to have a washing machine in their apartment, so as not to have to resort to the building's basement laundry room, or the indignities of a public laundromat. She had not operated it since they hired Martha.

Panting, she wadded the sheets into a ball and stuffed them into the machine, then, remembering her stained nightgown, pulled it off and shoved it in as well. She turned the dial every which way and pressed several buttons at once, until the machine whirred into life. Mrs. March returned to her bedroom naked, sweating and shivering, and had barely pulled on her bathrobe when she heard the front door open and Martha call out her usual lifeless greeting.

Her heartbeat a deep and painful poke against her ribs, Mrs. March stepped into the hallway in her robe. "Oh," she said, as if she had forgotten Martha worked here almost every day. "Good morning, Martha."

Martha stopped in her tracks, her little olive purse swinging from her wrist. "Did I forget to wash something?" she asked, looking past Mrs. March at the churning machine in the linen closet; Mrs. March had forgotten to close the door.

"Oh, no," said Mrs. March, wringing her hands, "I wanted to wash my sheets. I'll need you to put some new ones on. Because—well, it's not important why, really, I had—well, they were stained, you see, and my nightgown, well—"

Martha's face melted into an expression of complete understanding. "Of course, Mrs. March," she said. "I hope you chose the cold-water cycle—otherwise we can use white vinegar. That's best for bloodstains."

Flashes of the woman—the woman with her face—in the window returned to her. The bloody palms, bloody nightgown. How did Martha know?

"We were six women in my house growing up," added Martha, "so this happened all the time. It's no problem. I'll get those stains out." She nodded curtly—an attempt at motherly kindness, maybe—before retreating to the kitchen.

Mrs. March was left standing in the hallway, her bathrobe sagging open as it dawned on her that Martha had assumed she was menstruating. She flushed. Her period—"the curse," as her mother put it—had been irregular for some months, arriving further and further apart, and lately she was plagued by hot flashes and tender breasts. When she did have her period, it was milky and light, like a watercolor. She struggled to remember what it had been like before, this affliction that had once dominated her life. She had planned holidays and gatherings and even her own wedding around it, gobbling painkillers and pressing hot water bottles against her back all day. Not much was left now. So much of one evaporates through the years, she mused.

◆

THROUGHOUT THE DAY, Mrs. March checked on the building across the courtyard compulsively through her bedroom window. She'd peer from behind the drapes, in the hopes of surprising whoever it was in the act, yearning for any clue that might explain what she had seen. The window in question remained dark, the glass reflecting her own building back at her. There was no sign of the woman in the slip dress, or indeed of any woman—only a man in a suit, who was standing on a fire escape on a lower floor, eating a sandwich wrapped in foil.

The phone rang twice that day. The first time, Mrs. March picked up, only to be met with silence. When the phone rang the second time, Mrs. March went rigid as she saw Martha holding the phone to her ear. "What are they saying, Martha?" she asked, her voice hoarse. "Don't listen to them!" She rushed to Martha, who handed her the phone in bewilderment. Mrs. March clasped it with trembling hands and pressed the receiver to her temple. She could hear nothing on the other end of the line, not even an exhalation or a titter. "Whoever this is, stop calling!" she said before hanging up. Martha shook her head and said, "Telemarketers."

◆

THAT AFTERNOON, Mrs. March went upstairs to pick up Jonathan from the Millers' apartment. Sheila answered the door wearing a loose sweater and men's white athletic socks. "Oh! Hi! Come on in." Sheila seemed surprised to see her, even though Mrs. March had called to tell her she was on her way over.

Mrs. March stepped tentatively into the apartment. She had never been inside; usually Jonathan would greet her at the door when she picked him up.

"Can I get you anything?" asked Sheila. "Some coffee? Tea?"

Sheila wasn't pretty, per se, but she was attractive, with high freckled cheekbones and sleek blond hair that always seemed to shine. She was wearing reading glasses, which made her look interesting, and when she took them off she hung them casually from the neckline of her sweater. Mrs. March had never looked good in any type of glasses. They accentuated all her facial flaws. "Tea would be lovely," she said.

She followed Sheila into the kitchen, observing her tiny back, tiny waist. The nape of her neck so bare, the subtle blond down hardly perceptible under the lights. Mrs. March often felt as if she had been drawn out of proportion to other women's forms. Her own body, bloated and ungainly, had nothing in common with Sheila's svelte, angular frame.

She made good use of the short trip to the kitchen to make a mental note of everything in the apartment. Sheila's effortless style was apparent in her playful, modern take on Moroccan rugs, in the settee upholstered in gull-patterned mustard velvet. The Millers had fanciful cove lighting built into their ceilings, rather than sconces or overhead bulbs or floor lamps. The cheerful runner under her feet made the hallway appear brighter and shorter. Although the apartment had the same layout as hers, it looked different. More modern. Superior. She wondered whether any of the doormen had been inside, the judgmental day doorman, in particular. Whether he had compared it to her own.

"You moved the kitchen?" she asked Sheila as they entered it. The Marches' kitchen was near the entrance. The Millers' was further down the hall and on the opposite side of the apartment, where George's study was.

"Oh, yes. We wanted the extra space for the living room. We tore the old kitchen wall down and joined the two rooms. We get so much more light this way."

Mrs. March pursed her lips. She sat down awkwardly—her skirt riding up her thighs—on one of the high stools around the kitchen island as Sheila set about heating the kettle, flexing her thin, red-nailed fingers. Sheila always appeared to have had a recent manicure. It would be just like her (easygoing, informal) to do her nails herself, but they were so perfectly trimmed and polished that Mrs. March could only hope it was because Sheila spent hundreds of dollars at the salon. As she pondered this, Sheila took out two teacups from a cabinet. They were charmingly mismatched but clearly part of a set, which Mrs. March also noted.

"Milk?" Sheila asked.

"Please."

There was a slight clinking of glass bottles and jars as Sheila opened her refrigerator. Inside, everything was arranged in neatly stacked rows of labeled containers. Mrs. March marveled at such efficient, aesthetically pleasing storage before the refrigerator door closed. Rather than pour it into a creamer, Sheila unceremoniously plopped the milk carton in front of her, where it sat, perspiring on the glossy surface of the island, for the entirety of their tea session.

When Sheila poured the steaming water from the kettle over a bulb of dry tea leaves at the bottom of each teacup, Mrs. March leaned closer, astounded, as the tea leaves began blooming into flowers. Sheila saw her staring and smiled. "It's Chinese flowering tea," she said. "Isn't it beautiful? We got them in Beijing last month."

"That's lovely. Such a long journey, though. How did Alec handle it?"

"We didn't take Alec. It was just Bob and me."

"Oh," said Mrs. March, annoyed that living together apparently wasn't enough for Sheila and Bob. They had to take romantic trips around the world, even though they had been married for at least ten years. "How nice."

"Yes. We found this tea at the sweetest little shop right next to our hotel. I couldn't resist."

"Fancy," replied Mrs. March with just a touch of tartness. She racked her brain in an attempt to recall what Bob Miller did for a living to afford a trip to China.

They sipped in silence. Mrs. March glanced down at her unfurling tea blossom, looking more and more like a thick, knotted spider unfolding its legs. A drop of refrigerator sweat dribbled down the milk carton and onto the counter. Unexpectedly, Sheila began to take off her sweater. Mrs. March winced at what was coming: Sheila's smooth collarbone; her ribs poking through her T-shirt as she raised her hands above her head; her thin, muscular arms. Mrs. March fidgeted in her seat, involuntarily lowering her own sleeves further down her wrists. When she couldn't bear the silence any longer, she said, "I love what you've done with the place."

Sheila beamed at her, and Mrs. March spied the most subtle chip in one front tooth. "Oh, thank you. You should have seen the state of it before we moved in. It was *horrible*. This old lady had been living here forever. Barely went outside in the end."

"Did she die here?"

"Oh no, nothing like that. But it sure *smelled* as if she had. I was terrified to open the closets."

"Was there anything in them? Insects?" Mrs. March asked hopefully as she sipped her tea.

"You know what, I have no idea—we removed the closets without so much as a glance. And good *riddance*. We have a modern dressing room now. Pine."

Mrs. March's eyes narrowed.

"Haven't seen any insects, though, no," continued Sheila, lightly biting a fingernail, the red varnish inexplicably, infuriatingly, unchipped.

"We are lucky not to have cockroaches in the building," said Mrs. March.

"Oh goodness yes," said Sheila, "I would absolutely die if I saw one. Revolting little things."

"You definitely haven't seen any, right?" said Mrs. March.

"Oh, God no." Then, frowning: "But I mean, I wouldn't— I *clean*." She laughed, displaying her chipped tooth and nipple-pink gums. Mrs. March forced herself to laugh along, although her laughter carried a hint of hysteria.

"Oh, gosh, where are my manners?" said Sheila. "I haven't shown you the apartment! Want a tour?"

"Oh, thank you, but I can't today. I have some errands to run. I'm sorry." The thought of being confronted by yet one more beautiful thing in Sheila's apartment was too much to bear.

"No problem," said Sheila, picking up the teacups and setting them in the sink. Mrs. March edged off the stool and followed Sheila into the hallway. "Boys!" called Sheila. "*Jonathan*! Your mother's here."

As a door opened at the end of the hallway and the boys spilled out, Mrs. March turned to Sheila with a much-rehearsed smile, sinking her nails into the leather strap of her purse. "Well, thank you so much for tea, Sheila. It was lovely."

She took Jonathan's hand, who wriggled free from her grip. He didn't like his hand to be held in front of people (or at all, really). He ran into the shared hallway and she walked after him, feeling Sheila's eyes on the back of her head all the way to the elevator.

That night, Mrs. March locked all the doors and windows, including the small window high in the bathroom, even though it was impossible anybody could ever climb through it due to its size and its position, smack in the middle of the façade, out of reach from any pipes or ledges.

On impulse, she threw open Jonathan's bedroom door to find him sitting on the floor, facing the wall. Rushing toward him, his name a fizzled garble in her throat, she clasped his shoulders and turned him. It was just Jonathan, however: doleful Jonathan looking up at her with raised chin. "I'm on timeout," he explained. She checked on him again before dinner, then again while he slept.

No calamity befell either of them that night, or even the morning after. Regardless, Mrs. March went about her day in absolute tension, shoulders hunched, stiff-necked, bracing for impact.

She sat on the living room couch trying to skim through a magazine, looking at the photo of a model wearing outlandish makeup—pink eyelashes and drawn-on freckles—reading the caption, *Katarina wears a pink diamond tiara by Tiffany's*, over and over again, as she glanced repeatedly out the windows to the buildings opposite, which were much too far away to see into.

She turned the pages of the magazine listlessly, flipping past

the featured models posing openmouthed, big-eyed, and contorted into impossible positions. When she came across a woman
dressed as a Christmas present, it dawned on her, in a small
burst of panic, how terribly behind she was on her Christmas
shopping. The apartment was barely decorated—except for
the Christmas tree—as Mrs. March had been mindful of not
overdoing it until after George's party. They were due to host
Christmas Eve dinner this year; her sister and her husband and
George's widowed mother had confirmed attendance (Paula,
who was always somewhere exotic for the holiday, cavorting
with her beautiful foreign friends, couldn't make it). How
could she have let this slip?

Wringing her hands, she resolved to visit the department
store immediately. She would drop Jonathan off to see Santa
and meanwhile buy everything she needed. Over the years, she
really put all her energy into making Christmas a memorable,
magical event for everyone—arranging big centerpieces with
apples and fir cones, and buying the most considerate presents.
Gilded bookplates for George, after he had once mentioned to
her in an offhand way that his parents had denied him this simple luxury as a boy. Or an elegant fountain pen, his preferred
brand, engraved with the date of his first published novel. Prize
examples of her thoughtfulness, which she would have no time
for this year, not with her exhaustion and light-headedness.

The sudden certainty that if she didn't leave for the store
immediately something terrible would happen pervaded the
air like a stale, putrid smell. So she barged into Jonathan's
room, his eyes narrowing with reproach as she interrupted
him doing—well, *something*—and hurried them both out of
the apartment.

Outside, Salvation Army bells rang from every corner.

Crowds formed to admire lithe, faceless mannequins posed in the Fifth Avenue holiday displays, swathed in fur and velvet, against snowy backdrops or amidst Christmas dioramas. Behind one particular window, a faltering lightbulb flickered a bluish-white light, like an oncoming storm, while a mannequin stood brave and dignified in her organza dress and wide-brimmed hat.

Mrs. March and Jonathan exited their cab in haste, narrowly avoiding a little girl in an extravagant white mink coat, her hair in two topknots. She was walking a Labrador puppy that chewed at its leash in jerky movements, or rather it was walking her, as her mother followed a few steps behind, immersed in her leather planner. A squat, stained man wearing a ratty coat and fingerless gloves begged for money on the opposite corner.

"Mommy, can we give him money?" asked Jonathan, surprising Mrs. March out of her panic-fueled determination.

"Oh, Jonathan," she replied. Sometimes that sufficed.

Jonathan stared at the homeless man with intensity, craning his neck to look as they passed. "Can we?"

"No, I don't—I don't have any change."

The last homeless person to approach her on the street had been a woman wearing socks and sandals, her face creased as if it had been folded one too many times. There was a dry white crust around her nose, and her pockmarked cheeks were so rosy they looked plastered in thick theatre makeup. She had called out to Mrs. March, who told her, in truth, that she had no spare change. She could have ignored the woman, but she liked to think of herself as a very empathetic person; she had listed it as one of her best qualities on her university application.

"I don't want money," the woman said—"I just need medicine. Medicine's all I want, see. You don't have to give me money, but please buy me my medicine."

She convinced Mrs. March to purchase said medication at a nearby drugstore. It was around the corner, she said. Mrs. March had been on her way home from the market and was somewhat burdened by the weight of her bags, but she agreed to go to the drugstore. She had no real excuse, especially now that she had continued their dialogue, forging some type of unspoken agreement she feared was now too advanced to break. The pharmacist looked up and narrowed her eyes at the homeless woman, who limped in behind Mrs. March in her chunky sandals, sniffing rudely.

"What do you want?" Mrs. March asked.

The woman told the pharmacist, who glared at Mrs. March before bringing out a little box and placing it on the counter. "Nineteen-fifty," she said, and Mrs. March swallowed. Nineteen-fifty seemed like a lot of charity all of a sudden. And for a box of *what*, exactly? She looked down at the carton on the counter but failed to glean anything from it. She knew she had been manipulated, that she could stop this at any moment, could refuse to pay for whatever it was—but that would lead to a scene. She paid with her credit card through gritted teeth, then gripped the box, sitting in a paper bag, in her fist, and waited until they were out in the street to hand it over to the woman. She hesitated a little before parting with it—there was some redemption in the power shift, in the control she now had over the woman, who followed the paper bag not just with her eyes but with her whole body. Mrs. March was punishing the woman for embarrassing her in such an intimate way, and because she wanted the pharmacist, in case she was watching, to think she still had some control over the situation. She had paid for the medication because she wanted to, and she would hand it over if and when it suited her.

The next time she was ready. Weeks later, when approached by a homeless man with a paper cup in one hand (the other was a stump), she said: "I'm sorry, but my mother shot my father today, and I'm feeling rather strange about it."

The homeless man squinted at her—"eh?"—and she shrugged, and he walked away, mumbling to himself, still looking at her sideways, as if afraid she might follow him.

As Mrs. March and Jonathan approached the department store entrance, she gave the homeless man across the street a furtive glance. He turned his head to meet her eyes and smiled, displaying two surviving blackened teeth. Mrs. March quickened her pace, tugging Jonathan along behind her.

◆

MRS. MARCH held Jonathan's hand tightly as they entered the realm of crying children, harried clerks, and women tossing all manner of items into little mesh baskets, while a shrill chorus sang buoyant carols through the loudspeakers. One woman cried in a corner, her mascara running thickly down her cheeks, but no—she wasn't crying, only sweating profusely.

As a security guard ran past to intercept a teenager wreaking havoc on the perfume displays, Mrs. March felt someone take her spare hand, felt unfamiliar skin envelop her own, and with a surge of dread, looked down to discover a little girl had latched onto her. Breathing loudly through her mouth, the little girl looked up at her and, upon seeing that this wasn't her mother, dropped Mrs. March's hand as if stung (the nerve—as if it had been Mrs. March who had touched *her*). She stepped away from this adult stranger and burst into tears.

Mrs. March yanked at Jonathan and they made their way through the labyrinth of polished marble floors. They swerved around glass displays of jewelry and leather gloves and cashmere scarves, around lipsticks laid out like multicolored pieces of candy, before they reached, spread out before them—under a sign reading *Santa is IN*—a mass of mothers and their children roped in a coiling queue. Beyond them, at a disheartening distance, Santa sat on his wooden throne, posing for a photo as a little boy howled on his lap.

Mrs. March stood on tiptoes as they joined the line. Scanning the mothers in front of them, she approached the one in fur and pearls.

"Would it be a terrible imposition," she began, smiling as wide as humanly possible, "if I were to ask you to please keep an eye on my son for a minute—" The woman's eyebrows rose in haughty indignation, and Mrs. March hurried to say, in a low voice she hoped conveyed intimacy, "It would only be a few minutes, at the most, as I sneak off to buy some presents . . . We can't ruin his Christmas surprise, now, can we?" She attempted a wink, her makeup beginning to run down her face.

The woman seemed suspicious, raising the collar of her fur coat, to which Mrs. March also raised hers, defensively. "When exactly will you be coming back?" the woman asked, annoyed. Mrs. March took it as a promising sign that she hadn't been refused point-blank, and assured the woman she wouldn't be long as she slunk off to the elevators.

Upstairs, not even the most expensive counters were bereft of mayhem, and Mrs. March was dragged into the general state of panic and furor, feeling dozens of hands brushing past her and prodding her, the upbeat Christmas music on the speakers bleeding into the babble, the blaring lights disorienting her as she halfheartedly grabbed a sterling silver tie bar for George and a train set for Jonathan.

At the last minute, she also picked up materials to decorate the apartment: bundled cinnamon sticks, dried orange slices, pinecones sprayed gold, and wreaths of fresh pine adorned with tartan ribbons. She might still be able to prepare a beautiful Christmas.

After she paid and waited for the presents to be gift-wrapped at the checkout counter, she looked at her wristwatch to discover that she had left Jonathan downstairs for forty minutes. She ran toward the elevators, but one look at the impatient crowds jostling to get into the one available car prompted her to take the stairs. As she stepped back to change course, the swollen bags hanging heavily from her wrists, she bumped into someone. When she turned, flustered, to apologize, she came face-to-face—maddeningly—with the woman from the window. The woman seemed to be as frightened as she was—an identical look of wild-eyed terror in her eyes—when Mrs. March realized that she was standing in front of a full-length mirror. She took a deep breath, waiting for her reflection to blink or start, almost afraid to turn her back on it, before spinning on her heels and heading toward the stairs.

She arrived downstairs just in time: Jonathan was sliding off Santa's lap. He greeted her in his limp, unenthusiastic way after she'd managed her way through the crowd. Santa smiled up at her through his artificial beard as she thanked him.

"Thank *you!*" he said. "For coming to see me. We had a swell old time, didn't we?" He beamed at Jonathan—who had already lost interest, his thoughts far away—then grinned at Mrs. March, saying, "That's quite a boy you have there, Johanna."

Mrs. March locked eyes with him. "What did you say?"

"I said that's quite a boy you have there."

Mrs. March stared fixedly at Santa, who returned her gaze. "Ho, ho, ho," he said, still smiling.

Forgetting the photo, she grabbed Jonathan, squeezing his arm so firmly that he cried out—her mother used to do this, digging her sharp nails, like harpy talons, into her upper arm— and they trudged through the teeming hordes of mothers, their lipsticks gleaming and earrings flashing, the chemical smell of their hairspray catching at the back of Mrs. March's throat. She managed a nod at the mother in pearls who had watched after Jonathan, who returned the nod, stoic, as her own little boy, shrieking and wailing, snot running down his face, refused to sit on Santa's lap.

Mrs. March lugged Jonathan and herself out of the department store, her feet dragging under the weight of all the bags. Outside, she sucked in the cold winter air, which seemed to slap at her in return, and collapsed into the next available cab.

The doorman offered to carry her bags up to the apartment but she refused him, fearing he'd find her Christmas shopping stingy, or the opposite—too extravagant, proof that they were spoiled and materialistic—though now she worried that he had interpreted her refusal as pride, or even distrust, which would harden him further toward her.

As she burst into the apartment, her forearms striped red from all the bag handles, she found herself face-to-face with George.

"Oh," she said, stopping dead in the entryway. "You're back."

Jonathan, who had walked in behind her, granted his father a feeble hug before running off to his room. George smiled after him. He looked disheveled, she thought, his shirt untucked, his hair tousled. He had cut his trip short. "Oh, it was a waste of time," he said, wiping his glasses with the cuff of his shirt. "We got there late and couldn't find a single animal. We didn't even catch one lousy pheasant."

"Oh."

"The season isn't turning out so great."

"Maybe it'll turn around next year," said Mrs. March, still holding the bags.

"Maybe," said George.

"Did you hear," she asked, her eyes fixed on his, "about the missing woman?"

She had expected him to react somehow—to wince, to

stop smiling, or to smile like a maniac and confess the whole thing—but he barely blinked as he replied that, yes, of course, the flyers were all over the place. You couldn't even buy gas without getting asked about it by the police.

"The police asked *you* about her?"

"Well, sure, they asked everybody."

"What did you tell them?"

"What did I tell them? What do you mean? I told them I don't know anything about it and that I was in the area on a hunting trip."

He was looking at her in that peculiar unflinching manner, while standing in her way, and in that moment it occurred to her that perhaps he was doing this on purpose. As some kind of threat. Believe my story, his eyes said. Or else. She swallowed and set down her bags on the floor. They looked ridiculous—him facing her, hands in his pockets, and her standing idly by the door, still in her coat and hat, bags at her feet, when she should have just walked past him as they talked, taking the bags into the bedroom. That was what she wanted to do, except that now, the more she thought about it, the more incapable she felt of doing it naturally. It was like a muscle she had forgotten how to flex.

Finally, after what seemed like an artificially long pause, George said, "Well. I'm going to take a shower. I'm all grimy from the trip."

She nodded at him, and his eyes lingered on her, a hint of a smile on his face, as he retreated to the bedroom.

Mrs. March stood in the entryway a while longer, exploring these new sensations, trying to bury them. A sharp whining sound within the walls startled her. Lately, whenever the shower handle was turned, it was followed by this rattling shriek along the pipes.

A figure to her left made her jump. "Oh," she said. "Martha."

Martha had emerged from the kitchen, wiping her hands on a dishcloth.

"Can I take the bags, Mrs. March?"

"Yes, please. Store them in the trunk in the living room for now? Thank you."

Martha walked away with the bags as a hesitant Mrs. March followed behind her. She passed by George's study. The door was open, the red chinoiserie wallpaper eating up all the light, and his small suitcase was resting on the chesterfield, unlocked.

She never liked for Martha to see her in George's study. It was as if Martha knew she shouldn't be in there and patrolled the apartment accordingly. So she waited until Martha was back in the kitchen, and—reassured by the clanging of pans and rattle of plates—stepped into the room.

She approached the suitcase, lifting the lid with one timid finger. She didn't know what she was looking for, exactly, some incriminating proof that her husband was a rapist and a murderer? Absurd. And that somehow he'd gone back to the site of the crime to destroy the evidence?—oh, please. She'd know what she was looking for when she found it, she concluded, and this gave her some resolve. She checked the lining of the suitcase, wondering if it could possibly have something sewed into it. The lining was flat, however, and the stitches sewn so tightly into the leather that they refused to yield no matter how hard she pulled. She brushed past a scarf, gloves, and socks, a few toiletries and a lens cleaning cloth. One of his shirts caught her eye. It was stained. She pulled it out by the sleeve to examine it under the light. She scratched at the maroon smear—a wine stain, she reasoned. Or blood from an animal. Although George denied having caught any. Not even one lousy pheasant.

She went over to his desk, rooted around, nothing suspect, nothing misplaced. It was all arranged into a tidy mess. She recognized the notebook she'd been poking around in last time and opened it, looking for the newspaper clipping on Sylvia Gibbler. It wasn't there anymore. She flipped the pages, shook it a little to see if anything would fall out. She read a few words from the notebook—random annotations, it seemed like, ideas or phrases for future books. She opened the desk drawers, her hands feeling their way around pens, envelopes, loose paper clips, and small boxes of staples.

"Looking for something?"

She gave a startled little hoot and looked up from her crouched position over the desk at George, who stood in the doorframe, his arms crossed. His hair was wet from the shower and a single drop—water or sweat—sat lodged, unmoving, on his temple.

"Oh, I'm—" She looked down at the drawer and took out one of the little boxes of staples. "Jonathan needed to staple his homework and I found lots of these, but wherever is the stapler? I can't seem to find it, for the life of me—"

George approached, the drop on his temple still refusing to slide down his face. She quavered slightly as he brushed past her in reaching for the stapler, which was completely visible atop a small tower of books at one corner of the desk. He handed it to her but she hesitated. They were regarding each other in that dogged, disquieting way when she heard herself say, "I forgot." She paused before continuing. "I have to buy some milk. For Jonathan."

George cocked his head. "Ask Martha to get it."

"No, it's fine. She has a lot of ironing to do."

"But you just got here."

"I forgot. I forgot."

She made her way to the front door, opened the small closet in the foyer, searching for her coat and hat, until she realized she was still wearing them, then swung open the front door and slammed it shut behind her. In the hallway, she walked backward to the elevator, keeping the apartment door in sight, wondering if George might be watching her through the peephole, half expecting him to burst through it and come after her, in which case, she determined, she would run.

When the apartment door remained closed, however, she calmed considerably. She supposed she might as well go and buy the milk now. She would look silly if she came back empty-handed.

◆

IN THE SUPERMARKET, coated women pushed shopping carts up and down the aisles as a slow, jazzy, almost drunk version of "Dance of the Sugar Plum Fairy" played over the speakers.

She took a carton of milk from the humming refrigerator in the back of the store, observing the other shoppers. They appeared to be pushing around their carts aimlessly, walking in uniform straight lines, neatly, on an invisible grid—never colliding, never regarding each other as they filed past.

She strolled through the aisles, milk carton in hand, and came upon an unmanned cart in the canned foods section, parked in front of shelves stacked with can upon can of Campbell's soup. She approached the cart with suspicion, expecting the other shoppers to appear around a corner, shouting "You're it!," dooming her to roam about the supermarket, lifeless, in their stead until she eventually tricked someone into replacing *her*.

There was nothing unusual about the cart at first when she peered inside it. Sausages in their casings, canned beans, mesh bags of potatoes and onions, then—shockingly, cruelly— a copy of George's novel. She spun around, squeezing her eyes shut, and turned back to look at the book, hoping that it had somehow changed into another book. It hadn't. The red-and-white Campbell's walls closing around her, she reached for it and—before she knew what was happening—grabbed it and slid it into her coat, under her armpit.

She hurried to the cash register to pay for the milk, and while in line she felt sweat forming in her underarms and the book beginning to slip. When it was her turn, she took out her ostrich leather pocketbook as carefully as she could, while pinning the book tightly against her chest. She paid, smiling pastily at the cashier.

Outside, she turned the book over in her hand a few times, before throwing it into a trash can on the corner.

◆

THAT NIGHT, she retired early to bed but lay awake for hours, motionless in the darkness. Eventually, the bedroom door creaked open, then closed. She felt George slip into bed beside her, and she stiffened. Lately she was always asleep when he came into bed, and then he'd get up so early each morning she wondered if he had actually gotten into bed at all. Behind her closed eyes as she pretended to sleep, she imagined him suddenly choking her. Raping her. She could not recall the last time they had been intimate. Maybe after that party at Zelda's last spring? In the beginning their relationship had been quite sexual: George initiated it daily and she had surprised herself by being willing for a number of years. Sex with George had felt easy. Undemanding. Her mind emptied whenever they engaged in it, which Mrs. March found soothing. During one particular sexual encounter with George, back when Jonathan was a toddler, she became unsettled by a growing certainty that it wasn't George who was touching her. The hands on her shoulder felt thinner, hard-knuckled. The skin on his face, in the dark, was coarser—at that time George was clean-shaven, his beard not yet a staple. She grew agitated, wondering who this stranger was who was fondling her, imagining what his face looked like—sunken cheeks and light green eyes?—until she reached for the lamp switch. When she turned on the light, she saw that it was George on top of her (who else could it have been?), and she offered some flimsy excuse ("I thought I might knock over that vase with my foot . . .") and they resumed intercourse. She was so in love with George, she told herself later, that she couldn't even bear picturing herself with a different man.

Some years into their marriage, she adopted an increasingly ambivalent attitude toward sex. She eventually began to dread it. The sheer awkwardness of it, the clumsy mechanics, the damp, saline smell of him, the moist texture of him between her thighs. Her body would recoil, instinctively, from the very hint of sex, and over time George initiated it less and less. She hadn't wished to draw attention to it, and although she vaguely knew of the existence of professionals she could consult on these issues, she would never be able to bring herself to visit one. She had a hard enough time examining them herself, and she would rather die than confide in her husband.

George's snores ripped her from her thoughts with such force, she wondered whether she had been asleep. As his snoring continued, she relaxed—he would not kill her tonight.

A few particularly nasty snow days followed, or what the news described as a "historic blizzard." At least two feet of snow were scheduled to fall, closing schools, disrupting electricity in some areas, and severely hampering travel. All over the Northeast families stocked up on groceries as they prepared for a momentary lockdown.

Throughout the first night a whisper of snowflakes fell quietly—almost disappointing in their gentleness after the panic-stricken forecasts. But the snow proved constant, relentless, and soon it was no longer picturesque but draining in its persistence, burying the city and trapping them in their apartment alone, just the three of them.

By morning, the snow had swallowed parked cars and continued to fall slowly, thoughtfully. They went down to the lobby. The doorman had not been able to make it to work, and so it was chilly and quiet, the lights over the concierge desk switched off. They looked out at the street, at the bleached landscape enveloping them, like the glare of an atom bomb. The nearby trees were barely discernible against the white, branches pointing at them like fingers.

Jonathan's school had closed and so the Christmas play was canceled, which sent him into a sulk. It frustrated Mrs. March, too, that the costume she had worked so hard to get the seamstress to finish on time would never be seen by the other children's mothers, who surely hadn't made their sons' and daughters' costumes from three yards of the finest merino wool (Jonathan was to play a bear in an original play written by his ambitious English teacher about forest animals attempting to bolster the spirits of an insecure fir tree).

Christmas dinners were called off, and theirs was no exception. Mrs. March's sister called from the airport—all the flights from Washington were canceled—and promised to make it for New Year's Eve instead. George's mother, afraid to brave the storm, refused to attempt the trip from Park Slope.

The situation was further exacerbated by Martha's absence. Mrs. March tried coaxing her over the phone but Martha firmly insisted there was no way she could even make it to the nearest subway station. In an alarming bout of joviality, George offered to prepare Christmas Eve dinner for them. "There's a whole chicken in the fridge," he said cheerfully, as if this solved everything.

The chicken dripped pink into the sink as George held it by the drumsticks so that it looked like a headless baby dangling from its arms. Mrs. March watched her husband's fingers stroke the edges of the cavity, watched them tugging at the folds. He bent over the chicken greedily, almost intoxicated, biting his lower lip with something akin to arousal as his glasses reflected his fisted hand pushing its way into the cavity and wrenching out the purplish liver, the heart. Slick and bloated like leeches.

The three of them sat through a quiet Christmas Eve dinner, during which Mrs. March spit out half-chewed chicken discreetly into her napkin as she wiped her mouth with each bite. Afterwards she threw the soiled cloth into the trash.

Christmas Day came and went. Jonathan seemed happy enough with his train set, and George gave Mrs. March a very expensive-looking camel scarf. Vicuna wool, said George. As he handed it to her, their fingers brushed. She beamed at him while making a mental note to scour his book for any mention of Johanna wearing a camel vicuna wool scarf.

◆

To MAKE LIGHT of their predicament, they pretended that they were prisoners, ambling on all fours through the living room and hiding behind furniture from their mysterious captor (played by George). As the hours rolled on, like unabating waves, Mrs. March began to really consider herself a prisoner and a rash as red as watermelon pulp sprouted across her neck. There was no need for them to attempt to leave the building as they had all the provisions they could possibly need, and the blizzard was scheduled to clear in a couple of days, and yet with every passing hour she found it harder to believe that their confinement would end, that she would return to her reassuring routines—to the street, to the dry cleaner's, to buy olive bread.

She began to look forward to any event, no matter how small, to serve as a minor disruption in the monotony. Preparing afternoon tea was now one of the most exhilarating moments of the day. Sometimes she thought she saw spiders rustling inside the teabags—once she inspected a hairy leg poking through the muslin, which turned out to be a green tea leaf.

Jonathan periodically went up to the Millers' to play with Alec, or Alec came down to their apartment. Their giggles seeped under the closed door of Jonathan's bedroom, sometimes sounding like there were more people in there.

Meanwhile George spent hours alone in his study or watching television—Jimmy Stewart's bumbling words resonating across the apartment as he unraveled in black and white.

She recalled having read—in a curious little library book abandoned in one of the bathroom stalls of her dorm—about the *Peggy*, a sailboat stranded in the Atlantic in the eighteenth century. Drifting aimlessly at sea, all their provisions exhausted, eating buttons and leather, the men decided to draw lots. The "custom of the sea." She pictured the hunger, the claustrophobia, the hopelessness of it all. The truth dawning on the men that they were slowly going crazy, and there was nothing they could do to keep it at bay, their vision registering nothing but an endless sea and the same haunted, hollow faces of the remaining crew in the wooden bowels of the ship.

Mrs. March wondered, if it came to that, whether she and George would be capable of eating their own child in order to survive, or whether George and Jonathan would turn on her.

❖

SHE WAS SITTING on the edge of the bathtub one evening, swatting at an irritating fly she kept hearing but could never see. The buzzing was constant, the fly blowing raspberries at her failed attempts to find it.

She reached over to the faucet, paused. There was something in the tub. Unmoving. She blinked. A dead pigeon. Wings outstretched, its scaled, metallic-green neck twisted. Its eyes bright amber. She wanted to touch them. She didn't think she'd ever seen one this close before. Tenderly, she cooed at it.

Thrilled at the thought of this new, exciting thing, she scampered to the living room to inform George. "I'm afraid there's a dead pigeon in our bathtub, dear," she said, whispering in George's ear, for Jonathan was sprawled on the floor watching television, and she did not want him to overhear and tamper with the carcass.

"Really?" said George, closing his newspaper.

"Do you think you could get rid of it?" she asked. "I can't bear to touch it."

And so George rolled up his sleeves and headed toward their bedroom to take care of the bird.

"What are you watching, Jonathan?" Mrs. March asked. Jonathan shrugged, not even turning to look at her.

Mrs. March picked up the newspaper George had been reading and, folding it, saw it was dated the day before the snowstorm. "Honey," George called to her from their bedroom, "come here for a moment."

She found George standing, hands on his hips, over the bathtub. He turned to her. "There's nothing here."

Mrs. March stepped over and looked down. The tub was pristine white, clean, completely unblemished—not a drop of blood or a hint of feather remained. She looked up at the small window above the tub. It was closed. She tried to remember whether it had been open before.

She brought her hands to her face. "It . . . it was here just *seconds* ago."

"Maybe it flew back out."

"No, no—" She wanted to explain how that couldn't possibly be, how this all rather frightened her, but she stopped herself and looked over at George, who was scrutinizing her, his eyes beady behind his glasses, his hands in his pockets. She chewed her thumb.

"Maybe you're just tired," George said, with a hint of caution, "cooped up in here all this time."

She stared blankly at George. He stared back.

"Yes," she said. "Probably."

◆

SHE CONSIDERED the possibility that George was torturing her. Having his sick fun with her. Or maybe the pigeon had been a warning to her to back off.

On the last evening of their confinement, as she was making her way to the bedroom for the night, she heard a brusque laugh coming from the living room. She walked in cautiously to find George sitting by himself in his favorite armchair, drinking a glass of whisky.

"What's so funny?" she said, clenching in case he had been laughing at her.

"I was just remembering something my father used to say . . ."

"What did he used to say?"

He looked at her, shaking his whisky, the ice cubes rolling around, clinking against the glass. "I forgot," he said, smirking. "Oops."

She turned to leave, when George said, "He wasn't a very funny man, my father."

Relieved that this didn't seem to concern her, Mrs. March loosened the belt of her robe and, exhaling, decided to engage. "Well," she said. "Didn't he struggle with diabetes most of his life?"

"Yes. It was horrible. He didn't take care of it. Couldn't feel the gangrene setting in. His skin was like graphite. The infection spread to the bone. It came to a point where they just started cutting away at him, little by little. You know, the first story I ever wrote was about his first amputation. 'Handful of Toes.'" He chuckled, then his features darkened. "Sometimes I find inspiration in the most horrible things. Do you think that makes me a bad person?"

Mrs. March looked down at George, at his searching, unreadable eyes, at his ambiguous smile that always seemed to mock her intelligence. "No . . ." she said softly.

He took her hand, rubbing her wedding band.

"You always see the best in me," he said. He fiddled with a hangnail on her finger, then brought her hand to his lips and nibbled it off, gently.

When the snow at last melted, uncovering cars and revealing bikes tied to poles, slush clogged the streets, and the grit of the city seeped through it like an infection. In the newspaper, families in Red Hook posed gravely on the stairs of their flooded basements. A fallen branch had killed a man in Central Park.

The Marches were set to host New Year's Eve dinner for Mrs. March's sister Lisa, and her husband Fred. George's mother would be spending the evening with one of George's aunts, and Paula, predictably, was on a beach somewhere tanning her long toffee legs at the expense of some generous friend.

Everything was in place when Lisa and Fred knocked on the door. The table was set, tastefully, with a grandiose touch because, although it was a family dinner, Mrs. March couldn't tolerate her sister going back to her hotel afterwards and commenting to her husband how *their* table settings were better. The food had been ordered from Tartt's three weeks in advance, while the desserts prepared by Martha rested on the kitchen counter—blushing macarons lined up like debutantes in silk-ribboned dresses, waiting to make their entrance.

The apartment was bursting with an almost suffocating cheer: the tree perfectly trimmed, Bing Crosby crooning Hawaiian Christmas greetings on the stereo, and the holiday cards displayed artfully on the mantel. Today, she moved her sister's cheap, tacky card featuring a glittery snowman up in front of all the others.

Mrs. March paused before opening the front door, lest they think she had been loitering in the foyer, waiting for them. She had been sweating in anticipation—she didn't know in anticipation of what, but it made her anxious in any case.

As she welcomed the couple inside, greeting them warmly, Mrs. March was thrilled to see that Lisa's hips, tight under a hideous woolly skirt, had broadened. It always brought her joy, the sign of any physical deterioration in her sister, no matter how slight. From childhood their mother had compared the two, and found Mrs. March, invariably, to be lacking. "Why can't you behave? Look at Lisa, *her* grandmother has also died," she had hissed to a sobbing Mrs. March at their grandmother's funeral.

Indeed, Lisa had always been shellacked with a sort of sterilized calm, as if she wasn't really experiencing things, only looking upon them from a distance.

Their mother, Mrs. Kirby, had seemed to resent Mrs. March from the beginning—evidenced by naming her after her own mother, whom she detested. Her disdain was confirmed one evening when, drunk on sherry, she revealed that Mrs. March had been an accident, and that she had contemplated aborting her.

Mrs. March was glad that Jonathan was an only child with no siblings to compare him to—and that her mother had no other grandchild to compare him to. Her sister chose not to have children, often stating how happy she was to be able to travel around the world, and, besides, her hands were full with their mother. But Mrs. March suspected it was really because her sister had always been too thin to conceive a child. She doubted Lisa had been capable of menstruating after losing all that weight in college, and now she was too old to get pregnant.

Mrs. March had initially regarded her delivery of Jonathan as a victory over her sister—at last her mother would be proud of her for something Lisa couldn't do. Mrs. Kirby often said that having children and a family was the greatest achievement of a woman's life. By the time Mrs. March had Jonathan, however, her father had died, leaving her mother rather quiet, and soon after the baby arrived, Mrs. Kirby was already exhibiting signs of dementia. "Lovely Lisa," she said when she first held Jonathan.

"It's so cold outside," said Lisa, red-nosed. "Isn't this time of year just lovely?"

Lisa's husband Fred waddled toward Mrs. March with a vacuous smile. Insufferable, pompous, fat Fred. Mrs. March had disliked him from the moment she met him. He went out of his way to make her uncomfortable in social situations. The kind of man who would announce bumptiously that their antique cedar tea table was passé. "Eighteenth-century is so cheap now. How much did you pay for this?"

Fred had seen a good portion of the world. He had carved Mani stones with the Buddhist monks of a Tibetan monastery, he'd swum with sharks in Bali ("not that scary"), and he had of course, regrettably, made his own foie gras on a visit to a French farm. Mrs. March, remaining within the self-imposed boundaries of the United States and Europe, couldn't help but find his stories intimidating and tedious. None of these humbling, enlightening experiences, however, seemed to have humbled or enlightened Fred in any way.

He slapped George on the back and planted a kiss on Mrs.

March's cheek, moistening it with his sweaty jowls, which she would feel on her face—her hand itching to wipe it off—throughout the evening.

"Let's finally drink some decent wine in this place, Georgie-boy," said Fred, chuckling, as he produced a ridiculously over-sized bottle of wine, "and not whatever it was you served us last time. And this," he said, extracting a smaller bottle, "is some elderberry wine I made. For the ladies."

"We'd like to try the good wine too, dear," said Lisa, eyeing herself in the foyer mirror.

"No, no, you gals have the elderberry. You can't appreciate how good this wine is."

"We can too!" said Lisa, though her heart wasn't in it.

"You said it yourself—you can't tell the house red from the Vega Sicilia."

Mrs. March looked sideways at George, who laughed good-naturedly as he took the bottles. She pursed her lips. She and George had been cajoled into drinking some very sour wine the last time they had been at her sister and Fred's home in Maryland. There were impressive vintage reds in their kitchen wine rack, yet Fred had poured from a bottle that must have been sitting, opened, on their counter for at least four days.

She stared at Fred as he bragged about how little they had paid for their plane tickets. "Bargain, absolute bargain," he was saying. Then, "Thanks, darlin'," as Mrs. March took his coat. "Where's Martha? Where's that ball-busting old gal?"

"Martha has the day off," said Mrs. March, taking her sister's coat as well—a soft pink woolly thing, too cutesy for her taste—and hanging them in the small coat closet. "It's New Year's Eve, after all."

"Our help always stays on, New Year's Eve and Christmas,"

said Fred. "You have to work that sort of thing out straight off the bat, otherwise they'll take advantage."

"This is *beautiful*," said Lisa, admiring Mrs. March's brooch. She said it in such an exaggerated way that Mrs. March knew it was a lie. She had gifted Lisa a similar brooch for her birthday years ago and had never once seen her wear it.

"Oh wow," said Fred as they entered the living room— where Mrs. March had been trying, casually, to steer them ever since they stepped into the apartment—"that book must really be doing well, George. Look at this place."

"It *is* doing well, isn't it?" said Lisa. "I've read rave reviews. Haven't gotten around to reading it myself yet—"

"Lisa pretends she reads," snorted Fred, his cheeks flushed like those of an aproned Victorian baker-woman.

"I do too read," said Lisa, a flash of exasperation in her eyes.

"Whatever you say, honey. Is that an original Hopper? How much did *that* cost?"

"That's been there for years. You commented on it last time you were here," said Mrs. March, careful to appear helpful rather than defensive.

"I'm sure I've never seen this in my life."

"Really, you have."

"No, I would remember."

"Let's sit, shall we?" said George. "I'm starving."

They entered the dining room through the French doors. The table shone grandly, decked in a magnolia wreath centerpiece and hand-painted porcelain dishes and tureens and bearing a sumptuous banquet of seared scallops with brown butter and pineapple-glazed ham. Mrs. March was aware that Jonathan detested pineapple, but this was the most impressive dish she could have served (Tartt's roasted pineapple ham, in

all its apparent simplicity, was the pinnacle of gastronomic eru-
dition). She also appreciated the familiar coziness of the dish,
how it looked when George carved it for his family, as if posing for a Norman Rockwell painting. Jonathan would have to
make do with the scallops.

"Oh, the table is simply *lovely*," said Lisa.

"Be honest, now. How much of this did you cook yourself?"
asked Fred, in his detestable jocular way.

"Oh," said Mrs. March, "I had some help, of course."

"I'll say," said Fred, and he grinned, revealing rows of tiny,
neat teeth—like milk teeth.

They sat, and as the men tucked into the food with the speed
and silence often evoked by male hunger, the women filled
their stomachs with water and the random steamed vegetable.
Mrs. March studied Lisa, mimicking her habits throughout the
meal. She would only take a bite when Lisa did.

Fred, attempting no such restraint, attacked his plate loudly. He
had the revolting habit of breathing through his mouth between
bites, and every now and then he would emit a curt chortle.

"Leave some for the rest of us, dear," said Lisa, in a light tone
laced with caution.

Holding her wineglass as she anticipated her sister's next
nibble, Mrs. March noted how Lisa meticulously rationed her
bread, how she dabbed at the corner of her mouth with her
napkin—even when she hadn't eaten anything. She had been
prim since childhood, even when they played pretend as children, conjuring up images of their ideal future husbands. Lisa
invariably described the same man: tall, floppy-haired, European, a little awkward but sweet. A modest intellectual. Mrs.
March's gaze turned to Fred, cheerfully balding at the crown,
his clammy double chin streaked with razor burn, his hands

balled into fists on the table. She fantasized about going back in time, to their parents' apartment, to their bedrooms connected by the bathroom. Young Lisa would never believe the real husband that lay in store for her—Mrs. March could barely believe it herself. Lisa would be jealous to learn her younger sister's future husband would be a famous writer. Possibly a rapist and murderer, too. Mrs. March's smile faded.

"Pass the potatoes," said a small voice beside her. She looked down at Jonathan. She had forgotten he was at the table. She overcompensated with a dramatically large serving of potatoes, then pushed his hair back in what she hoped was an obviously loving gesture. Jonathan resumed eating.

"What's wrong with him?" asked Fred, who had been watching their interaction, Mrs. March now realized. Sometimes she caught Fred staring. At first she had assumed that he was attracted to her, but over the years she considered his intentions to be much more sinister.

"Nothing is *wrong* with him," said Mrs. March, a little too shrilly, because she had often wondered the same thing.

"I was much more lively at his age," said Fred, his small eyes gleaming, his cheeks bulging with ham. "Always getting into fights. Little boys have to get into fights, that's how they learn to be men."

Lisa raised some lazy objection, to which Fred said, "It's true. Otherwise they'll never know how to defend themselves."

"Well, maybe therapy would be good for him," said Lisa.

Mrs. March went cold at this betrayal and looked at her sister with what she could only hope was pure, unequivocal hatred. "I don't think that will be necessary," she said, helping herself to more vegetables, even though she hadn't finished the portion on her plate.

"Why not?" asked Lisa.

"I don't believe in therapy," Fred cut in. "Children have to face life on their own. Or they'll never learn to do it by themselves. They'll always need help from others."

"Really, why won't you send him to therapy?" continued Lisa, ignoring Fred. "Is it because of your experience? Did you not think it helped you?"

"Don't be silly," said Mrs. March, her face hot. "This has nothing to do with me. I hadn't even thought of that in ages. I forgot all about it."

Mrs. March had not, in fact, forgotten her sessions with Dr. Jacobson. The waiting room, its thumbed kids' magazines with already filled-out puzzles. The long corridor leading to his office, the closed door, the muffled voices behind it. The way Dr. Jacobson asked her how she felt about everything, the pressure to make up answers to please him.

"When did you go to a psychologist, honey?" asked George.

"Oh, a long time ago—as a child. It was nothing, just a session or two. Apparently I bit the maid once, so." She rolled her eyes, smiled.

"It wasn't just about biting the maid," said her sister. "You know that, right?"

Mrs. March looked away but could feel her sister's eyes boring into her. George went back to munching the leftover bacon-wrapped shrimp.

Fred, who was slumped over the table as if tired of bearing his own weight, proposed a toast to the new year and to their generous hosts, the Marches. His fat puckered lips shone wetly as he leered at Mrs. March. She tried to hold his gaze but couldn't.

◆

THE FOLLOWING morning—the first morning of a fresh new year—she brewed a cup of tea and blew on it gently as she stood by her bedroom window. "Rabbit rabbit rabbit," she breathed, looking out at the neighboring building, at its lifeless windows. She continued, her volume rising until she was screaming, her breath fogging up the glass, "Rabbit! Rabbit! RABBIT!"

XXIII

A week after school resumed, Jonathan's principal summoned Mrs. March to her office. "I'm afraid there's been an incident," the principal said. "It's a little . . . delicate to discuss over the phone."

And so Mrs. March prepped for the role of stylish, charismatic mother, one who would be concerned for her child but also intimidating to staff; enigmatic yet warm. She took a cab to the Upper West Side in high spirits, wearing her best clip-on earrings, but grew somewhat carsick from the driver's repeated abrupt braking all the way up Central Park West.

As a child she had been driven to school by her father's chauffeur. He ferried her back and forth for ten years yet she rarely ever saw his face. She remembered the nape of his neck, though—square and prickle-haired—visible through the gap in the headrest. On days when her father went into work a little later, he would be in the car with her, dressed in his tailored suit and reading the business sections of the morning papers, which would be waiting for him in the backseat, fanned out. The gasoline-like smell of the newspaper ink never failed to nauseate her. Once she'd vomited all over the leather interior and the door's wood trim (she'd been aiming for the window). The chauffeur had been comforting and discreet, as always, and she'd felt bad for him—but at least she'd had the good sense to wait until after her father's stop. The following morning the car arrived clean and fresh-smelling, as if nothing had ever happened.

Fanning herself to abate her current wooziness, she exited the cab in front of Jonathan's school, where the second graders were playing in the adjacent basketball court amidst cheers and the occasional shriek. They were all wearing the school's mandatory uniform.

She spotted a man hovering near the fence. She knew well what kind of men loitered around schools and parks. Her mother had warned her, very early on—when sending her off to confession for the first time, aged nine—from ever fully trusting a man. "What about Daddy?" Mrs. March asked, expecting some kind of exception to the rule, especially as her mother had only ever spoken words of praise about her father.

"Never let your guard down," her mother answered.

Inside the school, the air carried a scent of metal and damp wood. It didn't smell of children, which Mrs. March was grateful for. The walls, penitentiary green and treacle-colored, were disrupted here and there by colorful artwork on corkboards. It was reverently quiet, like a church, except for the low, monotone drone of a teacher that loudened as she made her way across the liver-spotted terrazzo flooring of the hallway.

The principal, whom she remembered vaguely from an initial tour of the grounds, was a woman with a tower of teased maroon hair, a thin smile, and a small sharp nose, like a sparrow's. She welcomed Mrs. March into her office—a cramped space adorned with colorful rugs and mismatched furniture. They sat, at the principal's suggestion, opposite each other in a pair of fat armchairs, one paisley, the other plaid.

"Thank you so much for coming in, Mrs. March," said the principal as Mrs. March sank into the bulbous chair. "Sorry for the inconvenience—I just felt that this discussion should be had in person."

There was silence. The principal smiled reassuringly, crow's-feet branching from her squinting eyes.

"Of course," said Mrs. March.

"As you know, I have never called you up here before, and I'm hopeful I won't have to again." She took a deep breath. "Is Jonathan under some sort of pressure at home? Did something—emotionally straining, perhaps—occur over the holidays?"

Mrs. March blinked. "No," she said.

"It could just be pure curiosity, you know, sometimes they're confused at this age, they want to . . . *explore*. They don't know that they can . . . hurt others." The principal sighed, folding her hands on her lap. "I'm afraid that Jonathan has acted out. Everything seemed fine when he returned from winter break—he seemed to be settling in all right, but then, well . . ."

As the principal talked, Mrs. March took in the tattered rug, upturned in one corner; the framed photographs of skiing trips on the desk; the child psychology books on the shelves. She had been sent to the principal's office only once as a child, after writing a nasty note to another little girl in her class. "Dear Jessica"—Mrs. March had hated the name ever since—"everyone hates you, and you shall soon die. It is God's will," the note read. "Signed, a fourth grader." It made no sense to her now why she had zeroed in on Jessica, an objectively unremarkable child. She used to observe Jessica in the playground, noticing with rage the way her socks slid down her calves, exposing her pink legs in the stark winter months, when all the other girls were layered in corduroy and woolly tights. She watched an unsuspecting Jessica play—dancing goofily, arms akimbo, as she laughed in a high-pitched squeal, her blond tresses bouncing on her chest. She studied Jessica in class—how she bit her nails, head bent over her notebook, her slightly parted lips revealing slightly parted teeth. How she'd overdo it when she raised her hand, her whole body swelling as she emitted little whines and *me, me, me*'s. She sat in the audience when Jessica performed at the school ballet recital. Watching Jessica dance, her white blond hair swept into a sweet bun, her tiny nipples poking through her pink leotard, had charged her with a searing envy that ran through her like a pulse. An envy that continued to thrive in her bloodstream when she sat down after math class and wrote that note, and without a second thought, slipped it into Jessica's book bag.

There had been a whole thing, of course, once the note was discovered. The concerned teacher photocopied it and passed it around to all the fourth-grade teachers. Mrs. March chided herself for identifying her grade level so smugly in the note, but then again, she hadn't expected Jessica to show it to anyone, the rat.

"I know Jonathan," the principal was saying, "and he's never done anything like this before, but you must understand that I can't have him *corrupting* my other students . . ."

Mrs. March quivered. She often felt nauseated when she was hungry, and she'd had very little breakfast. Why had she had so little breakfast? She struggled to remember.

"And so, you see," the principal continued, "we simply can't have this sort of behavior at the school. You do understand."

"Of course."

"Good, I'm glad. Of course Jonathan will be welcomed back as soon as his suspension is over—"

"Suspension?"

The principal frowned. "Well, yes, Mrs. March. As I was just saying, his behavior must not go unpunished. It wouldn't reflect well on the school. Or, frankly, me. It would also be unfair to the parents of the little girl involved. We must set an example."

"Yes, I understand," said Mrs. March, not understanding at all. She was sweating in her heavy coat, which she had not removed, and to do so after all this time indoors would be awkward, and she no doubt had patches of sweat on her shirt.

"As I said, Jonathan can finish the rest of the school day. We'll welcome him back next week."

The principal rose, which Mrs. March took to mean that the meeting was over, and stood up as well. Both women thanked each other, so repeatedly that Mrs. March wondered what they had each done for the other to be so thankful. The principal escorted her to the door and smiled her out.

In the act of hailing a cab on Columbus Avenue, a homeless man accosted her. "You're unfuckable!" he yelled as she scurried into a cab and slammed the door behind her.

XXIV

As she approached her apartment building, Mrs. March came upon a cluster of people on the sidewalk, huddled together against the cold. One was pacing in circles, while another stood a bit further away, smoking a cigarette. It was difficult to see any of their faces or to determine their genders, as all were strapped into puffy winter coats and wore winter hats pulled low over their eyebrows. Most, if not all, were carrying the same book—George's new novel. The glossy cover winked in the light at Mrs. March from the gloved hands of one, from the coat pocket of another. One of them must have sought George out, she surmised, or spotted him going into the building—and now they were all waiting around for him, hoping to get a picture or an autograph.

A few of them eyed her as she dashed into the building. The doorman stood silent and stiff as he held the door for her.

"Good afternoon," she said, to no response. She crossed the lobby, blinking in bewilderment. Had she uttered the words aloud or had she just imagined it?

◆

THAT EVENING, the March family sat together at the dinner table. Across from Mrs. March, Jonathan quietly picked at his food. She sneaked glances at him, studying his sunken, dark-rimmed eyes, his reserved demeanor, and concluded that there was simply no way there could be any truth in what the principal had said about him. The word *corrupt* hung limply inside her like a rotting organ. Maybe, she theorized, grasping at straws, it was *Jonathan* who had been corrupted. Led to dark acts by a classmate, or by . . . she looked over at George, who was consuming his meal in noisy gulps. He has corrupted him, she thought. This monster has corrupted my baby.

"Potatoes, dear," said George, not bothering to look up from his plate.

"Yes, potatoes," echoed Jonathan.

Mrs. March slid the serving dish toward them, now perceiving, with a sudden electric clarity, the ways in which the two were alike. She had never really considered it before (Jonathan seemed to have sprung, self-formed, bearing no genetic material from either of them), but she saw now a definite likeness— the curve of the forehead, the hairline, the arch of the eyebrows. Their eyes were different, though, and she was relieved—for if they were indeed windows to the soul, it stood to reason that their souls must be quite different. Jonathan's heavily lashed, big, empty eyes shone in stark contrast to George's small, piercing, knowing ones. But maybe George's came from near-sightedness, from years of squinting at his books through his glasses. As a child he may have been just as big-eyed and inexpressive as Jonathan. He had been an unusually intelligent boy, according to his mother. George had always been idolized by his mother. They had developed a special bond, Mrs. March supposed bitterly, after George's father died. United in their grief. Even though his father, according to George himself, had been strict. Aloof. Perhaps it wasn't losing him that had traumatized George, Mrs. March suddenly considered. Perhaps, unbeknownst to everyone, George's father had been abusive.

A drunk. Beating young George into submission. She berated George in her mind for hiding his painful past. He must be embarrassed by it, she supposed, or he blamed himself, as many abused children do. Or maybe, maybe George had *liked* it. She stifled a gasp at the mere thought, and the asparagus she was attempting to swallow caught in her throat. Maybe his father had turned George into a monster, too, and now George was doing the same to Jonathan. Grandfather, father, son: a legacy of monsters.

She stared at George, then at Jonathan. Neither of them acknowledged her. She wondered for a fleeting instant whether she was even there at all. They had asked her for the potatoes, hadn't they? Wanting to speak—needing to speak, to have them look at her, to confirm her presence—she cleared her throat and said, "Well, Jonathan. Aren't you going to tell your father what happened at school today?"

Jonathan raised his eyes, his face inscrutable, eyebrows puckering into a frown. George peered at him over his glasses. "Poe?" he said.

"I got suspended," said Jonathan, looking down at his plate.

George sighed, more in resignation than surprise.

"He did something," said Mrs. March with a dry mouth, "to a little girl."

George eyed Jonathan over his glasses. "Well, that simply won't do. We have taught you how to behave," he said, his voice stern. "I will not accept this kind of behavior from you. Frankly, I'm disappointed, as is your mother. You know better than this."

"It wasn't my fault," said Jonathan, now with a wisp of regret in his voice. "Alec was daring the other boys to do it—"

"Alec?" said Mrs. March, hope returning as she relished the

possibility that Sheila Miller might be going through the same ordeal upstairs. "Was Alec suspended, too?"

Jonathan shook his head, still staring into his plate. "No, he wasn't even sent to the principal's office, but it was all his fault—"

George slammed his hand against the table. Mrs. March jumped.

"This is unacceptable!" yelled George. "Suspended at age eight, and not even able to admit responsibility for something you've done! This is your fault, and yours only. You better think about this long and hard, Jonathan, and don't you *ever* let this happen again."

Mrs. March watched, bewildered, as the scene unfolded before her eyes. George's jaw was set, his nostrils flared. The saltshaker lay on its side. She couldn't recall the last time she'd seen him like this, if ever. George had never been the stern disciplinarian with Jonathan. She imagined a seething George with Sylvia—Sylvia begging for her life, splayed on her bedroom floor, and George, towering over her, telling her that what was about to happen was her own fault, that she had to take responsibility for her actions. For teasing him. For provoking him. Later, as the life seeped from her violated body, she would have used her last breath to beg for mercy a final time while George laughed at her. Mrs. March shuddered at the monstrous tableau she had conjured. Inside her mouth, the lining of her cheeks bled from her chewing.

"Go to your room. You're finished," said George. Jonathan rose from his chair and ran out, refusing to look at either of them.

Mrs. March looked sideways at her husband, who carried on with his meal. She watched him cut into an asparagus spear, bit by bit. When he swallowed the last piece, he frowned and said, "Wasn't it somebody's birthday today? Your sister's?"

"No," she answered. Fearing he'd think she was being curt, she added, "September."

"Oh, right. Well, it's *somebody's* birthday. Can't remember whose."

Sylvia's, thought Mrs. March.

"Can I have the rest of that?" said George, nodding at her unfinished plate. "If you don't want it."

She pushed her plate toward him. He usually enjoyed light dinners, as a heavy meal made him too sluggish to write. Perhaps his anger had awakened a hunger, she thought. Maybe he thrived on it, on sucking the discomfort out of the air, like a bee sucking dew off a petal.

◆

THAT NIGHT, George sat down on the bed as she slept, but it wasn't George. It was the devil. "I won't believe anything you say," she told him. He stroked her cheek with a long yellow fingernail and said, "You have so many demons, my dear."

"Yes."

"They've found their way in."

"The exterminator is coming on Monday," she said. "There's an infestation, you see."

"What happened to your ear?" the devil said, tracing her earlobe with the same yellow nail.

"Oh, I burned it, but it's all right now."

"Is it?"

She brought her fingers to her earlobe and felt the crust. "Oh," she said, "that's funny. I thought it had healed."

The crackling earlobe came off, like a wobbly tooth from its socket. She offered it to him to examine, and he popped it into his mouth, chewed on it, and swallowed it, which she found rather rude. "Excuse me," she said loudly, "someone's calling for me."

He gave her a curious look. "No one's calling you," he said.

"Yes, in the hallway."

"There's no one in the hallway."

Her eyes fluttered open, and she was standing in her bedroom, her hand closed around the doorknob. It was mostly dark, except for the diluted moonlight entering through the poorly drawn curtains and a line of light from the hallway sneaking in under the bedroom door.

Slowly, she turned the knob and opened the bedroom door. There was someone just outside—a dark figure standing in shadows, facing her, motionless. She took a step back, gasping for breath, then squinted as her eyes adjusted to the darkness. Jonathan. He was strangely erect, his large vacant eyes staring past her.

She knelt before him in his open-eyed blindness and shook him. He blinked, startled, and began to cry. She hugged him, or rather he hugged her, and as his shaking little body began to settle against hers, she noticed the light on in George's study. They stood like that for a while, Jonathan and her, hugging each other as she looked at the light under the study door.

Mrs. March spent the next few days jumping in surprise whenever Jonathan appeared, always apparently out of nowhere. She'd then remember his suspension, and she'd try, in her way, to talk to him, but Jonathan, like his mother, wasn't a natural conversationalist. He often avoided eye contact, but when he did look at her she considered the things the principal had hinted at. How well could one really know an eight-year-old child, she pondered.

Not knowing quite what to do with him, she bought him colored pencils and illustrated books and asked Martha to deliver sandwich- and fruit-laden trays to his bedroom. One morning she took him ice skating at Wollman Rink. It was a cool, clean January day, the azure sky seemingly dyeing the buildings blue.

As she waited for Jonathan to put on his skates, a voice erupted nearby, and when a man, bellowing madly, burst out of the surrounding trees and ran toward her, she froze, clutching her ermine stole. Realizing he was holding his infant son in his arms, growling in play as the child screeched with delight, she smiled at them, heart pounding so violently her ribs felt bruised. It was an effort to collect herself and loosen her grip on the strangled fur as Jonathan wobbled onto the rink.

As she watched him from the sidelines, she recognized a

familiar face among the onlookers—the mother of one of Jonathan's classmates. At first Mrs. March tried to shield herself from the woman, cupping her hand against her forehead as if she were shading her eyes from the sun, but alas, she had been spotted.

"It's me! Margaret, Margaret Melrose? I'm Peter's mother." Squat Margaret was there with her toddler and husband. Mrs. March's mood lightened at this, for the husband's weekday appearance at Central Park possibly meant that he had been laid off.

"John took the day off work to spend some time with us," Margaret said, beaming with pride.

"That's lovely," said Mrs. March.

"Is that Jonathan? Why's he here on a school day?"

"Well," sighed Mrs. March, "his grandmother is quite ill. He's rather close to her. I thought I'd give him a few days off school." She leaned into Margaret and said in a low voice, "We don't think she'll make it past Sunday, so"—nodding at Margaret's gratifying gasp—"this may be the last week he gets with her."

"Oh, gosh," said Margaret, looking horrified. "I'm *so* sorry. How sweet of you to give him this. I'm sure he really appreciates it."

Mrs. March smiled and lowered her eyes in a show of modesty. She pictured Margaret Melrose welcoming her son home from school that evening, telling him that she'd seen Jonathan at the rink and informing him gravely of the sickly grandmother, trying to impress on her son how important it was that he treat Jonathan kindly over the next few weeks. The son, puzzled, would shyly tell his mother the truth. Perhaps, with any luck, he wouldn't know the exact reason for Jonathan's suspension, but children, Mrs. March knew, were cruel gossips and not to be trusted with rumors.

"Where is George?" asked Margaret, brightly shifting the subject. "Working, I expect?"

"Ah. Yes. He's having an intense publication, what with all the press and everything. You know."

"I really loved his new book."

"Oh, I've yet to read it," blurted Mrs. March. She was too exhausted by her previous lie to utter yet another.

"Oh, you should," said Margaret, winking. "You really, really should."

You really, really should. Mrs. March studied Margaret's winter-cracked lips as they formed the words. As Margaret walked back to her family Mrs. March turned to the rink. Everyone had stopped skating. They stood, unblinking, looking at her—not just the skaters but the onlookers as well, had craned their necks to stare at her, locking eyes, one after the other, like the portraits in the museum, refusing to break their gazes. Jonathan, in the center of the rink, smiled at her with all his teeth.

Mrs. March stumbled backward and buried her face in her hands. She breathed loudly in her mint green gloves—where it was dark and soft and safe—until her breath began to sound like that of a stranger.

At the sound of the chirping of birds and the scratching of blades on ice, she removed her hands. The ice rink was as it had been before—bustling and loud, indifferent to her, the background music festive. Overcome with relief, she motioned to get Jonathan's attention. "It's time to go home!" she called out.

As they left—Jonathan sulky and refusing to wear his hat—Margaret called out to them, but Mrs. March pretended not to hear.

They made their way through the park, past promenading tourists and amateur watercolorists. Jonathan pointed to a fractured, empty bottle of Veuve Clicquot in a trash can, which Mrs. March warned him not to touch.

Mrs. March sensed, out of the corner of her eye, a shadowy figure following them—standing a few feet away, just out of sight—but every time she turned to look, she spotted no one. She panted, her deepening anxiety slowing her pace like a twisted ankle. She was just being paranoid, she told herself. She had dreaded his return for years, had seeded her subconscious with the expectation that she would bump into him at the grocery store, at the florist's, anywhere, really. She could still see him sometimes, behind closed eyelids—a dark silhouette, hands in his pockets, standing against the sun.

"Can we come back tomorrow?" asked Jonathan, somewhere below her.

"We'll see."

The man had worn a short-sleeved shirt adorned with tiny embroidered tennis rackets. Could she have seen the shirt now, among the trees? Surely he wouldn't be wearing the same shirt in the cold, she reasoned. Or did he want her to recognize him?

"Can we have hot dogs for dinner?"

"Not tonight, Jonathan."

"Alec has them all the time."

Mrs. March flinched at a crunch to her left—twigs breaking under a heavy shoe?—and walked faster, ignoring Jonathan's complaints as he struggled to keep up.

She had been about thirteen. She didn't remember much about herself at that age, except for her legs. What a funny thing to remember about oneself, she thought, but there it was. Before puberty altered her shape, a young Mrs. March had long, spindly legs—daddy-longlegs legs. They were especially tan that summer in the south of Spain, coated in a soft blond down. She remembered Cádiz as if she had dreamt it or seen it on a movie screen—bush-topped dunes cupping the beach, loud barefoot men selling shrimp on the shore, and a bitterly crashing sea that glittered. The sound of the waves was constant and inescapable, deep and rough like breathing, and would not quiet, even at night.

In Cádiz the days were long and Mrs. March grew bored and restless. Her parents had traveled over thirty-five hundred miles to discover that they did not in fact much care for the beach. They took the occasional halfhearted walk up and down the shoreline—Mrs. March lagging moodily behind—but spent most days lounging at the pool in silence, sipping margaritas and concealing any trace of enjoyment under large sunglasses. They had urged her to make friends but she was at that age when making friends was tricky, when one wasn't as uninhibited as a younger child nor welcomed yet among adults, where the rules of etiquette at least guaranteed a minimum politeness. So she spent the majority of her days moping, burdened with a heavy emptiness, taking uneasy dips by herself in the sea, worried about what lurked underneath—not just scales and pincers and stingers, but the evidence of other bathers: stained Band-Aids and warm patches of urine. The wind carried the chatter and intermittent shouts of nearby swimmers. In the afternoons she'd take shelter from the sun in her hotel room, occasionally venturing into the lobby to inspect the books left by other guests on the shelves or to try on the straw hats on the wire display racks in the gift shop. All the television channels in her room were in German, and indeed all the tourists seemed to be German—the men sported tight, revealing briefs, and the women had hair so blond it was almost white, and their backs and thighs were painfully pink from the sun, streaked through by bikini-strap tan lines.

At night when the fishing boats emerged, lights blinking across salmon-pink and lavender horizons, she thought she could see a big-breasted figure bobbing up and down in the ocean at an alarming distance from the shore, and every time she would realize, as if for the first time, that it was just a buoy.

She had first seen the man looking at her on the hotel deck (later she concluded that she had actually seen him all over before that, but she had only become aware of it afterwards). The deck overlooked the beach, surrounded by palm trees, their pineapple-skin trunks lit from below. She'd finished her dinner but her parents were still enjoying the buffet, where a group of flamenco musicians sang and clapped as a woman with big hair and a pained expression danced and stamped on the floor. There was laughter and festivity in the air, and the spectacle made her feel as if everyone around her had been drugged or hypnotized into compliance. Her parents had befriended a young married couple and had been drinking merrily with them for days. It irritated her how her mother, usually so cold and distant, could manage to appear friendly enough to make such close friends in less than a week.

Unwilling to make an effort to join in the fun, she had sulked off to the deck, where other guests were smoking and drinking cocktails. She ordered herself a Virgin San Francisco and stood against the handrail sucking on the maraschino cherry when she noticed the man in the shirt with the tiny tennis rackets. He was watching her, his lips pursed into an expression she couldn't decipher. "Sorry," she said, and threw the cherry over the handrail into the sand, assuming that he'd found her rude for sucking on it so loudly.

"Does that have alcohol in it?" the man asked, jutting his chin toward the peach-colored cocktail in her hand.

"No," she said, her voice emotional with that need teenagers have, sometimes, to be believed. "No, of course not."

"Figures," he said, somehow closer to her, although she hadn't seen him move. He was leaning on the handrail, resting on his elbows. "Kind of a boring party, don't you think?"

She nodded and sipped. His eyes bore into her as she desperately thought of something clever to say, when he suddenly stood up straight and turned away from her. Fearing that he had lost interest, she blurted, "Well, I'm going to the beach to see the fireworks."

"Fireworks?"

She nodded. "Every night at ten. You can see them much better from down below. They reflect off the ocean. It's very powerful." She once heard a museum tour guide describe a painting as powerful. It struck her as a very mature way to describe something.

The man looked at her, hands in his pockets.

"Well," she said, "I'm going now."

She abandoned her unfinished cocktail and made her way across the deck, toward the long wooden bridge that led down to the beach. She hoped that he would follow her. She was tired of being alone, and she'd have to pretend to be happy looking at the fireworks by herself in case he could see her from the deck. The whole scene would be rather humiliating.

He did follow her, however, and they both walked down the bridge together. Once they reached the sand, she allowed herself a closer look at him. It was a dark night—the sky an inky black against the stars and moon—but they were dimly illuminated by the yellow lights strung around the bridge's handrail. They stopped when they got to the beach and threw subtle glances at each other. He had sunken cheeks and light green eyes. She looked at his forearms, noticing gray hairs interspersed with the black ones.

A couple strolled past them, hand in hand. The woman was smoking a cigarette and, in a brief fit of bravado, Mrs. March skipped up to her and asked her for one. The woman handed her a cigarette and lit it for her, and Mrs. March sauntered back toward her new acquaintance feeling like a real adult.

"Tell me your name," he said.

"My friends call me Kiki," she said.

"How exotic. Exactly how old are you?" he asked her.

"Sixteen, seventeen next month," she said, coughing.

"Are you excited for college?"

She contemplated his question as if she were appraising jewelry, and, exhaling a cloud of smoke into his face, she answered, "Oh, yes. Although, you know, I'm going more for the adventure of it than anything else."

He grinned at that, his jaw dimpling, his nostrils flaring, and her stomach looped. "Sure," he said. "I don't remember much of my college days. I think I drank them all away."

She dropped her cigarette butt into the sand and said grandly, "That's a pity."

"Yes. It is."

They had been slowly making their way along the dunes, leaving the bridge lights behind. For once the sea seemed mercifully quiet, the waves lapping the shore softly.

His arm brushed against hers as they walked, but she pretended not to notice. She blew a puff of air upward and her bangs fluttered up in what she hoped was a playful yet charming manner, and he laughed, and she giggled. He leaned over and blew into her face, making her bangs flutter again. "Don't," she said, laughing.

"Are you here with your parents?"

"Yes."

"What do you do here all day?"

"I'm writing a novel," she said.

"Are you really?" His astonishment was a burst of sweet, surprising pleasure, like biting into a liqueur-filled truffle.

"Yes. I'm sure it isn't any good," she said, looking at the ground, "but I will finish it sometime next year. By spring, I think."

"That's impressive," he said. "I wish I had time to write a book."

"One has to make time for things that are important." She smiled.

The man moved closer to the water, and when she saw him removing his shoes, she asked, "What are you doing?"

"I want to feel the sand and the sea on my feet," he said, swaying as he pulled off his shoes. "I'm afraid I'm a little drunk. There." He placed his rolled-up socks inside the shoes. "I hate walking on the beach in shoes, don't you? I feel so constrained."

She nodded in agreement and bent down to remove her own shoes—new white tennis shoes her mother had bought for this trip, dismissing her petition for flip-flops as an unrefined fad. As she unlaced them, she could somehow sense how intensely he was looking at her. In response, she sported a furtive pose as she slowly peeled off her socks.

"You have incredibly dainty feet," he said, and when she had straightened up, he placed a hand on her shoulder. "Do you know how attractive you are?" he said. He leaned into her, his eyes like the green parchment of cats' eyes. "Don't," she said as the lightness she had only just experienced transformed into a heaviness that rooted her to the ground.

They were alone in a shadowy corner of the dunes between hotels, the water creeping nearer with the changing tide. The sand was cold and hard, unresponsive under her feet, so different from how it presented itself during the daytime.

It wasn't that she couldn't recall what had happened that night under the fireworks, it was just that she had preferred to remember it as having happened to somebody else. Some girl from her school or even a friend of her sister's. Or it might not have happened to anyone. Maybe it was a cautionary tale she'd heard, a story of a foolish girl playing grown-up.

Dragging Jonathan out of Central Park, she cut through the long line of carriage horses. Despite the blinders, their eyes of polished mahogany followed her, bulging, the whites streaked with vessels.

The devil had gotten inside her that night in Cádiz, she decided with surprising aplomb, and somehow he was working his way into her home, like the cockroaches, through some imperceptible gap. He'd found the opening, and soon he would get in.

XXVI

She had not slept well. She'd endured a series of dreams in which she borrowed other women's reflections from mirrors and stole into their homes and lives, desperate to keep up the pace of their marriages and social standings. At one point she had gotten up to go to the bathroom and realized, with crushing disappointment and pained bladder, that she had dreamed the trip and would have to make the effort all over again.

And so the following day, when Mrs. March came to find herself standing, coat and hat on, in the foyer, she did not know whether she was about to leave or whether she had just returned. She heard Martha behind her in the belly of the apartment, moving furniture and opening windows. She attempted to construct a rough timeline of her day so far—breakfast, a shower, a conversation with Martha about beef carpaccio, all fragments—but there were too many blanks. She looked into the gilded mirror next to the coat closet. Her reflection stared back, frightened. Jazz music danced through the wall from the neighbors'—the tinkling of a piano and a cocky, elaborate saxophone. On a whim, she decided she had been about to leave, and she stepped out of the apartment.

The day was strangely lit, like a movie set under simulated daylight, and Mrs. March briefly feared that at any moment the scenery would move and reveal itself as flat cardboard.

She walked to the grocery store on autopilot and stepped

through its automatic doors in a daze. Inside, weekly sales offered themselves loudly on star-shaped neon signs, while staff were summoned through the crackling loudspeakers and the dead fish stared at her, mouths agape, in their beds of ice. Mrs. March strolled through the cereal aisle as if she were sightseeing along the Champs-Élysées. It had always seemed to her the most curious of aisles, with all the garish colors on the otherwise uniform boxes, the cartoons threatening to leap out at you, screaming for you to choose them.

She turned into an adjacent aisle and stopped short in front of a woman. Her back was turned to Mrs. March but there was something familiar about the woman's fur coat, the ample shoulders slightly hunched beneath it, arms bent and elbows out, as if the woman was wringing her hands. A sharp tap on her shoulder made her jump, and she spun around to face one of her neighbors, but she could not—for the life of her—remember her name.

"How've you been, dear? How's George? We haven't talked in ages!" the woman said in rapid succession, no room for a reply of any kind. "I think the last time I saw you was at Milly Greenberg's party . . . no, I don't think you went to that. But anyway speaking of the Greenbergs, I don't know if you've heard . . ."

Mrs. March knew the Greenbergs only superficially, but as the woman proceeded to gossip, she learned that Milly Greenberg was in the midst of a shameful divorce because her husband had cheated on her (deservedly, apparently, seeing as she'd cheated on *her* ex-husband with her current one while he was married to his first wife). The woman—whatever her name was—gesticulated wildly as she spoke, and Mrs. March caught glimpses of her arm hair, black and thick, sprouting from under her sleeves and onto her wrists, where some of it caught on her wristwatch. This was the neighbor, she now recalled, who thrust apples at crestfallen trick-or-treaters under the pretense of preserving their dental health. The kind of neighbor who reported neighbors' dogs for aggression solely based on their size.

"And so *that's* what's happening, if you can believe it."

"But they always seemed so happy together," said Mrs. March.

"Oh, don't be so naive," snapped the woman. "I know plenty of couples who seem like they're so *in love*, but they're all lying, all of them. Now I knew Anne, or at least I thought I did, and it hurts me deeply that she wouldn't confide in me about her troubles."

"Perhaps she wanted to but couldn't."

"Nonsense. I told her all *my* troubles, about my mother-in-law's operation—a ghastly affair—and about how I get the blues on Tuesdays because my father used to drink on Tuesdays and spit on us."

"Goodness."

"Right? Serious stuff. I bared my soul to that woman. And what did she give me in return?"

There was a pause during which Mrs. March wondered, alarmed, whether it wasn't in fact meant as a rhetorical question. But then the woman tutted and, thankfully, continued—"And now Anne has had to move to a much smaller apartment, and she's really depressed and talks to nobody, apparently. Well, if you push people out, people will stay out, you know. That's what my sister always says."

"How can Anne afford her new apartment?" asked Mrs. March, prompted by a genuine curiosity. "I thought she didn't work?"

"Oh, she's had to find a job all right. She's working part time at a lawyer's office. Apparently her husband had the decency to set her up with a job there."

"How nice of him," offered Mrs. March.

"Oh no. Everyone there *knows*, you see, about her husband's affair. In fact, you wait and see if his mistress isn't working at that very office."

"Oh dear. I should hope not."

"I don't think Anne will know how to recover from this. She could have been a great artist, you know, she is quite the painter. But she gave everything up. For *him*."

Mrs. March now wondered if she, too, could have been something. Something other than a wife and mother. She pictured herself alone in a sad, dank apartment, heading to a dreary office in the mornings, not buying her olive bread for anyone. Not knowing, really, where to go, what to do, who to be. "Poor Anne," she said.

"Hmph. You never know. You spend your life pitying people, and it turns out they don't deserve your pity. Some of them are as ungrateful as they come. My sister knows this woman, about Anne's age, who was doing very well at her advertising job. Well paid, all the perks. Anyway she decided to *quit* her job to pursue an acting career. Imagine that, at her age!"

"Did it work out for her?"

"As if!" She said this with relish, and Mrs. March, who herself had been hoping for a negative outcome to the story, savored a surge of delicious satisfaction. "What did she expect? And my sister heard rumors that she may have resorted to . . . you know." The woman's eyes widened and she leaned into Mrs. March conspiratorially. She smelled like steak and Shalimar.

"She's been seen with much older men," the woman said, sotto voce. "Wealthy old men, one after the other. Listen, I don't like to gossip, but I doubt she's finding love with any of these men, is all I'm going to say." She pulled back and paused. "So, your George's book," she said, looking at Mrs. March for the first time with any real attention after talking in her general direction for several minutes.

"Yes?" Mrs. March was so unprepared for the intensity of the woman's focus, thrown upon her so unexpectedly, that she almost lost her balance.

"You know, it's funny," said the woman. "I left my copy right here in my cart the other day while I went to get some more sausages—Dean does love his pork—and can you believe it, somebody stole the book. Right from the cart!"

"My goodness!" Mrs. March shook her head somberly.

"I know! The book is certainly in demand, but for people to actually go around *stealing* it—"

"I'll speak with George and get you another copy—"

"I already bought another copy. I read it so quickly I'm almost finished." The woman's eyes narrowed, her brows furrowed, as if she were weighing what next to say. "It's a . . . it's quite a special book, isn't it."

"Yes."

The woman stared at Mrs. March in silence, while Mrs. March's skin itched in anticipation of the dreaded question. Given the insulting nature of the inquiry, and that the woman was a neighbor, it was safe to assume she wouldn't risk it. It would be like congratulating a woman who wasn't actually pregnant. Mrs. March stared back, smiling weakly.

"Well, I won't keep you any longer," the woman said at once. "I'm sure you're busy. Aren't we all, though? I'll be sure to congratulate George if I see him around."

"Thank you. I'll tell him you liked it," said Mrs. March.

Mrs. March walked out of the store without buying anything and braced herself against the wind on her way home, pulling her coat collar over her face as she walked past a square brick building overlooking the park with LOVE THY NEIGHBOR AS THYSELF engraved into the limestone over the entrance.

◆

IN THE ELEVATOR, she pressed the button for her floor. The doors closed and—slowly, almost dreamily—she pressed all the other buttons in one measured swoop of her hand. The panel lit up like a Christmas tree.

A special book, the woman had said. It *was* quite special for an author to degrade his wife so publicly, she supposed. To expose her innermost secrets like a greedy Asmodeus ripping off roofs. She fisted her hands so tightly her knuckles protruded like molars. He should be punished for it. Taken into custody for Sylvia Gibbler's murder, for starters. That would whip the smug smile right off his face.

Inside 606, George sat by himself in the living room, reading a newspaper. An opera aria—Puccini—bellowed on the turntable.

Mrs. March frowned at him from the doorway. "How are lamb chops for dinner," she said.

"Just fine," he replied.

She lingered a few more seconds before walking off to the bedroom, where she removed her heavy earrings and paced, arms crossed, eyeing the telephone on George's nightstand. She picked up the receiver, dialed 911. Before it could ring she hung up. Ridiculous, she thought. I have nothing to go on. What would I say, that I found a newspaper clipping in his notebook? She picked up the receiver again, looping a finger from her free hand around the plastic cord, and debated over whether to dial.

She was still holding the receiver to her ear, oblivious to the confused beeping of the line, when the floorboards creaked behind her. She turned to find George at the door and suppressed a scream.

"Have you by any chance seen my gloves?" he said. "I'll need them for my trip to London."

"London?"

"Yes. Remember? There's a charity event with several other authors, and a really important television interview? It'll just be a few days." His tone was flat, rehearsed.

"Oh. That's right." She didn't really remember them discussing anything about it, but thought it more astute to play along.

"Who are you calling?" asked George.

She gave him a puzzled look, then realized that she was still holding the phone to her ear. "Nobody," she said.

He looked at her curiously, half smiling. "All right then."

"I'm trying to reach my sister, but she's not picking up." She returned the receiver to the cradle so clumsily and with such force that the bell rang. George continued to stare at her and, feeling the need to do something with her hands, she began folding the clothes she had tossed onto the armchair when she had entered—scarf, mint green gloves, heavy sweater—and stacked them in an orderly pile.

"You'll be all right here all on your own?" asked George, watching her fuss with the clothes.

"Well, it's not like I haven't done it before."

"I know, I know. I'd ask you to come with me, but I'd feel better if someone was home with Jonathan, now that he's going back to school. Don't you agree?"

"Of course," said Mrs. March. "I wouldn't feel right about it either."

Mrs. March pictured how she would spend the next few days with Jonathan back in school. Visiting museums alone, eating lunch in silence in the empty dining room. But wasn't that what she always did, she reminded herself.

"Besides," said George, "I wouldn't want to put you through such an exhausting trip. You'd barely have time to get over your jet lag before we'd have to fly back."

It occurred to her that George had never used the term *jet lag* before. A heavy, steely certainty descended upon her: this man wasn't George. But who was he? There was something off about this man. It was George—it had his face and wore his cardigan—yet her gut told her that it wasn't.

"It does sound much better to stay at home," she said carefully, overenunciating every word.

He smiled, hands in his pockets—he didn't normally walk around with his hands in his pockets, did he?—"I thought it might." He raised a hand to scratch a spot behind his ear, saying, "I'll be in my study. Call me when the lamb chops are ready."

He turned to leave and, on impulse, she called out to him— "Wait!" He looked back at her as words tumbled from her mouth. "I've been meaning to ask you . . . what was the name of that little town . . . you know, when we summered in the south of Italy, and we had no air-conditioning, and we could see the ocean from the hotel room, and you used to stay up late smoking cigars on the terrace . . . Remember?"

"What? Why are you asking me this now?" he said. Buying time, she thought.

"Well," said Mrs. March, "the Millers upstairs are thinking of taking a trip to Italy. They love traveling together," she added, "and I told Sheila about our holiday and she asked me the name of the place."

George looked down at the floor, and for a moment she thought she'd caught him, this stranger, but he snapped his fingers, looked up at her, and said, in a triumphant tone, "Bramosia!"

They've really done a good job, whoever they are, she thought. Such attention to detail. As the stranger left the bedroom, she contemplated this new, dangerous idea with care. It was a queer sort of thought, but also an oddly logical one. The possibility that she might be right, that George had been replaced by an impostor, led her to an especially frightening notion: If there was another George walking around, might there be another *her* as well? But then, she concluded, her head jerking involuntarily toward the window, she had known that already.

XXVII

Martha's presence had a very palpable effect on Mrs. March. She wouldn't have made the effort to get out of bed and dress on the few days that George was away if Martha wasn't due to arrive each morning. The prospect of Martha's silent judgment of her sloth was incentive enough to get her up. In fact, Mrs. March had gotten into the recent habit of clearing away anything Martha might have to clean. Each morning before Martha's arrival, Mrs. March would get on all fours, peering under the furniture and in the corners of the bathrooms in search of cockroaches, wiping away any traces of ashes from Gabriella's cigarettes (she still occasionally smoked in secret, savoring the dwindling stash as she would a box of chocolate truffles), and removing any wineglasses she may have left atop dressers or night tables without coasters, where they left dark rings. She would sweep the sheets for crumbs—she had taken to nibbling late-night snacks in bed, a masochistic habit given the roaches. Lately, her clothes stretched a little tighter than was comfortable over her midsection. She now enjoyed longer, hotter baths so that the room filled up with steam, misting the mirror and obscuring her naked form when she stepped out of the tub.

She went about her daily routine in a daze, an endless series of cold walks to buy olive bread from subpar alternatives to Patricia's patisserie, or to visit the museum. One day she forgot her gloves, and her fingers went so numb that she was unable to unlock her own apartment door when she arrived home. She stood in the hallway for a few minutes until she could feel her cracked, pink hands return to life in painful pricks.

It was on one of her frigid walks one morning, heading down 75th Street, when she chanced upon the headband in a shopwindow. It was just like the one Sylvia Gibbler wore in the most recent photo released by the press. Sitting on a blanket in a wooded area, the dead girl smiled at the camera (she seemed always to be smiling), holding a peach and wearing a simple, black velvet headband.

Mrs. March contemplated buying it. Trying it on at home. Looking at her suddenly more attractive reflection in the mirror. Perhaps Sylvia would look back at her. She studied the possibility as she strolled past the shop, leaving the headband behind, navigating the masses on Third Avenue.

She joined the ranks of pedestrians at the crosswalk, all standing bravely against the whirlwind stirred by the passing M86 bus. It was then, as she was about to cross the street, that she noticed the woman in front of her. The woman wore a fur coat and polished tassel loafers, her hair arranged into a thin, limp bun. Mrs. March stared at the back of her head until the light turned green and she was jostled into the crosswalk so violently that she lost the woman in the blur of bobbing hats and swinging bags. After a few seconds she spotted her again, walking past the luncheonette on the corner. Mrs. March hastened after her, careful to keep a few steps behind. At present they were heading in the same direction, so Mrs. March reasoned that there was no harm in continuing this little game of Follow the Leader. The woman walked at a steady pace, the clacking of her loafers matching the rhythm of Mrs. March's own. When the woman turned her head to look into a shop-window, Mrs. March's heart fluttered as she studied the familiar rise of the woman's cheekbones, the patrician curve of her nose. They walked like this for a while, one Mrs. March following the other, like ducklings, until the woman turned the corner and Mrs. March, who was meant to go in the opposite direction, stopped in her tracks. She stood staring at the woman's back as she made her way down the street, and, invaded with a liberating, buoyant feeling—like red wine warming her chest and blooming into what could almost be described as happiness—decided that she simply couldn't walk away now. She swerved to the left, narrowly avoiding a passerby hidden behind a massive floral bouquet.

Mrs. March followed the woman in the fur coat to a street lined with identical townhouses. She kept her distance and watched the woman walk up the stone steps to one of the brownstones. The woman did not fumble around for any keys, instead turning the doorknob and pushing the front door open. She stepped inside and closed the door behind her. Mrs. March stood watching the front door a while longer, looking up and down the quiet street, before deciding to approach. It seemed so inviting, this sleepy brownish-purple building, with its arched front door and windows that curved under bracketed cornices. It looked so friendly. She went up the front steps slowly, her loafers tapping on the sandstone, her hands clasped in front of her as if in prayer. When she reached the top step, she placed her gloved hands against the heavily varnished wood, feeling for a pulse, then pushed. The door swung open with a satisfying creak, her reflection on the glossy veneer swinging along with it. She closed the door behind her, as softly as she could, and stepped into the foyer.

Inside, the air felt different. She walked across the black and white mosaic tiles, and thought she recognized her own mirror and the narrow coat closet in her own entrance hall. She walked further and encountered, to her right, a large, bright living room. Framed pictures gleamed from the white marble mantel. Strangers' smiles beamed at her from their silver frames. She surveyed the living room. Velvet fringed cushions lay propped up on an antique sofa, and a large gilded edition of *Jane Eyre* sat upon a quaint rolltop desk. She felt comfortable, soothed even, as if she'd been here before. Perhaps, she told herself, she had. She proceeded to a mirror, and thought she could distinguish, rather than a reflection of this woman's room, her own living room with its Hopper under the brass picture light and the bookshelves on each side of the fireplace.

She took a few measured deep breaths as she returned to the foyer, sensitive to any footsteps from upstairs, but she refused to flee, almost as if she was waiting for someone to discover her.

When no one descended the staircase, she opened the front door and left, taking a flowered umbrella from the porcelain umbrella stand on her way out.

◆

SHE WAS in a dreamy sort of mood when she arrived home. She left the stolen umbrella in the coat closet, along with her coat and hat. Martha was in the bedroom—she usually turned down the beds at this hour—and Mrs. March sneaked into the kitchen to make herself a cup of tea. She loitered awkwardly by the stove as the water boiled, then took her cup of tea and an embroidered napkin to the living room. She set the tea down on a side table, turned on the television, and was just sitting down when there was a knock on the front door. She froze mid-sit, hovering over the couch, listening for a second knock to confirm that someone was indeed at the door. When it came, much louder, more insistent, than the first, she sprang to open the door, forgoing the peephole in favor of speed.

There was no one there. The hallway, adorned in its familiar wallpaper, its sconces casting a warm, reassuring light, was empty. She glanced at the open elevator, its buttons unlit.

Slowly, she closed the door. A third knock, quick and light, almost shy in its hesitance, was barely audible through the door. She swung the door open with force and held it open, looking up and down the hallway, seeing no one. One of the children in the building, perhaps, playing a prank?

When she heard George's voice behind her she started. His voice was emanating from the living room into the foyer, where it seemed to poke at her mockingly. She closed the front door and followed the voice. Had George returned from London early? Her breath wavered, jagged, and she stepped gingerly into the living room to find it empty, but George's voice continued, uninterrupted. Puzzled, she stuck her head through the French doors into the dining room, only to realize that the voice was behind her, issuing from the television speakers. George was on TV.

"I do believe Johanna is regarded with a definite sort of derision in the book, particularly by the narrator," he was saying, eyes focused downward as he did when he was trying to appear thoughtful. "It was absolutely unintentional, but I did find myself gradually growing to dislike her, detest her even." Tittering erupted from the audience.

"What is it about her, do you think, that readers seem to be finding so compelling?" asked the interviewer.

"Well, to start with I think that she's very real." George

looked directly at the camera, at Mrs. March, his gaze boring into her like a deliberate, almost erotically slow stab. He looked back to the interviewer. "Or at least I hope she comes across that way."

"She certainly does. You've crafted a rather clever story around such a tragic creature."

"And to answer your previous question, I *would* consider selling the movie rights, yes. I think the book does lend itself to what I'd call cinematographic language."

"Do any actresses come to mind for Johanna?" asked the interviewer.

"You'll not catch me on that question, sir. I wouldn't want to offend any actress by naming her directly." George laughed.

"Well, I can guarantee there would be a long line of actresses willing to ugly themselves up to play this part. It has all the makings of an award-winning role."

Mrs. March envisioned a line of prospective Johannas, all looking like her, moving like her, like hundreds of mad reflections. She reached for the remote in the deliberate manner of one reaching for a hidden weapon, and turned the television off. She drank her cup of tea in silence, looking at her reflection on the screen.

XXVIII

The night before George was due home, Mrs. March grew tipsy on red wine and settled into a fragrant bubble bath. She and Jonathan had dined on their beefsteaks in silence, neither regarding the other, as the Chopin record played to its end. After they finished and Martha had left, Mrs. March took one of the good wineglasses—the ones reserved for formal affairs and stored in the dining room china cabinet—and filled it to the brim with Bordeaux.

Mrs. March sent Jonathan to bed but she could still hear him prancing about and talking to himself in his room. She closed her bedroom door and inspected the bathroom tiles for vermin. Finding none, she poured a thick stream of scented soap into the tub.

She undressed, dodging her reflection in the mirror the way one avoids a neighbor at the supermarket. She left her clothes folded neatly on the toilet seat and stepped delicately into the bathtub, adjusting to the temperature before submerging herself into the plush aromatic froth. The water pressed down on her chest with a weight that was almost crushing.

The events of the past few days nagged at her like flies on a corpse. She had explored George's study down to the last paper clip, searching for any souvenirs of his crimes, expecting to stumble across Sylvia's teeth in a porcelain snuffbox (the way she stored Jonathan's baby teeth). She had rifled through multiple notebooks and velvet-lined fountain pen cases and drawers filled with loose typewriter ribbons, but in the end had found nothing—only a telephone number scribbled on a notepad. She had called the number, and a woman had answered, but Mrs. March had not been able to come up with a convincing ruse to extract information and had hung up in a panic.

Earlier that morning, as she was still fending off the idea of getting out of bed, she was startled out of her lethargy by the devastating realization that she'd forgotten to tip the day doorman for Christmas. She'd raced down to the lobby, her hair undone, dressed sloppily in a loose shirt that bunched over her midriff and George's much-too-large trench coat, and had pressed a thick, sweaty wad of cash into the unsuspecting doorman's hands as he backed away from her.

She gulped her wine in the tub in an attempt to stifle the memory of her voice breaking as she pleaded, "Take it, please take it!" Like some kind of madwoman. Her purse had fallen from her shaking wrist, scattering its contents all over the lobby floor. The shriveled chestnuts from her long-forgotten visit to the museum rolled across the marble.

Going forward, she would have to wait until after the doorman's shift change at three o'clock to leave the apartment.

She bent her left leg, exposing her knee, and watched the steam rise off her skin in smoky wisps. As she squinted at her wrinkled fingertips, a string of blood dripped into the water. It moved across the tub like a water snake, diluting in a light pink near her toes. She sat up, ready to flee the tub, when she realized that she'd spilled some wine into her bath. She relaxed, leaned back into the water, and took another sip. Had Sylvia bled a lot as she was murdered? Could she feel the blood leaking out of her, trickling down her skin, as she was beaten and violated? The medical examiners had advised the public that rape was difficult to determine in this case, as the body had been subject to the elements, but the idea of Sylvia's rape was firmly instilled in everybody's minds, including Mrs. March's. At this point it would be disappointing if she *hadn't* been raped, if they had all been wasting their time mourning a simple murder. Certainly the contextual clues pointed to rape. The body had been found half-naked from the waist down, and Sylvia's panties had been discarded nearby as if in haste. Mrs. March tried to imagine what Sylvia's naked form had looked like. While she regarded her own body under the translucent water, she pictured Sylvia's pubic hair, imagining her killer marveling at it before raping her. A forgotten sensation blossomed inside Mrs. March—arousal. She immediately felt guilty, a familiar pattern burned into her psyche from her teenage days, when she had explored her body in the bathtub. The first time she'd done it, she imagined that Kiki had watched her, and that she had judged her for it. She finally put an end to Kiki, once and for all, the winter after that strange summer in Cádiz. When Kiki stepped into the bathtub with her that night, Mrs. March felt a wave of fury wash over her, followed by something altogether more desperate. She implored Kiki to leave, to never return, but a stubborn Kiki had refused. Angrily, Mrs. March reached out her hands toward Kiki's throat, pressing so hard that her nails dug into her palms and her arms trembled, shaking the air as if Kiki were fighting for her life. As her imaginary friend sank into the water, she pictured her neck hanging limp and her eyes going white. Satisfied, she pulled the stopper and the water circled the drain, taking Kiki with it.

As she grew drunker on her wine, the glass balanced precariously on the edge of the tub, she could sense something just out of her line of vision. She looked to her left without moving her head to see that it was a woman standing, naked, next to the bathtub. She gripped the edge of the tub, bracing herself to turn her head, and she saw that it was herself, looking down at her. Mrs. March held her gaze, trying to will them into cohesion, as her twin raised a leg over the tub and slipped inside, looking squarely at Mrs. March. It was then that she realized it must be a dream. The woman that was herself regarded her somewhat quizzically, then leaned forward, her too-dark, too-big nipples grazing the surface of the water, and extended her hands, her fingers searching, toward Mrs. March. She placed them under the water and Mrs. March could see them advancing between her open legs. "Don't," she said.

She woke up in tepid water, a greasy film on its surface, to find Jonathan standing over her. He was wearing his bear costume. "Are you dead, Mommy?" he asked. She tried to smile but her lips cracked painfully, dried out from the wine. "Mommy's only sleepy," she said. "Why don't you go along and play for a bit."

"It's after my bedtime."

She looked to the little window above the bathtub and saw that it was dark, although hadn't it already been dark when she first drew the bath? "Of course it is," she said. "Why are you up then?"

"I had a nightmare."

"Go back to bed."

"Can I sleep in your bed tonight?"

"You're too big for that. You know that."

She waited as Jonathan silently debated with himself. She couldn't move or the remaining foam would dissolve and he would see her breasts. She couldn't remember the last time he had seen her naked body. She didn't think he ever had. She herself had only ever seen her mother naked once, and she remembered it vividly. The black, woolly patch of coarse hair between her legs as she sat on the toilet in front of a young Mrs. March, and doing so inexplicably casually, even though nudity had been considered inappropriate in their household.

"Mommy . . ." began Jonathan, rubbing at his eyes, his dark heavy eyelashes crusted with sleep. "I can't find the lady inside the other lady."

"What are you saying?" said Mrs. March, alarmed.

"The lady inside the other lady . . ." repeated Jonathan. "You know, the Russian one!"

"Oh," said Mrs. March, with relief. He was referring to her mother's collection of wooden Russian dolls. "Have you been going through my things? You know you're not allowed in there."

"I couldn't find her . . . the last one, the tiniest one."

As a child, Mrs. March herself had played with these dolls in secret, twisting them open, revealing smaller versions of themselves. She would sometimes replace the innermost doll—the smallest, purest one—with another object. A folded bit of paper with a doodle on it, an ivory chess pawn, or one of her baby teeth. She'd thought it marvelously relatable that her mother even *had* dolls. It was at last something she could understand about her, something that might bond them. Her mother, upon discovering that she'd been tampering with them, scolded her and relegated the dolls to the highest shelf above her bedroom dresser. The dolls possessed an aura of unattainability, which prompted Mrs. March to take them for herself after her mother had been shipped off to Bethesda and the apartment had been emptied.

When Jonathan finally left the bathroom after much cajoling and, ultimately, the threat of punishment, Mrs. March rose from her awkward position in the tub—the water now cold—and pulled the drain stopper. Water drained from her body, too, dribbling out thinly from between her legs.

◆

SHE'D TAKEN the herbal pills that had worked on other occasions, but this time they failed. Sleep managed to elude her.

She got up from bed and pulled on some socks, grabbing her robe and making her way to the living room. Softly illuminated by streetlamp light, the room was silent, save for the occasional car on the street below.

Years ago, on a trip to Venice, George had gifted Mrs. March with an old mask. It sported a long beak, like the ones worn by plague doctors, except this mask had been painted a brilliant yellow, with white and gold feathers around the eyeholes, making it further resemble a bird. Perturbed by it, Mrs. March had hidden the mask on a high shelf among decades-old travel guides. Now, she stepped onto a chair, feeling for it blindly with her hands. She recognized it immediately upon touching it.

She walked with no real purpose around the apartment, her breath hot and loud inside the mask, her vision adjusting to the small eye cutouts. As a child, when she couldn't sleep, she hadn't dared to wander about like this. There had been something forbidding about her parents' living room in the dead of night, with its stiff sofas and heavy coffee table.

She walked into the dining room, running her hand along the table, tracing a finger on the portraits. She spotted something silver in one of the frames, glinting against the dark

Victorian palette. She peered closer, as close as her beak would allow, and saw that it was a silverfish, trapped under the glass, searching blindly for an exit. The insect creeped up toward the Victorian woman's face, whose entreating eyes seemed to be asking her to do something about it.

The silverfish raised its tiny head, as if to look at Mrs. March. She tapped on the glass gently and the insect skittered off, retreating under the frame and out of sight.

XXIX

With George scheduled to return in the evening and Jonathan at the Millers', Mrs. March set out to pick up the family's dry cleaning. This had once been a task for Martha until one of George's suits returned missing a tie. Rather than reprimand her for failing to notice, Mrs. March decided to take care of the dry cleaning herself from then on. She tended to wait until the weekend, when Martha had a day off, so as to avoid any awkwardness.

Mrs. March had gathered, on the many occasions she'd witnessed the doorman with the neighbors' dry cleaning, that it was considered appropriate to have him retrieve it, but that was out of the question. As she rushed past him in the lobby, she pulled her hat lower over her face to avoid interaction. He held the door open for her and called out "Good morning, Mrs. March!," to which she flushed a deep crimson, and mumbled an unintelligible reply.

The dry cleaner's was a deceptively small place tucked into a building on Third Avenue. Their delivery service wasn't reliable, and Mrs. March had noticed that she was charged at varying rates depending on what she happened to be wearing when she dropped off the dry cleaning (her fur coat coincided with the highest prices). However, the quality of the cleaning itself was beyond reproach. They could, as advertised, get any stain out. Today she was eager to pick up the clothes George had worn on his trip to Edgar's cabin. George had, strangely, insisted on dropping them off himself.

"Did you find anything, say, funny? On the clothes?" she asked the dry cleaner after he slapped the plastic-wrapped clothing onto the counter.

The man squinted at her for a minute, one edge of his mouth pulled into a sneer she hoped was involuntary. "Whad-dya mean?" he asked through a rancid cloud of cigar breath. His shirt had a small burn hole in the collar.

"Oh, nothing. Never mind," she said. "Did you get every-thing out all right?" She pressed her hands against the plastic, inspecting the clothes underneath.

"Everything all right, everything usual. Ain't no stain too hard for the stain professionals. Receipt's in the bag."

Mrs. March fumbled with her pocketbook as the man tended to another customer. From the back room, amidst the hissing of steam from the irons, a tinny radio announced: "*The little town of Gentry, still distraught over the discovery of Sylvia Gibbler's body . . .*"

She thrust a few bills at the dry cleaner, and as he made change, she leaned over the counter, straining to hear. "*There are currently no suspects, and friends and family believe the brutal crime may have been committed by a passing stranger. Authorities urge anyone who has any information to call the anonymous tip hotline at—*"

Mrs. March toyed with the idea of calling, of turning George in. She couldn't, for fear he was innocent. But from the dread in her stomach, she knew that he wasn't.

"Thanks, come again," the dry cleaner recited in a gruff singsong as he handed her the change.

On her way back home, her hands sweaty against the

plastic, a plan began to take shape in her mind. She would travel to Gentry herself. Search for clues, confirm her suspicions. No, that's ludicrous, she said to herself. Why would I go all the way to Maine on a silly hunch? But this objection proved to be halfhearted as she imagined herself gaining the trust of the locals, uncovering overlooked clues, even being lauded by the police for her bravery and tenacity. She resolved to make the trip, to ascertain once and for all if she was married to a violent murderer.

She was walking past a bookstore on Madison, turning her nose up at old editions of George's books that lay in carts outside the store, pages splayed like the legs of beckoning prostitutes. She stopped when she saw his latest novel on display in the store window. Through the glass she could see the warm-lit café, the brass-railed ladders attached to the bookshelves, books from floor to ceiling. Standing in front of the section labeled "Bestsellers," Mrs. March thought she recognized the gossipy woman from the supermarket, whose name still eluded her. The one whose copy of George's book Mrs. March had stolen from her sausage-laden cart. Mrs. March couldn't hear through the glass, but it looked as if the woman was reading aloud from George's book and laughing. And laughing beside her . . . was that Sheila Miller? Short-haired and slim, decked in a boyish parka and colorful scarf, and holding her stomach as if trying to contain the convulsive laughter within.

Mrs. March glared at them through the window, her heaving chest rustling the dry cleaning bag. A cab sped by behind her, its reflection a yellow blur across the bookstore window, slicing through the women's necks as it splashed gutter water onto the pavement.

The supermarket gossip pointed at something inside the

book. Sheila bent over for a closer look, her face expectant. Whatever she read made her still-smiling mouth drop open in cheerful shock, and she covered it with her hand, her eyes wide. The women turned toward each other in delighted mischief, like witches over a cauldron.

Mrs. March began to traverse, slowly, the length of window. Eventually her eyes met those of the two laughing women. She waited for their faces to collapse into an expression of contrition. Instead, to her dismay, the women's lips stretched into cold, greedy smiles. Mrs. March continued home.

When she arrived at her apartment building, she spied a small group huddled outside. Another gathering of George's fans, she assumed. As she neared the entrance, a few of them glanced at her curiously.

She had barely stepped inside her apartment when the intercom rang—a harsh, ugly bray that startled her. She picked up the receiver. "Yes?"

"Is George there?"

"No, I'm afraid he's out. Who is speaking?"

"Could we come in? We'd really like an autograph."

"That's not possible. Like I said, my husband isn't home."

"We're huge fans of the book. We only want to see where he lives. Please?"

"No, I—"

"We'll be out of your hair in five minutes, tops."

"Where is the doorman?" she said, her mouth dry.

"I'm writing my thesis on his new novel," said another voice. "It'll just take a moment. To see Johanna's birthplace would be invaluable to my research."

"I really can't let you in. Please leave."

Through the static of the intercom, she could hear

whispering. "Stop bothering us," pleaded Mrs. March, the dry cleaning still clutched in one hand, sweat forming at her temples. "Hello?" she said. "Hello?"

"Yes?" came a voice, so loud and clear she recoiled. "This is the doorman."

"Oh, thank God," she said. "This is Mrs. March, in 606. Are they gone?"

"Are who gone?"

"The fans, George's fans, the group outside . . ." She stopped, her sweat now cold, as she theorized that this wasn't, in fact, the doorman speaking at all. And now they had her apartment number.

As if in confirmation, something slammed against her front door with such force the hinges rattled. Mrs. March gasped, the dry cleaning dropping to the floor, as if shot. She swallowed, gathering her courage to peer through the peephole, when another violent slam threatened to knock the door from its very frame. She held her face in her hands, and as the banging continued, pressed her back against the door as a kind of buttress. The relentless pounding rang through her chest as she leaned on the door. "Leave me alone!" she cried between anguished sobs as she slid down to the floor.

And just like that the knocking stopped.

◆

SHE REMAINED in a heap on the floor, propped against the door, until well after dark. When the doorbell rang she twitched, and a voice on the other side announced: "Mrs. March, it's me, Sheila! I've brought Jonathan."

Jonathan—she was bringing Jonathan back from upstairs.

Mrs. March got up off the floor and checked herself in the mirror. Her face was puffy and her mascara had streaked down her cheeks. She fixed it—smeared it more or less—with her fingers, as Sheila knocked again. Shadows shuffled underneath the door, and Mrs. March suspected for a second that it was all a ruse: George's fans were getting creative. She put one eye to the peephole and saw Sheila, her blond head warped, looking directly at her. She pulled back hastily, then bit her thumb and unlocked the door.

Sheila smiled, her hand on Jonathan's shoulder. If she had seen Mrs. March outside the bookstore, her face betrayed nothing. Jonathan ran into the apartment, and Sheila was about to walk off after uttering a generic "Have a great day!" when Mrs. March cleared her throat and said, "I would appreciate it, Sheila, when Jonathan is in your care, if you wouldn't go out and leave him unsupervised."

Sheila's face projected bewilderment, her neck flushing. "Of course not," she said. "I would never—"

"But didn't I see you on Madison? Just a couple of hours ago?"

Sheila frowned in such an exaggerated manner it could only be taken as mock contemplation. "No, I . . . I didn't go out at all today. The boys watched a movie, I made some lemonade and cookies . . ."

"Well, I must be mistaken then."

Sheila scratched at her collarbone. "Are you all right?" she asked.

"I'm perfectly fine," answered Mrs. March. She blinked, and it was like flipping a switch: her posture straightened and she smiled so widely her face threatened to bubble and melt and slide off the side of her head. "Thank you *so* very much for taking care of Jonathan," she gushed. "We'll see you again soon,

I hope. Have a *lovely* evening." And with that she closed the door in Sheila's face.

◆

WHEN GEORGE returned, Mrs. March—ever dutiful—asked him how his trip went.

"Splendidly," he answered, which annoyed her greatly. "Everything went without a hitch. I think I nailed the interview—did you watch it?"

"I recorded it so that we could watch it together, with Jonathan," she said, her eyes darting to the television and the empty tapes in the console.

"They seem to really love the book over there," George said as he sat on the floor attempting to fix Jonathan's train set, which had stopped working the previous evening.

"They love it everywhere, darling," she said in such a breathless way that even Jonathan, who was lying on the floor watching television, gave her an odd look.

"Regardless," continued George, "I'm thankful for everything." He shook his head as if in disbelief. "I'm thankful," he repeated, reaching out to squeeze Mrs. March's hand.

She was supposed to be pleased for him, she thought, pulling her hand from his, but she wasn't. She had been left alone despite wanting to accompany him (had she really? a small voice inside her asked). She wanted to punish him, to make him feel guilty for leaving her behind. To make him think twice before doing it again. As George rattled on about some prize his book had been longlisted for, she examined him for any traces of the stranger who had stood before her in their bedroom packing his suitcase. She took in the blackheads on the tip of his nose, a wiry white hair sprouting from an eyebrow, his slightly lopsided glasses, and she concluded—with disappointment—that her theory was flawed. George was George, as he had always been and always would be, and her insistence on fantastical theories to excuse his violent crime would simply not do. No, she thought, feeling herself physically harden as she watched George fumble with Jonathan's train set with the same hands that had strangled Sylvia—she would get to the bottom of this once and for all. She would tell George that she was visiting her sister and mother in Bethesda, but instead she would go to Gentry. When George cut his finger on a train track, Mrs. March headed to the bathroom for a Band-Aid, smiling to herself all the way.

It's a funny concept, guilt. The first emotion Mrs. March could ever remember feeling. She had been around three years old, toilet trained but not yet proficient in the art of wiping. Her parents were hosting a luncheon. She couldn't recall exactly who was present, or why she and her sister Lisa were allowed to sit at the dining table, but in the midst of eating her pureed vegetables—perhaps through some Freudian connection—she felt the unavoidable call of nature. She looked to her mother, who was presiding at the table a few chairs away. Pushing her chair back noisily, her linen napkin falling to the floor, she made her way to her mother, her pudgy hands gripping onto chair finials. She reached Mrs. Kirby in the middle of a shrill, rippling laugh, of a kind never heard in the apartment unless guests were present. On tiptoes, Mrs. March cupped her hand and whispered into her mother's ear, her nose brushing one Chanel clip-on: "I have to go to the bathroom."

Her mother sighed, asking "Can't you hold it *in*?" through gritted teeth. When Mrs. March shook her head, her mother dismissed her with a flick of her hand.

Mrs. March still dreamed of it some nights—the shadows of her dangling feet on the tan marble as she perched on the guest bathroom toilet. She had used that particular bathroom, presumably, because it was nearest to the dining room. So that her mother could hear her when she called out to her—"Mommy!

I'm ready, Mommy!" After what felt like an impossibly long time (*what if she never came?*), her mother appeared, furious, muttering under her breath, "Couldn't you have *waited*? . . . shouldn't be *my* job . . . *Lisa* never . . ." She wiped her daughter's behind with such force it left her raw. Afterwards, whenever Mrs. March called for her mother from the bathroom to come and wipe her, the help would appear in her stead.

That was Mrs. March's first experience with guilt.

Then, aged four, she had received a lavish dollhouse on Christmas, bursting into tears upon tearing off the gift wrap.

"What is it?" her mother asked. "Isn't it what you wanted?"

She nodded and continued to cry, snot running down to her lips.

"Ugh, she's so spoiled," her sister Lisa said, holding her own present—an elaborate chemistry set—with mature dispassion.

Mrs. March hadn't, at that moment, been able to explain that she *had* in fact wanted that particular dollhouse, that she had fantasized about it ever since first glimpsing it in the FAO Schwarz catalog. And now here it was, a mammoth Victorian, complete with miniature paintings in gilded frames and working light fixtures and a porcelain bathroom. She'd done nothing to deserve it, hadn't worked for it the way she would for a gold star sticker in her preschool class. She had merely asked for it, and now here it was, in her undeserving hands.

Lisa rolled her eyes, saying, "Jeez, it's not that big a deal. You'll get what you want *next* year," as Mrs. March wept quietly.

Guilt was for the brave. Denial was for the rest.

XXXI

The only problem now, Mrs. March thought, was the possibility that her sister might call while she was away, asking after her. She didn't think Lisa *would* call; in fact she rarely ever bothered to pick up the phone outside of holidays and birthdays. However, she had been known to call randomly with updates about their mother. Once she phoned with the pressing news that their mother had stuck glitter to a handmade Christmas tree ornament at the nursing home.

Another lie was necessary. She was on a serious mission, after all. She'd cover her tracks and, depending on what she found, nobody need ever know she'd even made the trip to Maine. The prospect of having a little secret to herself, known only to her, possibly forever, thrilled her.

The following evening, after Martha had departed and George had sequestered himself in his study, Mrs. March telephoned her sister. "I wanted to tell you that I'll be away for a few days, so in case you were thinking of calling, well, don't. I won't be here. Neither will George," she added on a whim, "we're going to a—a spa."

"Oh, how lovely. I didn't know you were into that sort of thing."

"Well, that's ridiculous, who wouldn't be?"

"True, I suppose," Lisa said. "Where is it? This spa."

"Oh . . . I don't know."

"You mean you don't know where you're going?"

"No, it's a surprise . . . from George," she said, impressed with herself.

"Oh. Lucky you," Lisa said—tartly, Mrs. March thought. "What about Jonathan?"

"He'll be staying with the upstairs neighbors."

"Want me to call in and check on him?"

"No, no, I'll be doing that myself. Again, I only called to let you know I won't be home. I'll ring you as soon as I get back."

"All right then, dear. Have fun."

Next, she called the airline and bought an open-ended ticket to Augusta.

"Thank you, ma'am, enjoy your trip! Maine is lovely this time of year," said the saleswoman before the line went dead. Mrs. March went over to the closet and opened the doors solemnly—there seemed to be a grand purpose behind all her actions now—and pulled down a small tartan suitcase from a high shelf.

She was packing her tawny winter slippers when George walked in, and it was like living a scene she had experienced before, but from the other point of view. "I'm going to visit my mother," she said as he had barely stepped over the threshold. "I spoke to my sister, and Mother's not feeling well."

She peered at George from the corners of her eyes as she pretended to busy herself with packing. He looked somewhat perplexed as he scratched his chin and said, "I'm sorry to hear that, honey. Is there anything you need?"

"No, it's all settled," she said, folding a few silk headscarves into the suitcase (her idea of traveling incognito).

"How long are you staying then?"

"Well, I bought an open-ended ticket, because I'm not sure

how long they'll be needing me. I told her I would stay as long as necessary." She said this with an air of martyr-like pride, leaving George to reply, "Of course. Do what you need to do."

"I'll call you every so often to let you know how she's doing."

"Well, it looks like you have everything under control, as usual," he said. It infuriated her, this deep lack of interest in her sudden trip. He walked over to her, and she tensed as he pecked her softly on the cheek. Like Judas, she thought. When he pulled his head back, she could detect the hint of a smile on his face.

"I'm going to take a shower," he said.

As soon as the shower was on she rushed into George's study. He kept the keys to Edgar's cabin in a small ceramic bowl on his desk, where she now spotted them in a bed of chewing gum wrappers and loose change. She took them gently, delicately, waiting to be caught in the act, but no one interrupted her as she pocketed them, and slipped out as quietly as she had entered.

◆

MRS. MARCH kissed George goodbye and bade Martha farewell (Jonathan was in school). She stepped into the elevator, looking back at apartment 606. The door was closed.

In the elevator she took a deep breath. She hummed a little, looking down at her suitcase. She'd written her address on a leather name tag and the ink had smudged across her first name.

The elevator doors opened with their usual jolt. She walked out into the lobby, rolling the little suitcase behind her. She approached the glass doors, expecting George, at any moment, to appear behind her. She dared not turn around as she stepped closer, ever closer, to the exit.

The doorman hailed her a cab, and she waited dumbly as he fit her suitcase into the trunk with more fuss than was necessary. She thanked him and slid into the backseat, the door shutting after her. She glanced up at the apartment building, at the square windows and the square air-conditioning units.

As the cab took off, turning the corner so that she lost sight of the building, she was blindsided by a pang of guilt. She hadn't visited her mother since Jonathan was a baby. Inside her lay the grim certainty that it was her mother who should have died—not her father. Her father, with his tanned, rotund belly she had only ever seen in Cádiz that summer. Her father, who always made their dinner reservations and knew who to call when their suitcases were lost in Greece. She had once prepared a repulsive dish of grapes and crumbled chocolate chip cookies and peanuts, garnished with salt and sugar and pepper, and had presented it proudly to her parents, encouraged by a beaming Alma. Her mother refused to try it, another reminder to her daughters that she wasn't their friend and never would be. Her father had declined politely at first, but after some gentle prodding by Alma, he volunteered to give it a taste. He bent over the plate and shoveled a generous spoonful of the disagreeable mix into his mouth. He munched on it silently, no doubt regretting it. Despite the scalding sheepishness she had felt at the time, Mrs. March had also been thankful, and for the first time, perhaps, truly appreciative of her father.

Sitting on the cab's odorous, cracked leather seat, she justified her neglect of her mother, reassuring herself that if her father were the one living out his last days, she would be visiting him plenty in Bethesda. In fact, she decided with sudden conviction, she wouldn't even have allowed him to be taken so far away in the first place. She would have kept him as close to her as possible. Dear old Mr. Kirby. She wondered what he looked like now in his coffin. She usually pictured him as a floating newspaper with legs. He would have rotted away by now, leaving nothing but bones.

The trip to the airport was uneventful—nobody in pursuit, nobody stopping her. The cabdriver didn't suddenly swerve off the expressway to murder her at some deserted location on George's instruction.

Similarly, her flight was on time and there were no delays getting through security. She donned a comically large pair of sunglasses and a headscarf and avoided the airport bookstore, where George's book taunted her on a revolving display.

As she queued up at the gate, she overheard a man talking loudly on a nearby pay phone. He was dressed in a trench coat and held a briefcase in one hand, the receiver lodged between his head and his shoulder. "Yes, Delmonico's? Hello, this is John Burnett. Right. I'd like to make a reservation for dinner, for next Saturday. Yes. For two. Seven o'clock would be swell."

Mrs. March displayed her boarding pass to the gate agent and walked onto the gangway, leaving the man to make his dinner reservation. How curious, she thought, that she knew where this stranger would be at seven o'clock next Saturday. She toyed with the idea of showing up at Delmonico's, maybe even greeting him with familiarity, reveling in his surprise. Would he pretend to know her? Or was John an honest man? As she stepped onto the plane, she wondered who John's dinner date was. Was this a romantic dinner with his wife? Or perhaps he was treating his lover to a bottle of champagne and oysters. But if that were the case, would he be making plans so brazenly on a public pay phone?

She sat by the window, her legs cramped, the seat belt slicing across her midriff. The takeoff was clumsy, and as soon as the seat belt sign was off she asked the stewardess for red wine. Forgoing the plastic cup and drinking straight from the tiny bottle, she imagined, should the plane crash, how long it would take George to find her. Once he spoke with her sister, he might assume she was having an affair, and when the days passed he might think she had run off with the man. She liked the thought of him fearing he had lost her, feeling remorse for how he had taken her for granted, for writing that abominable book.

◆

After a one-hour stopover in Boston, she flew to Augusta. The whole trip took a little over three hours. Since it would have taken half the time to get to Bethesda, she called George from a pay phone at the airport to say that she had arrived at her sister's after an unforeseen flight delay. George seemed uninterested in her update, distracted even, and she could hear muffled giggles in the background.

"Who's that?" she asked.

"Oh, it's just Jonathan being silly."

She wrinkled her nose, staring down at her shoes. She had never known Jonathan to be *silly*. "And you're both all right then?"

"Yes, yes. We'll miss you, but we'll be fine. Don't worry, honey. We'll make do without you."

"Very well. Don't forget to tell Martha to make the lamb tonight. Otherwise it'll go bad."

"Will do," said George. "Have fun! Give my best to everyone." George hung up.

Mrs. March stood at the pay phone, blinking, the phone still clutched to her ear, and said, loudly, "I love you, too, darling. I'll see you soon," for the benefit of the woman next in line.

Under the pay phone scattered business cards listed numbers for local restaurants and cab companies. She called one of the taxi services. It took a few rings for them to pick up, and the man on the other end seemed surprised to be fielding a call, but he assured her that she'd have a cab in five minutes.

She stepped, with determination, into the freezing air, which slammed into her like a wave.

XXXII

Edgar's cabin was about a forty-minute drive from the airport. Mrs. March had copied the address from George's Rolodex onto a slip of yellow paper she'd been rubbing inside her coat pocket the entire trip. She'd also brought along a notebook (one of George's) and a pen to jot down notes.

The cab had arrived promptly as promised. The logo on the back door featured a cartoon moose in sunglasses on its hind legs, giving a thumbs-up. The driver was friendly and overly chatty, which irked Mrs. March, who saw it as a mark of unprofessionalism, even when he offered to get the door—pronouncing it *doah*.

On the drive to Edgar's cabin, cemeteries spread out on either side of the road, the gravestones casting their shadows on the snow. On the bridge over the Kennebec River, the driver pointed out large frozen patches of water, explaining they were set to be broken up by the Coast Guard.

He alerted her when they entered the quiet town of Gentry. She looked out her window at the deserted streets—so deserted she wondered why the cabdriver bothered using a turn signal. She noticed two scrapbooking stores and a wilted wreath hanging on the front door of the town hall.

Once through what passed for a downtown, the cab swerved onto a road lined with massive fir trees where the buildings were spaced further apart. Here the stores looked like houses—

squat clapboard buildings with signs in the windows or yards, announcing such local businesses as "Diana's Hair Emporium" and "Muffin Madness" and "Lester's Dog Grooming." The locals looked to be proud of their town, but all Mrs. March saw was an ugly, lonely little place. She was mystified as to what Edgar had ever seen in it to inspire a property purchase. Maybe it was the remoteness that appealed to him, as it facilitated his and George's dark habits. She tried to remember if George had known Edgar when he bought the cabin all those years ago.

They passed a diner with a massive parking lot. She noted how close it was to the cabin when the cab pulled into Edgar's dirt driveway.

Mrs. March paid in cash and refused the driver's repeated offers to lug her suitcase up to the house. He threw up his hands and drove off, bidding farewell with a good-natured honk, which made her drop her luggage onto a patch of ice. The wooden cabin was bigger than she had anticipated, with steps leading up to a deck that ringed the house and a stone chimney.

When she unlocked the front door with the stolen key and stepped inside—knocking over a pair of snowshoes propped up on the wall by the door—she was taken aback by the sheer amount of wood. Wooden floors, wooden walls, wooden furniture, wooden shelves, stacks of wood by the fireplace. Wood, much of it plainly varnished, was everywhere, giving the place an unfinished look. The walls, Mrs. March thought, were screaming for a layer of paint.

She closed the door behind her, feeling as if she were closing the lid of her own pinewood coffin. Lowering her suitcase to the floor, she proceeded to explore, her arms crossed at her chest. The ceilings were crisscrossed by exposed beams. There was a fieldstone fireplace, and on the mantel a taxidermied fox—possibly one Edgar himself had caught—posed as if prowling on a wooden branch, one marble eye missing from its socket.

She surveyed the large built-in bookcase, dreading what she knew she'd find there: George's complete bibliography, arranged in order of publication date, their glossy jackets shining. She slid one out at random, disturbing a thin layer of dust on the shelf, and opened it up to read the handwritten note on the first page. "To Edgar, Editor Extraordinaire. George." She took out another one and flipped to the same page—"To Edgar. This book wouldn't be what it is without you, and neither would this author. George"—then another—"To Edgar, my friend, my editor, my partner in crime. George." At this, Mrs. March licked the page savagely before closing the book and returning it to the shelf. George had only ever signed his books for her at the beginning. There was really no point anymore, she supposed, to signing or dedicating any more books to her, when she had lived with their author for so long. Besides, she had always assumed it was implied that all his works were dedicated to her, the person to whom George had chosen to dedicate his *life*.

The term *partner in crime* nagged at her as she walked through the cabin, opening doors that led into barely furnished bedrooms and musty closets, failing to find traces of a specific kind of life lived here. Ratty blankets and old coats and faded swimming trunks told no stories—at least the kinds of stories Mrs. March was looking to uncover.

She opened another door and found the kitchen—rustic, with copper pans hanging over an ancient six-burner stove. There was some food in the fridge, its edibility suspect, and she thought it best to eat out at the diner.

There was a key box mounted on the kitchen wall by the back door, lined with keys. She took the key labeled "Garage" and stepped outside. Parked inside the garage, like a hibernating bear, sat an old Jeep, dark green with bald tires. She pictured Edgar driving it, George in the passenger seat, both of them silent on the ride back to the cabin after murdering Sylvia, possibly with her body stuffed into the trunk. She cupped her hands around her face, which she pressed against the driver's side window. On a lark, she pulled on the door handle. It clicked open with such ease that Mrs. March yelped. Her cry still echoing inside the garage walls, she crawled into the car and sniffed at the tree-shaped air freshener—no longer smelling of pine—hanging from the rearview mirror. She lifted the floor mats and opened the glove compartment, where she found a sloppily folded calendar detailing the current hunting season. "1 deer per year," "2 bear per year." Several dates were circled in red. She popped opened the trunk, searching for traces of blood, long brown hairs, a monogrammed bracelet or a necklace, anything that could have belonged to Sylvia, but she found nothing.

She contemplated taking the car keys and driving into town. She was nervous about drawing attention to herself by calling more cabs and giving fake names, but the thought of driving a car on the open road unnerved her—her last foray behind the wheel had been at her father's club in a golf cart.

She resolved, then, that it would be prudent to walk whenever possible, and she would start by walking to the diner for dinner.

◆

WRAPPING HER scarf around her face, Mrs. March walked among the trees just off the main road to avoid detection, glancing back frequently at the garage—barely visible now. She chided herself for her stupidity. Surely she would die of hypothermia in these woods, and her body would be hidden for weeks before a hiker or a hunter found her, just as they'd discovered Sylvia's frozen corpse.

The pine trees swayed in the wind as she made her way to the diner. Trees from this very area might have been cut down to make the paper in George's books. How many trees, she wondered, to print all of those copies? A whole forest stood waiting to be sacrificed for future editions. The trees around her seemed to shiver. She imagined them screaming in women's voices, and as their branches began flailing, she hurried on toward the diner's neon sign, flashing in the distance.

◆

THE DINER was almost empty, except for an elderly couple and a man reading a newspaper in a corner. It wasn't a dive, although it certainly wouldn't be mistaken for a fine-dining establishment with its maroon vinyl booths. Plastic-coated menus sat between ketchup and mustard bottles on every table. The place felt cozy, safe even, and Mrs. March imagined herself coming here for dinner every night, getting to know the waitstaff, eventually becoming their favorite customer.

She picked a booth next to a window overlooking the parking lot, and a small squeak of flatulence from the plastic cushion announced her arrival. At the sound, a waiter looked up from behind the bar and nodded at her. Not wishing to raise her voice, she responded with a queenly wave of her hand.

She sniffed at her wrists and realized that she had forgotten to pack her perfume. She felt like a stranger to herself without it—a scentless ghost. She smiled at the thought. If scent was an identity, not having one opened up new, exciting possibilities. She could stay here in Gentry, her slate wiped clean, and start over. She could be anyone she wanted.

She felt a sudden draft and turned to see two men entering the diner. The door slowly closed behind them as they proceeded to sit on stools at the counter. One of them looked over at her. She smiled. He ignored her, turning his back to her as a waiter took their order.

Her face growing hot, Mrs. March looked down at her menu. It was probably mannerless brutes like these who had murdered Sylvia, not her husband. They had spotted her, a nubile young creature, eating alone at this very diner, and had abducted her in the parking lot. She glared at their backs, stung by the certainty that these men would never leer at her the way they surely had at Sylvia.

The waiter approached her table, and as he took her order she tried to purse her lips seductively, as she decided on a lobster roll and a hot tea. He never once met her eye, however, between scribbles on his notepad.

By the time she finished her dinner, only the two men at the counter and Mrs. March remained. She sat in her booth, rehearsing in her head the different ways she might reject the men's advances if they were to approach her. In the end they did not come anywhere near her, and when they put their coats and hats on, she threw a few crumpled bills onto the table and hurried to the exit, giving the men one last chance to assail her as they all walked out. The men did not acknowledge her, let alone hold the door open for her, and her face burned as she stepped out into the cold.

Crossing the parking lot, she ran into a dog, or rather the dog ran into her. She never had managed to figure dogs out, and having lived, as a child, with a cat and its erratic whims, she had learned to fear the unpredictable nature of animals in general. The dog pressed its snout against her leg and sniffed, blinking serenely. She'd read somewhere that dogs often smelled those who were ill or suffering. Had it sensed her anguish? She knelt down beside the dog in a grand gesture of appreciation (its owner, indifferent to the exchange, held the leash limply as he readjusted his scarf). She petted the dog, sensing a great connection. She curled her fingers around its wiry gray coat and whispered to it, "Yes. Yes. It's going to be all right, isn't it?" as the dog yawned with its tongue out, its wet black eyes focused on a point in the distance (why did dogs never seem to look her in the eye?).

The owner cleared his throat, and Mrs. March gave a quiet little laugh, sniffed, and stood up. "Thank you," she said to the owner. "*Thank* you." Not waiting for a reply, she walked off across the parking lot, her tasseled loafers—the leather now ruined by snow and salt—clicking on the cement, her shadow slicing through the lights cast by the streetlamps.

◆

THAT NIGHT, as Mrs. March attempted to sleep in the cabin, she was distracted by a series of unfamiliar noises. The wood walls and floors creaked and a hidden clock ticked away the minutes. Outside, the wind pealed, the endless rumble identical to that of the ocean in Cádiz. As she drifted to sleep, she wondered whether she might drown.

At some point in the night she lurched awake, disoriented, to find herself in a darkness unknown to her, so black it rung in her ears. The wavelike wind had ceased its crashing, slowing into a kind of relaxed breathing. Listening closer, Mrs. March could detect actual breathing, deep and heavy, almost wet. It's only Kiki. Good old Kiki who misses you.

Unsure if she was squeezing her eyes shut or whether it was just the darkness, Mrs. March covered her ears with a blanket.

XXXIII

A wooden mallard sat on the edge of the bathtub. Mrs. March blinked at it, praying that it wouldn't blink back as she dabbed at her underarms and between her legs with a threadbare towel she had found under the sink.

She squinted at the harsh morning light pouring through the bathroom window. It was so bright it was almost white.

She had slept on the couch in front of the fireplace, so as to disturb as little as possible. For warmth she'd draped herself with a thick blanket that most likely had been used by Edgar's basset hound; immediately upon waking, she returned it to the floor near the dog bed where she had found it and conducted a more thorough search of the cabin.

Mrs. March looked under beds, in flower vases, behind toilets, and even in the sugar and flour jars in the kitchen. She knocked on walls, listening for the telltale hollowness of a secret room. She was in search of anything that might seem suspicious or out of place, anything that might contradict George and Edgar's description of the cabin. She found nothing.

That morning she walked over to Gentry's Main Street—a long, bitterly cold forty-minute walk, the backs of her ruined loafers digging into her heels by the end of it. The grocery was a dirty-white clapboard building with a tattered American flag and a blue mailbox. A sign over the entrance read "Gentry General Store."

Walking inside, Mrs. March passed a revolving display crammed with postcards, piles of local winter produce—potatoes mostly—and an ice cream freezer, its motor shivering, freezer-burned cartons piled up inside it.

She wandered the narrow aisles, lifted a few scented candles to sniff them. No matter the label, each one smelled of dust.

"Can I help you?"

She turned around to see the store clerk, a pudgy bald man with hairy arms and hairy knuckles, and tufts of hair on the nape of his neck and in his ears. It was as if his body were trying to apologize for his hair loss, Mrs. March thought. "Oh, hello," she said. She set the candle—"Turkey Stuffing"—back on the shelf and walked over to the counter where he stood. *Hunting and fishing licenses sold here!* proclaimed a sign on the wall behind the cash register. "I was—I was just looking around."

"Looking around at a store with only three aisles? That's mighty peculiar. Most folks come here with a list, if they're out of milk and eggs, say." Mrs. March stared at him blankly until he said, "Well, look around all you want. Nobody's rushing you. Let me know if you need anything."

"Well, actually—" she said, wringing her chapped hands, "I was curious to know whether you knew anything about what happened, about that girl who was killed."

The clerk raised his eyebrows, eyes widening.

"I know it's lurid to be curious," Mrs. March hurried to explain, "only I'm not from around here, I was just passing through, and the story struck me because, well, I'm a mother," she said, bravely, gaining conviction as she went on, "and I have a daughter and she—Sylvia—reminds me so much of my Susan."

The clerk's eyebrows relaxed and his face formed an expression resembling tenderness. He looked from left to right rather dramatically before leaning over the counter on his elbows. "*Well*," he said, "it's been really hard for folks these past few weeks. Especially for me—I mean, I knew her personally."

Now it was Mrs. March's turn to raise her eyebrows. "Really?" she said, breathless.

"I mean, you know, she came in here sometimes. For milk and batteries and whatnot."

"Oh," said Mrs. March, deflating.

"But let me tell you, that girl was friends with everybody. Real friendly like. One of the kindest people I ever met. She was the type to give the less fortunate canned goods and her old clothes. And not just on Christmas."

"My goodness," said Mrs. March. "What a terrible waste."

Isn't it funny, she thought, how one's status invariably soars after one's death. She had pictured her own funeral many times: Jonathan, always so imperturbable, finally breaking down into heaving sobs as he clutched his mother's casket, George at his side in a shocked silence most would misjudge as stoicism but was actually repentance. People would remember her fondly, feeling closer to her than they ever had in life. She liked to imagine another author writing George's biography, who would include a very large section on her premature death. It sounded wonderful until she pictured the biographer snooping into her past, digging away at the quiet corners of her life, coming up with a less flattering portrait of her, another version of sad, pathetic Johanna.

"Shouldn't have been out so late," the clerk said. "Isn't safe. Even in a town like this, where everyone knows each other. It's a shame, but even in Gentry it isn't safe. My daughter always says to me, it's not fair women have to be careful when it's dark out. Well, look, it might not be fair, but that's how this world works. Your daughter ever say that to you?"

It took Mrs. March a second to realize he was asking after her fabricated daughter. "My Susan's more of a homebody," she said, "because she's very studious, you see. She just got into Harvard." Even in fantasy, Mrs. March was compelled to keep up appearances.

"Harvard, eh? Wowee, you got a good one there, dontcha?"

"Yes, we like to think so," said Mrs. March, forgetting her modesty.

"Ayuh. Lucky, very lucky, indeed."

"Well, yes, of course luck comes into it," she said, attempting to correct course, "but one does wonder whether our *parenting* had anything to do with how she turned out . . ."

"Sure, sure. But you never know. Our daughter makes no sense to us, even as a baby—we just can't figure out who she takes after. Wild thing, you know the type. She settled down a bit after they found Sylvia, though—"

"Who were the hunters who found her? Do you know them?"

"Naw, they were just visiting. One hell of a trip, eh, one minute you're looking for birds to shoot and the next minute you're staring down a dead body."

"How awful," said Mrs. March. "I wonder who could have done such a thing?"

"Oh, there's all sorts of crazies and weirdos out there. Hate to say it but they mostly target women. What you gonna do, though?"

"Is it possible that Sylvia knew her attacker personally?"

"Naw, the people of Gentry would have noticed something funny"—he snapped his fingers—"like *that*. It's a small town. Very small town. Had to be an outsider for sure."

"Mmm."

"She's just down the street, if you want to pay your respects. Laid to rest at Gentry Township Cemetery."

"Yes, I think I will. And—is her store somewhere nearby? The store where she worked? I want to buy a present for my daughter there, you know, in solidarity. It must have been such a blow to her coworkers."

"Ayuh, 'specially to Amy, they were very close. Amy Bryant?" he said when Mrs. March frowned at the name. "She's the daughter of some friends of mine. Very close to Sylvia. Went everywhere together. I saw them pass by the store every morning on their way to work," he said, pointing his thumb at the window by the counter. "I heard they were thinking of moving in together. Sylvia lived with her grandmother, see. Girl her age *would* need her independence."

"You know, I think I will visit the store, talk to poor Amy," said Mrs. March.

"Oh, Amy hasn't been working since it happened," said the clerk. "Stays at home, isn't really doing anything. She's in a bad state."

"That's a shame, really. How sad."

"It's been quite a rough couple of months around here, I'll tell you that."

"So this Amy, she—she lives near here?"

"Yessiree, but as you may or may not understand, I'm not gonna give you her address," the clerk said.

"Oh, I wasn't—"

"Gentry's a small town and we're very protective of our own."

Mrs. March was offended at his assumption that she wanted to pry the friend's address out of him—even though that was exactly what she had intended. She fought the urge to tell the clerk that for a town so protective they'd sure allowed a terrible murder, and instead she said, curtly, "You could direct me to the store, at least, I assume?"

◆

SHE RECOGNIZED the purple shop front immediately from the news footage. *The Hope Chest* was painted over the door in old-style gold-leaf lettering. It clashed frustratingly with the more modern style of the items in the window display, many of them posing as antiques but most likely vulgar imitations shipped from China. The display, Mrs. March noted, remained wholly unchanged from when they'd shown it on the news—except for the decorative holiday tinsel, which had been removed.

"This tight-knit community is in mourning, having lost all hope of ever seeing Sylvia alive again," Mrs. March quoted to herself under her breath, as she pushed the purple door open.

Inside, the store was dark and cramped; trinkets lined the walls while shelves erupted with stuffed animals and handmade soaps, flower-patterned crockery interspersed throughout.

Mrs. March walked quietly, squeezing through the shelves and around the furniture, suppressing a cough from the churning dust. She stopped at a chest marked with the initials "G.M.M." and a date—"1798." It looked to be a wedding chest. The blue wood was badly splintered and faded, but Mrs. March could make out the traces of a green and yellow bouquet painted on one side. On top of it lay a couple of beautiful leather-bound books tied together with string. Noticing the store assistant loitering nervously nearby, she picked up the books and asked how much they were. The girl—dumpy, with a piggish nose and thin hair the color of a robin's breast—

blushed. "Oh, those aren't for sale," she said, "those are on loan from the bookstore down the street, they're just decorative—"

"I assumed as much," said Mrs. March. Meanwhile, she felt her neck aflame under her scarf.

"Is there anything else I can help you with?" the assistant asked.

"Actually, yes. I'm looking for a coworker of yours, Amy Bryant, who works here, I believe?"

"Amy? Oh—she's not in today."

"I see. Well, I need to speak with her," said Mrs. March, possessed of a calm authority previously unknown to her. "It's rather important. Do you know where she lives?"

"Well . . . I mean I would *like* to help you, but I don't think—"

"I'm from the *New York Times*. I'm writing an article on Sylvia, and it would be of the utmost importance to get an interview with Amy Bryant, seeing as how they were so close. They were close, right?"

"Oh," said the girl, her dull, freckled face arranging itself into an expression of unadulterated clarity. "Oh, wow, I understand—of course—Amy's actually staying at Sylvia's grandmother's, they're keeping each other company, you know, after what's happened—so you'd have to visit her there."

"The house where Sylvia used to live?" Mrs. March swallowed, her head reeling at the thought that she might be about to venture into the actual house Sylvia slept in, ate in, breathed in . . .

"Is that all right?" the girl asked, seemingly anxious that she had lost Mrs. March's interest with this new piece of information. "I can write the address down for you."

Mrs. March was tempted to call the whole thing off and confess, but the lure of entering Sylvia's home was too much to resist, and, quashing any remaining moral objections, she said, "Yes, thank you, that will do," in an accurate imitation of her mother's transatlantic accent.

She set off for the house clutching the piece of paper on which the address was written in loopy schoolgirl cursive. Giddy, she wondered what she would find there, and asked herself whether she was taking her suspicions too far, or— remembering Johanna—not far enough.

XXXIV

Mrs. March knocked on the door to Sylvia's home—a dull, beige structure just off the main road, on a street that ended in a cul-de-sac presided over by a light blue steepled church.

She had just taken off her headscarf and stuffed it into her purse, suspecting it was not something a *New York Times* reporter would wear on assignment, when Amy Bryant answered. Mrs. March considered it rude to open a front door that wasn't one's own, but she supposed Sylvia's grandmother was too affected by the whole tragic ordeal to muster the strength to answer it herself.

Amy Bryant was sharp-nosed, with a small mouth and chin and hard, beady eyes. No doubt Sylvia had befriended her because she was so plain, Mrs. March reflected. Although she most likely had been the more intelligent of the two, Amy would always have paled in comparison to the beautiful Sylvia, who must have used the discrepancy to her advantage.

"Hello, I'm a reporter with the *New York Times*. I'm writing a piece on Sylvia Gibbler and I'm hoping I could just ask you some questions. I'd only take a few minutes of your time. I know how hard this must be for you, but you and I have a duty to the public to bring her killers to justice. Sylvia would want that." Mrs. March fiddled with her purse as she said this, figuring it looked more authentic—a busy *Times* writer with a busy schedule—if she were searching for a pen.

Amy Bryant held the door open. "Of course, yes. Come in."

Mrs. March was thrilled at how easy it was to get people to talk once you said you were with the *New York Times*. Nobody asked to see any proof, not even a business card, at the merest possibility of being featured in a *Times* article. Would she open the door to herself, just as Amy was doing now? She supposed she would. She pictured herself sitting across from the reporter—also herself—in her living room in New York, offering herself a macaron from a dessert plate.

"Nothing you don't want to talk about," she said to Amy as she crossed the threshold of Sylvia Gibbler's house. "I'm just trying to get as much information as possible. To really write the truth, you know. I want to paint as objective—and truthful—a picture as possible."

"I understand, ma'am. I'll try to be as objective as I can—"

"Oh, don't you worry about that, Miss Bryant, that's my job. You just focus on telling me what you remember. You've been through enough already." She directed her most sincere, most compassionate gaze at Amy, whose weak chin quivered and beady eyes watered with self-pity upon hearing this.

Mrs. March was led into the living room, which she couldn't help but eye critically. The house—from what she'd seen of it—was cluttered and mismatched. The curtains were stained, the floors unmopped, doilies yellowed, the air musty. She itched to open the windows.

"Please—" said Amy, motioning toward a particularly haggard-looking couch sheathed in plastic. Mrs. March managed a quick scan before she sat, attempting a surreptitious brush of her hand to swipe away a smattering of crumbs and white animal hairs.

Amy sat in a nearby chair and said, loud enough to wake

the dead, "Oh, Babka, come and sit with us." An old, smiling woman shuffled soundlessly from a shadowy corner of the living room like an apparition.

"This is a reporter, Babka. She came all the way from New York City," said Amy, almost at a yell. "She wants to talk about Sylvia."

Mrs. March pulled her notebook and pen from her bag. She clicked the pen repeatedly, watching the point pop in and out, in and out, as Babka continued smiling.

"Sylvia's parents died when she was little," explained Amy, "and she lived with her grandmother ever since. Babka is from Poland. She moved to the States when she got married."

"I'm so sorry for your loss," said Mrs. March, and the grandmother's smile faded into a frown as she cocked her head sideways, offering Mrs. March her left ear—the good ear, presumably.

"Sorry for your loss!" repeated Mrs. March, louder this time.

Babka straightened up as much as her bent frame would allow, and gestured with one hand, as if to thank Mrs. March for her condolences. Mrs. March attempted to smile back.

"Sylvia . . ." began the grandmother—nearly a whole life living in the United States had evidently done nothing to dilute her thick Polish accent—"such a good girl. But . . . life . . . so many things can happen."

"Yes," said Mrs. March, scribbling gobbledygook in her notebook in a pantomime of what she hoped came off as shorthand.

"Life is like this. Tricky, yes, but . . . one must move forward."

"That's a very brave way of looking at it," said Mrs. March, and the old woman closed her eyes, pursed her thin lips, and shook her head, as if in disagreement. Mrs. March wondered if she had misheard her.

"Do you want something to drink?" asked Amy. "Some coffee maybe?"

"Yes, I bring out coffee!" exclaimed Babka, and she set off, surprisingly spry, toward the kitchen.

Mrs. March smiled weakly at Amy as they both sat waiting for Babka's return.

"*Babka* is Polish for 'grandmother,'" said Amy, into the silence.

"Ah."

A small mauve dust ball rolled toward them and came to rest against the leg of a chair.

"She can't hear very well out of her right ear. She's very insecure about it."

Babka returned bearing chipped, coffee-stained mugs and a cheesecake she had made "with own hands," of which she was obviously very proud. Mrs. March's heart sank when she came to the grim realization that she was not to be let out of the house without first tasting the homemade cheesecake. Babka served a huge portion and thrust the cracked pink plate at her until Mrs. March took it, along with the tarnished dessert spoon, and, smiling all around, bit into the viscid cheesecake. The tang of room-temperature dairy on her tongue disgusted her. She struggled to suppress images of Babka handling the cream cheese and raw eggs with her papery, liver-spotted hands. But Mrs. March chewed on the cake stoically.

"I mean we got some nationwide attention," Amy was saying, "but it's barely been a couple of months since they found her. Her *body*," she amended awkwardly, "and it seems like everyone's already moved on, but we still don't know who did it. Do you really think this article can bring the attention we need?"

Mrs. March nodded, chewing loudly, breathing through her

mouth, cheesecake stuck to her palate. The grandmother had retired to the kitchen again, either uninterested in this interview or unable to hear it or both. Mrs. March was grateful for this—the old woman made her uncomfortable, and her absence meant she wouldn't have to eat any more cheesecake. "No suspects, then?" she asked around the mound of dessert on her tongue. She would need to swallow it. There was no avoiding it. Meanwhile, Amy was explaining how Sylvia's boyfriend had been the first suspect, as boyfriends usually were, but that he was ruled out when multiple witnesses placed his whereabouts throughout the night of Sylvia's disappearance, as well as the days around it. "But honestly," said Amy, "everybody just assumes it was someone passing through. An outsider." At this, Mrs. March swallowed her cheesecake.

"Mmm, I see. Was there anything on the body that would suggest it was an outsider?"

"Just the violence and the—the rape," said Amy. "We don't have anyone capable of that here. We all know each other."

"Well, you can never really know anyone," said Mrs. March. Amy Bryant narrowed her eyes at her, and Mrs. March went on, "So Sylvia didn't know anyone remotely suspicious? Capable of such violence? Perhaps someone she met in the days preceding her disappearance? Someone from out of town?"

Amy shook her head. "I've been thinking back on all the people we met in the weeks before. But I just can't picture anyone." She sighed, looking down at the floor. "Sylvia and I, we'd go out sometimes," she said, quietly. "It was always my idea. We'd meet men, but I really don't think any of them would do anything like . . ."

The guilt radiating off Amy Bryant, and her not-so-subtle attempt to solicit some kind of absolution from this confession, filled Mrs. March with such pride in her interviewing skills that she began to believe in the possibility of a real article. "We would meet a lot of men," Amy said in a trembling voice, her eyes watering, "but nothing ever came of it; it was innocent, you have to believe me."

Mrs. March's eyes softened in sympathy and she nodded, writing "*slut*" in her notebook, then, remembering her imaginary oath to journalistic objectivity, added a question mark at the end. "It is so very difficult," she said, "to form a real picture of the case. To form a picture of Sylvia, just as she truly was."

There was a small pause before Amy said, timidly, "You can see her room, if you like."

Mrs. March, feigning initial reluctance, agreed, and asked Amy to accompany her, because that seemed like something a reporter would do to maintain integrity (but really it was so that Amy would continue to reveal more things about her dead friend).

They climbed the worn staircase, following a framed timeline of Sylvia through the years. Composed mostly of yearbook pictures, the series included the first photograph released by the press—the one Mrs. March had found in George's notebook. Mrs. March imagined George creeping up these very stairs in the dead of night for a lovers' rendezvous, the creaking of the steps muffled by the pilled lead-gray carpet. Had he traced the raised grain of the banister with his fingers as she was doing now?

Sylvia's bedroom was unremarkable, yet entering it felt almost spiritual, like stepping into a church. Ethereal light slanted into the room through the window, spotlighting the dust floating above the cedar vanity.

In the sanctum of Sylvia's bedroom, she strived for archaeological detachment as she observed the modest bed coverlet in hues of blue; the graying white frilly drapes; the peach lipstick on the dresser next to a half-empty bottle of perfume—she noted the name in her notebook, for purchasing later.

The wall nearest the door was covered in newspaper clippings, all featuring loud headlines about Sylvia and her disappearance. Babka, Amy said, had cut them out and pasted them up in the nerve-racking weeks before the grisly discovery of the body, when they still held on to the hope that Sylvia would be found alive. Below them was a childish-looking pine writing desk, littered with coloring books, star-shaped sticky notes, feathered pens, and vials of glitter.

"I suppose Sylvia didn't keep a diary?" asked Mrs. March, breaking out into an anticipatory sweat at the prospect.

"If she did, nobody ever found one," said Amy matter-of-factly. Her arms were crossed and she was surveying the bedroom as if she were the keeper of this domain. When her eyes fell upon a small handkerchief folded neatly on a corner of the pine desk, she picked it up slowly, inspecting it, debating what to do with it. Finally, she said, "Look. This was her handkerchief. She always carried it around. It wasn't on her, though, on the day . . . the day she disappeared."

Mrs. March took the white handkerchief in her hands. It was bordered in lace and embroidered with Sylvia's initials. "Did they test the clothes she was wearing? For fingerprints?" she asked.

"Yes, they tested everything, but they didn't find anything . . . I guess because she'd been lying outside for so long."

Amy crossed her arms again and turned toward the window, and Mrs. March took advantage of her inattention to slip the handkerchief into her pocket. She dawdled, her eyes hovering over colorful stacks of records and a pink plastic rotary phone, until she stopped short at the bookshelf—an entire row of which was dedicated to George's books. Her vision momentarily fogged, then sharpened, the "George March" on the spines coming into focus as keen as a whetted blade. She wiped the moisture that had formed above her upper lip. Almost salivating with expectation, she pulled one of the books from the shelf and opened it. It was signed. Authentic. She'd recognize George's lazy signature anywhere. Swallowing, her throat dry, she pressed her stubby finger against the ink, half expecting it to pulsate, like a poisoned vein. She traced the signature across the page. She conjured up an image of the pair of them meeting at a reading, Sylvia queuing to get her book signed, George stopping in mid-sentence with another fan to look at her over his glasses. The two talking and laughing and flirting, leaving the remaining book buyers feeling snubbed. Maybe Sylvia had left her scarf behind—to stoke his escalating infatuation with her—which he had taken to sniffing, only recently having gotten rid of it to hide evidence of their meeting—or had he? What if it was somewhere in her own house, the dead girl's scarf? Where would he have hidden it? Stuffed behind some books on a shelf in his study. Or—in a fit of mad hubris—in plain sight on his desk. Maybe Martha had come across it and, mistaking it for one of Mrs. March's, tucked it away in one of her closet drawers, where it now lived next to her own clothes?

When Amy turned back from the window, Mrs. March was still holding the book in her hands. "Oh, yeah, the George March books," she said. "Sylvia was a big fan. She had an old copy that belonged to her father, I think? And she loved it. I bet I saw her reading it like a hundred times." She paused before saying, "She was a really good reader." She pondered over the sentiment, perhaps needing a little moment to recover from bestowing the compliment. "Then when he got really famous she read somewhere that he summered here or something. I think he has a cabin around here. A lot of people have seen him around town—"

"It's his editor who has a cabin here," said Mrs. March, confident that an important *New York Times* journalist would certainly know this.

"Right, well, anyway, last summer she would wait around in restaurants or whatever, hoping to get a glimpse of him."

"And did she?" Mrs. March said as the last of her breath seemed to leave her body.

Amy shook her head. "No. She never managed it."

Mrs. March inhaled greedily. "But this one is signed." She thrust the book, open to the signature page, at Amy.

"Oh, yeah, that must have been her dad's, then. She never met George March. Trust me, she would have told me the second it happened. She was obsessed with those books." Amy explained how she herself never quite cared for them, considering them novels for "old people with nothing to do," but Mrs. March had stopped listening. She flipped through the book, looking for any type of clue—a handwritten note or a secret code consisting of randomly circled letters—but the only thing in its pages was a pressed and faded flower that crumbled at her touch. She turned to the author photograph on the back flap. It was an old studio portrait of George, which indicated that this edition had been released before Sylvia was born. Not long after, his team convinced him to sit for a new photo because readers were commenting that he looked—in polite terms —"intense." Indeed, his hunched shoulders, his raised eyebrows, those narrowed eyes peering over his glasses did give off a rather sinister portrait of her husband, who, at least in person, looked nowhere near as menacing. Mrs. March stared into those eyes, made darker in black and white, and wondered whether they were the last thing Sylvia ever saw.

Amy showed Mrs. March a few sketches Sylvia had done. Girly things like ponies and flowers along with a botched portrait of her grandmother, but Mrs. March made sure to appreciate them, while appearing to describe them in great detail in her notebook.

Mrs. March was about to propose they look through other rooms—she thought there might be something especially juicy waiting to be discovered in the bathroom medicine cabinet—when Amy said, "I think you've got all you need."

Downstairs, she thanked Babka and Amy for their time, and told them she was going to make a big push to get the article published, but one could never know, she warned, as her editors were fickle and slaves to passing fancies. She opened the front door—seeing as how nobody had moved to open it for her—when Amy said, "Can I please have the handkerchief back?"

Mrs. March stopped in the doorway. "Oh," she said, "I left it upstairs."

"No, it's in your pocket."

A stillness descended as Mrs. March looked at Amy—at her stern, unimpressed expression, akin to George Washington's—and heard herself say, as she took the handkerchief out of her pocket, "You know, it's funny, I seem to have confused it for my own. I must have left *mine* upstairs. How absentminded of me."

"I'm sorry, what did you say your name was?"

Mrs. March straightened her posture, catching her breath.

"Johanna," she said, and put on her sunglasses before walking out the door.

◆

HER FIRST DAY in Gentry had been so fruitful that it was hardly a surprise when the next few days went by without much progress. On the second day she bought a few plastic-wrapped sandwiches and packets of saltines for nibbling when she was peckish, so as not to disturb anything in Edgar's kitchen. She ate them voraciously, cleaning up the crumbs with a moist fingertip.

She continued to root through cupboards and drawers for clues. She took walks and napped. She trapped a spider under a glass and giggled, imagining what Edgar would make of it.

On the third day she discovered a narrow wooden box hidden under a stack of blankets in the master bedroom closet. It was locked shut with a heavy padlock. Adrenaline surging, she rummaged through the toolbox in the garage and managed to break the lock with a hammer. Instead of a series of illicit letters between Sylvia and George, or Sylvia's diary, or Sylvia's fingers, Mrs. March was disappointed to find Edgar's hunting rifles. She replaced the padlock immediately, buying one just like it at the general store, telling the clerk that her daughter needed one for her bicycle at Harvard.

On her walk back from the store, she came across a doe in a clearing. It was dining on a dead rabbit, the crunch of the rabbit's bones between the doe's teeth indistinguishable from the crunching of the snow beneath the boots she had borrowed from the cabin. Snow was falling, collecting on the doe's back. Cupping a hand against her temple, she continued on her way. The doe, undisturbed, carried on eating.

✦

On the fourth day Mrs. March visited Sylvia's grave. She spotted it easily, as people had left flowers and stuffed animals and letters at her tombstone, all of it decaying. A teddy bear's eye dangled by a thread from its socket. Mrs. March tried sketching it in her notebook.

That evening she called George and told him she'd be home the following afternoon. "All right," he said. "How did it go? How's your mother?"

"Not as well as I'd hoped."

"I'm sorry, honey."

"Yes, well, what can one do but bear it. I'll see you tomorrow, dear."

"I'll be here."

✦

On her last night in Gentry, notebook in her purse, she visited the town pub—a cheap place with wood panels and sticky floors and a couple of battered bowling lanes to one side. Stools topped with ripped vinyl lined the bar. The felt on the pool table was pocked with cigarette burns. The air, palpable and stagnant with the smell of smoke, beer, and bodies, clung to her the instant she stepped inside.

Mrs. March sat alone in a booth wearing her sunglasses and headscarf, sipping from a glass of sour red wine, which the bartender had poured from a two-liter bottle. As he screwed the cap back on, she asked, "Did you ever see that famous writer around town? George March? Did he ever have a drink here?" and his reply—"I don't read, lady"—had been discouraging. When she then asked him about Sylvia, assuming this to be

one of the spots she and Amy had frequented while out prowling for men, the barman didn't answer her. Instead, he looked
beyond her and said, "Why don't you ask her boyfriend? He's
right there." She turned to see a young man drinking by himself at a table in the back.

She didn't dare approach but she did choose a spot facing
him. She studied him for a while as she sipped her wine through
a straw to avoid placing her lips on the wineglass, which was
spotted with fingerprints. The boyfriend sat, sweaty and pale,
chin stippled with acne, drinking beer after beer while muttering to himself, until he finally stood up, helping himself along
by leaning on tables, and staggered to a small clearing by the
bar. He began to sway gently, rocking his body back and forth
and knocking his head back—eyes closed, mouth hanging
open. At first Mrs. March thought he was having a seizure,
until it became clear that he was on a little dance floor of his
own making. She stood up, her mouth feeling like a clump of
rancid yarn from the wine, and teetered over to him. Still wearing her sunglasses and headscarf, she hugged him. He didn't
seem to notice, nor did he return her embrace. His arms hung
limply by his sides, but he didn't push her away, either—and
Mrs. March swayed with him, rocking him like a baby, feeling
his warm body against her own. Under the stench of beer he
smelled like fabric softener and cereal milk, like a boy who is
well cared for by his mother. She envisioned Sylvia hugging
him, taking in his scent and listening to his heartbeat through
his sweater.

They swung gently from side to side, out of rhythm with
the music, until the place emptied out and the bartender
announced last call.

◆

Night had fallen when the cab pulled up at the Marches' apartment building. As the evening doorman rushed out from under the green awning to greet her, Mrs. March glanced up at the familiar façade. Home. Tall and imposing in dim winter night, its windows shadowed like hundreds of lidded eyes.

The sixth-floor hallway betrayed nothing unusual as she made her way across the carpeted floor to 606. The brass keys jangled on the key ring as she unlocked the door, entered, and locked it behind her. The apartment was completely dark yet she felt it was expecting her, salivating and alert in its stillness, like a bad oyster. She patted the wall, searching for the light switch, and suddenly a loud exhalation—more like a prolonged gasp—burst out in the darkness. She wanted to open the front door to let in the hallway light but found that she couldn't move. The breathing continued, a little louder now, almost hissing at her. At the sound of a toilet flushing next door, Mrs. March relaxed, her shoulders dropping—it was just the sound of old pipes. She found the switch on the wall and flicked it quickly, in case she was wrong and could surprise whatever might be lurking there. The empty hallway stared back at her, inscrutable. Where was George? Where was Jonathan?

She poked her head into empty rooms, calling their names into the dark, half expecting them to jump out and scare her. A chilling possibility occurred to her: George was onto her and had fled, abducting Jonathan as leverage. She was flinging open closets when she heard a key turning in the lock and the front door opened behind her, letting in a slight draft and cheerful voices.

"Honey! You're home," said George as Mrs. March found

herself rushing toward her son, wiping away with one mint green gloved finger a single tear.

"We saw a movie, Mommy!"

She kneeled to receive Jonathan's little body in hers, and as they hugged, she settled her gaze unwaveringly upon George's face, and she told him, with her eyes, with her cold, slight grin, that she knew everything. Was it her imagination, or at that moment did something—fear, perhaps, or remorse—stir in George's eyes?

After her trip to Maine, from which she'd brought back nothing more than a toothache, Mrs. March found it hard to believe that she had actually done all that—that she had lied, taken a plane by herself, manipulated a grieving family into granting her a fake interview, danced against the chest of a man who had been the main suspect in a murder investigation. She must surely have dreamed it.

One thing she was more and more certain of was her husband's guilt. She fed this conviction daily by foraging for the hidden meanings in the things he did, in the things he said. A casual allusion to his latest novel was a taunt. His retiring to his study after a mention of Sylvia on the news was glaring proof of his crime.

At some point, she resolved, he will mess up, drop a clue. A letter to Sylvia still in its sealed envelope, left in one of his desk drawers. There would be other victims, too. Someone who commits such an act develops a compulsion—she knew that much. But she needed to remain observant, stay patient. Doing the police's job, really. Then, when the time was right, she would honorably hand him over to the authorities. George would be arrested, and she would be cast by the media as the admirable, innocent wife—naive at first but quick to catch on, and brave enough, smart enough, to investigate (what nerve! what pluck!) and bring him to justice single-handedly. She could already visualize the speech she would give in front of the flashing cameras, all looking to *her* for once. "In the name of the victims," she would say—wearing her sunglasses and a headscarf in a show of humility, for it would seem vulgar and insensitive to willingly attract more attention than the victims—and then she would ask for forgiveness, but the media and public would agree unanimously that she had nothing to be forgiven for.

She would testify at George's trial with a dignified air. George would go to prison. She'd give only a handful of interviews, then she would live out the rest of her days under the radar, knitting scarves for her grandchildren.

An altogether darker alternative scene in which she calmly coaxed a confession out of George, in which he then begged her to become his partner in crime, had also occurred to her, followed by images of her selecting and trailing his victims for him. She was proud to admit she had banished these from her mind more or less immediately. She had also considered the possibility that George might flee when confronted. Fleeting images of George as a fugitive: shaving his beard, dyeing his hair blond, eating greasy cheeseburgers in dingy motel rooms, searching the news for his face, and eventually losing himself in the bleakest, grittiest corners of the American criminal landscape, never to be heard from again, except the occasional untraceable phone call on Jonathan's birthday.

She would often dwell on the morality of her choices, of living with—and exposing her son to—a dangerous psychopath, but she reasoned that there was no use in leaving George now, when nobody would believe her claims without sufficient proof. Especially when his literary status had been cemented around the world. In the past Mrs. March had reveled in his burgeoning fame, when strangers would approach them in restaurants to shake his hand and ask him to sign their books. Nowadays, however, every time a stranger approached—which she was experiencing less often now because they rarely ever went out together—she steeled herself for fear this would be the person who'd finally ask George about Johanna in front of her. And George would snicker and stall and get away with it. Just like he'd gotten away with murder.

◆

SHE WAS on her way home from running errands one morning, clutching a paper bag of olive bread and sucking on an ice chip to ease her toothache. George's birthday party was coming up, and she was contemplating the ways in which she might surpass the previous soirée—string quartets, a menu inspired by the political dinners hosted by Jackie Kennedy—and also how she might snub all those guests who had disrespected her that last time.

There was a hint of green on the trees, despite the cold, and she was clasping her fur coat shut with one hand. She had left it unbuttoned in a bout of optimism; that morning had felt fresh, ripening. The sky was a deeper, stronger blue; it had finally lost the sad, bruised look of faded linen that has been washed too many times.

She dawdled as she neared one particular establishment. It boasted a large window with lush burgundy curtains that were often drawn. She had passed by it many times, and had often played with the thought of going in. The word *Psychic* hung on the brick façade in golden cursive. She didn't believe in this fortune-telling thing, of course. When a young Mrs. March had confessed to her mother that she thought a ghost was haunting her at night (referring to Kiki, although she hadn't specified at the time), she was taught to dismiss concepts beyond those taught by the church. Her mother had tutted and held her by the shoulders and said to her as she leaned over: "There is no such thing. You understand, right? Don't start believing in such silly things or everyone will laugh at you." She said this as if the knowledge came from experience, leaving Mrs. March to wonder whether it was her mother who had been laughed at, or whether she'd been the one to laugh at somebody else (a much more likely scenario; it was impossible to picture her mother being victimized).

Still, as she stood in front of the psychic's shop, she let out a small sigh. It might be fun, to receive some good news about the future.

She clutched the crinkled bag of bread to her chest, the oil from the olives staining her coat through the paper, and pushed open the shop's French door.

Inside, it was quiet and strangely bright despite the thick curtains. She stood for a moment in silence, contemplating the crystal ball on a small round table. She closed her eyes, and for a few seconds experienced something she hadn't felt for so long that the exact word escaped her.

"Good day," said a scratchy voice beside her.

Mrs. March turned to face a short woman with absurdly long, thick black hair. It coiled around her head in several braids, then slithered down around her neck, falling all the way down her spine, where it ended at her waist in a burst of split ends.

"I would like my fortune told," said Mrs. March, who had decided that the best way to go about this was to employ the same concise, commanding tone she would at the butcher's.

"Certainly," said the psychic, in an exaggerated Eastern European accent. "Hands? Deck?"

"Ah . . . deck."

"Any preference? Rider-Waite?"

Mrs. March didn't understand the question, so she answered, simply, "Yes."

"This way, please."

The short woman led Mrs. March through a pair of velvet curtains into a smaller, darker space. The walls were papered in a screaming shade—somewhere between red and fuchsia—patterned with ornate flowers. Mrs. March avoided focusing her vision there, for fear of the migraine it would no doubt give her.

The psychic drew the curtains closed and they were left in near darkness, illuminated only by a few scattered candles. The abrupt light change caused Mrs. March's vision to blacken momentarily, as if she were on the verge of fainting.

With a dramatic air the fortune-teller gestured to a small table topped with green felt, like a poker table, and Mrs. March sat on a tiny wooden chair crowned with a plush embroidered cushion, leaving her purse and olive bread on a nearby stool. The slight chair didn't so much as groan as she sat down, which relaxed her considerably.

The psychic sat down opposite, in a chair draped with a paisley sheet. Her left hand was malformed: several of its fingers were underdeveloped, twisting into each other like tree roots. Her right hand was flawless, stemmed with long, elegant fingers. She used both hands to shuffle the deck, clearing her throat as she did so. She looked at Mrs. March and said, "You have been on a trip recently, yes?"

Mrs. March, refusing to feel impressed or to show

amazement—both amateur mistakes—shifted a little in her chair and said, as dispassionately as she could, "Yes."

"It has given you what you were looking for, this trip."

"I expected a little more from it, I think," Mrs. March said, choosing her words carefully.

"You know in your heart that you did find what you were looking for on this trip," said the psychic. Had she just winked at her? Mrs. March's thoughts flashed to the signed copy of George's book on Sylvia's shelf.

"Maybe you wished to find something else, but the truth is hard to face sometimes." After a pause, she continued, "But there is more to discover, and you will discover it. Your instincts, your suspicions, were correct."

How full Mrs. March felt at receiving those words. She had cramps all over, as if she'd just eaten too much baked Alaska. The wallpaper loomed over her in all its bordello-like glory, and she looked down at her hands, which had begun to sweat. Her breathing grew louder.

The psychic finished shuffling the deck and began placing the cards facedown on the table. The backs of the cards were printed with a crackled brown design to mimic smashed glass. Mrs. March wrung her wet hands as, one by one, the twenty-two cards of the Rider-Waite Major Arcana were arranged before her.

The psychic took a deep breath, then closed her eyes. Her hands hovered over the cards as she hummed (to Mrs. March's growing embarrassment). She continued producing sounds for a few more uncomfortable seconds, before opening her eyes and saying, "Please choose a card."

Mrs. March, who had not been expecting to be an active participant, fussed in her chair. At random, she patted the card nearest to her. The psychic slid the sleeves of her caftan up her arms and, with exaggerated importance, turned it over. The card portrayed a squatting monster composed of a human upper body and hairy goat legs. It was flanked by two chained, naked humans, both sporting horns and tails. THE DEVIL, said the card, matter-of-factly, in big block letters.

"Well, I believe I'm in trouble," said Mrs. March, hoping for a humorous tone. When the psychic remained silent, she leaned forward and in a whisper asked, "What does it mean?"

"Well, you see the card is reversed," said the psychic. "The reverse devil can appear when you are retreating into your deepest, darkest places, or when you're hiding your deepest, darkest self from others. You don't want to trust your soul to others because you're embarrassed, filled with shame, so it's grown deformed in the darkness inside you"—Mrs. March envisioned her soul as a hairy, misshapen creature chained in a dark cellar, and pitied herself—"and now you think it's too late for anybody to see your true self."

What followed was a silence so powerful it almost reverberated off the hysterical red walls. "Well, that's silly," Mrs. March said.

Undeterred, the psychic continued. "I am going to tell you how to fix this. Usually I don't use two cards. Very unusual for me. I use the one, only. But you need all the advice you can get. Special moment, yes? You understand? I help you."

She cleared her throat again, and again closed her eyes, and once she had performed her humming theatrics, she asked Mrs. March to choose another card. The card the fortune-teller turned around this time was THE HIGH PRIESTESS. The dark-haired figure, severe-looking in her horned crown, sat with her hands in her lap, a large cross on her chest. Behind her hung a tapestry embroidered with lush palm trees and pomegranates.

"High priestess is guardian of the subconscious," said the fortune-teller. "Everything you do not say, everything you keep deep inside here and here"—she tapped her chest and her temple simultaneously—"is guarded by her fiercely. She appears when you need to access this knowledge deep inside your subconscious mind."

Mrs. March looked at the two cards—one reversed, the other upright—on the table. They were cartoonish, like drawings for children. "Aren't you going to turn a third one?" she asked.

"She is telling you how to fix it," said the psychic, tapping the high priestess's face with one twisted finger. "There is no need for third card. Don't you understand?" When Mrs. March did not respond, the psychic sighed and said, "You are in danger. The danger is getting stronger. See?"

Mrs. March, who *was* beginning to see, leaned forward, pinching at the skin on her throat.

"If you're not careful . . ." the psychic continued, "this danger, this will be terrible for you. You understand what I mean?"

"Yes, oh yes," said Mrs. March, forgetting all her mother had warned. "What can I do?"

"You have to protect yourself. Separate yourself from what is hurting you."

"He *will* hurt me, you mean?"

The palm reader looked at her with her dark brown eyes. "You are hurting already. But . . . maybe it's not too late. Don't let it hurt you more. More hurt is—dangerous. Over the limit." She held her hand flatly in the air and waved it upward, representing the limit that was not to be passed. "You understand? Don't let it hurt you."

"I won't," said Mrs. March. "I won't."

"If you sense the danger, ask for help."

"Help?" Mrs. March looked down at her ugly, cracked hands and ugly, cracked nails, and wondered why no amount of French hydrating cream ever seemed to do the trick. Even the psychic's mangled fingers seemed prettier than hers.

"If you sense that the danger is crossing that line," continued the psychic, her voice louder as she noticed her client's attention dwindling, "ask for help immediately."

◆

MRS. MARCH had expected to leave feeling uplifted, and she did indeed feel relief—a relief brought about by the unwavering conviction that her husband was guilty, and that she was right to suspect him, and that, most importantly, she was not at all crazy. As she closed the French door behind her, shocked by the sudden sunlight, she felt she had been granted permission, in a way, to continue harboring these feelings of rage and mistrust toward him. She did not dwell on the fact that the fortune-teller might just as well have been talking about a tumor, for all the vagueness of her words. She would not question it later in the apartment either, where she quietly took a butcher knife from one of the kitchen drawers and hid it under her pillow.

XXXVI

It was rather exhausting, shadowing George. After trying to keep up with him for a few days, she promised herself she wouldn't follow him out into the street anymore, trailing him up and down Manhattan—carefully stalking him in and out of bookstores where he signed stock, hiding behind clothes racks at the department store where he purchased a new cardigan, and pressing herself against a brick building in the numbing cold for hours, waiting for George to finish a leisurely meal with his private banker.

She resorted to observing him whenever he was at home with her. She tensed as a reflex whenever he entered a room or said a word; she studied the way he spoke to Jonathan, the way he generally avoided Martha. She looked through his study for clues as often as possible and one time even listened in on a telephone conversation with Edgar (during which, to Mrs. March's frustration, they only discussed news of George's film deal).

Whenever George stepped out, Mrs. March adopted another role: Sylvia. Within days of returning from Maine, she had gone back to the store on 75th and Lexington to buy the black velvet headband. She'd also purchased Sylvia's brand of perfume—the one she had seen on her bedroom dresser—at the department store. It was on sale, so she could hardly pass up the opportunity. To complete the transformation, she'd bought a wig from a costume shop downtown, and once a week she'd buy peaches, the same size and color as the one Sylvia was holding in the newspaper photo.

At home, with her bedroom door locked, she had taken to becoming Sylvia. She'd walk, back straight, feet pointed, across the carpet. She'd eat the peaches in front of the bathroom mirror, trying on smiles in between bites, watching the juice stream down her chin. She read beauty magazines as she imagined Sylvia would, licking her finger to turn the page, or just lounged, looking at the wall, contemplating her own death. She discovered that Sylvia grew bored and impatient when she lounged, that she felt more sensual when wearing a silk slip than when fully undressed. Sometimes she'd smoke, too—the last of the cigarettes from the stolen cigarette case—tilting her hand the way Gabriella did, holding the cigarette languidly between her index and middle fingers.

She aired out the room afterwards to eradicate the smoke and perfume. No matter how vigorously she soaped herself afterwards, Mrs. March could still smell Sylvia on her throughout the day—a stinging, provocatively sweet scent that seemed to hide an underlying rot, like when her mother sprayed Chanel No. 5 in the bathroom to disguise the reek of a leaking pipe.

Mrs. March would wash her neck and wrists in her bathroom—suds falling between her breasts and down her back, the delicate skin on the inside of her wrists peeling from the repeated rubbing—refilling daily the gilded soap dispenser (which she'd been assured by a pushy antiques dealer once belonged to Babe Paley). Then she'd sniff herself repeatedly, stopping on her way down the hall to wash herself again in the guest bathroom.

It was on one such occasion, after washing her increasingly cracked hands in the guest bathroom with a round soap

George had brought back from the London Ritz—that she noticed the painting. The painting, which once depicted several naked women bathing in a stream and peering shyly in a half-turn, now showed the women with their backs completely turned.

The towel dropped from Mrs. March's hands. She stepped closer to the painting. They were the same women—she knew their hairstyles and coloring by heart—and yet their smiling, rosy faces and their plump, pastel breasts had disappeared. On display now were their pale backs and dented buttocks. She stared at it, confounded. Had they bought the two paintings as a set and she had somehow forgotten all about this one? But even if that were true (which was unlikely), where was the one that had been hanging in this bathroom for ten years? She studied the painting for several minutes, touching it softly with one fingertip, willing it to change back.

She stepped out into the hallway, debating whether to tell George about the painting, contemplating the possibility that he would laugh at her. As she approached her bedroom, she heard voices. Whispers. She stopped dead in the middle of the hall and cocked her head to listen. The voices were coming from Jonathan's room. "This game is boring," she heard Alec say. "Let's play something else?"

Mrs. March tiptoed to the door, pressed her ear to it. On the other side Alec said, "I wanna be the cop."

"Okay. I'll be the criminal then," Jonathan answered.

"A robber?"

"Naw, something better. Like a murderer."

"A murderer, gee."

"Would you turn in a murderer to the police?" asked Jonathan. "Even if you knew 'em?"

Mrs. March covered her mouth with her hand, her wedding band cold against her lips.

"How do you mean?" asked Alec.

"Like, say it was your brother?"

"But I don't *have* any brothers."

"Well, say it was your mother then."

"I couldn't rat out my *mother*," said Alec firmly, with a touch of pride that prompted a surge of envy inside Mrs. March.

"But if it was the right thing to do?" said Jonathan.

"I don't know. Can we just play now?"

The voices quieted, replaced by light thumping sounds. Armed with a new determination, Mrs. March sought George out—he was reading in the living room, the television on in the background—and asked him, straight out: "Who changed the painting in the bathroom?"

He frowned but kept his eyes on his book. She rubbed her wrists, then turned off the television for something to do.

"Mmm?" said George, more at his book than at her.

"The painting in the guest bathroom. Who changed it?"

George appeared to continue his reading as he said, "Honey, I'm sure the painting is the same as it's been all these years."

When she didn't answer, he peered at her over his glasses in that George-like way that irked her. "Are you all right?" he asked.

"Of course I am," she said. "I thought I remembered it differently, is all."

"Well, it's been up there for so long, you probably just never really noticed the details."

"Yes," she said, looking at him. "That certainly seems to be the trouble."

Gritting her teeth, she retired to her bedroom and closed

the door, her hands trembling with rage so that her finger-nails tapped on the panels. He was denying it, just like he had done with the dead pigeon in the bathtub. Like he had done with everything.

She slipped on the wig, fingering the brunette tresses, admiring herself in the bathroom mirror. He didn't consider her worthy of murdering, of possessing in such a fervent, urgent way. He thought she was stupid, plain, boring, only deserving of humiliation in the pages of a book. A joke.

She slid the black headband over the wig, the velvet like soft down under her fingertips. Her pupils dilated in the mirror. "It's me you want, George March," she whispered.

◆

SHE WAS waiting for George in the dark when he entered the bedroom that night. She sat, whoever she was, in shadows in the armchair in the corner. "George," she said. Her voice was different, like her larynx had been restrung.

George turned toward her, squinting. The moonlight through the window only illuminated her hands, crossed in her lap, in faint streaks. "Can't sleep?" he asked.

She slunk toward him and embraced him as she imagined a young girl who was having a yearning, long-distance affair would: feeling every wrinkle in his shirt between her fingers, taking in the scent of him (whisky, old wooden drawers). George touched the tips of the wig tentatively. "You changed your hair," he said, as if admiring the effort. The room seemed to darken further around them in response.

That night, Mrs. March seduced her husband. Familiarly at first, then strangely—laughing, biting herself. George seemed curious, politely responsive, then ultimately appreciative, his pine-needle beard grazing her neck, his heart beating against her chest. She could feel her shoulder blades protruding more than usual, threatening to slice through her skin.

There was a quick, sharp pain between her legs as he pressed his way into her. She pictured a closed ear piercing, the skin grown over it like the stump of an amputated limb.

Pounding the mattress with her fists, she felt a trail of maggots—Sylvia's maggots—tickling her from the inside before dripping out of her in wet, writhing knots.

She rocked back and forth, humming softly, Sylvia's chocolate locks brushing her clavicles, until Johanna was no more.

XXXVII

Gabriella's stolen cigarette case was gone. Mrs. March searched for it, feverishly, among her drawers: scarves flying across the room like streamers, her sweat leaking into her silk chemises. Gripping the closet doors, fearing the worst, she crossed the hallway and went looking for it in Jonathan's closet.

She was setting aside cartoon underwear between pinched fingers when she came across the drawings. Disturbing, hand-drawn images of birds pecking at the naked, bleeding bodies of women, the waxy crayon lines spread thin over dark scribbles of pubic hair.

Tucked among the drawings she found not one but several newspaper clippings concerning Sylvia's disappearance and murder. They were stained with grease and flecked with coffee grounds, indicating that they had been salvaged from the garbage can in the kitchen. The missing article from George's study was among them. As Mrs. March dug deeper into the closet, she retrieved, from under a navy sweater, one of George's notebooks. She rejoiced at this reversal of fortune, but as she flipped through it she realized that it was the notebook she had taken with her to Maine. It was *her* notebook.

As Jonathan entered the room to find his mother clutching all these secrets in her ugly, trembling hands, a wave of anger swelled within Mrs. March, as sudden and visceral as a bout of nausea. The truth was, she didn't want to face the implications of Jonathan reading these horrible things—*rape* and *strangled* and *slut?*—written in his mother's handwriting. The fear that Jonathan may have also found her brown wig—may have even tried it *on*—so unmoored her that she gagged, hiding her face in the coats hanging in Jonathan's closet.

When she had composed herself enough to face her son, he was standing so close to her she jumped, and fell deeper into the closet. "Where did you find this?" she asked, waving in his face the news clipping from George's study. *"Where?"*

Jonathan shrugged.

"Have you been into Daddy's study? Answer me!"

"I don't know. Sometimes."

"What else did you find?" she asked, eyes wide and beginning to water. "Did you find anything else?"

When he didn't answer, she shook him. "Why did you draw these?" she asked, crumpling the drawings. "Did Daddy tell you to?"

Jonathan, upset, also crying now, shook his head. "No!"

"He did, didn't he? Don't lie to me!"

"No, it was, it was—" Jonathan's eyes failed to meet her own as his little mind searched for an answer. "Alec."

"Don't just say it was Alec, if it wasn't. If it was Daddy, you have to tell me."

"It wasn't!" He hugged her, his arms around her midriff, as he sniffled. "Please don't be mad at Daddy."

Mrs. March didn't return her son's embrace, but rather continued her inquisition, bile rising in her throat. "Then tell me, Jonathan, why did Alec want you to draw these?"

When Jonathan didn't answer, she offered, "Does Alec want you to get in trouble?"

"Yes!"

"Why?"

"He . . . he's jealous because Daddy's famous."

Mrs. March kneeled down in front of her son and he hugged her, resting his head on her shoulder. She let him. "Jonathan, is Alec really jealous about that?" she asked, stroking his hair.

"Yes," Jonathan answered, his breath hot in the furl of her neck. "He told me you're really mad about Daddy's book and everyone knows."

Mrs. March buckled, cradling Jonathan's head with one hand, holding his body against hers with the other. There was a silence, then she heard, feverish and moist inside her ear: "*Johanna*," in a drawn-out breath.

In one quick movement Mrs. March pushed Jonathan away from her, and he stumbled backward with huge, shocked eyes.

Resolute, Mrs. March stood up, grabbed Jonathan by the wrist, and pulled him out of the room. She dragged him through the apartment, out the front door across the carpeted hallway, and into the grand elevator.

A few floors up, she knocked on the Millers' door, and Sheila had barely opened the door when Mrs. March said, "I'm afraid the children are not to be friends anymore."

Sheila stared at her with such a pantomimic display of surprise—all knotted eyebrows and concerned blinking—that Mrs. March felt the urge to slap her.

"I don't want Alec to see Jonathan anymore," Mrs. March said, and—not getting a reaction—grew more hysterical. "Alec is not good for him! He is *corrupting* my child!"

Now Sheila piped up. "*Excuse* me?" she said, her low voice restrained, her eyes diverting to Jonathan, who was held, firmly, in his mother's grip. The look of concern on her face for Jonathan further enraged Mrs. March, who yelled, "You heard me!" Her words echoed down the hallway.

"Well," said Sheila, her shoulders dropping, relieved of an unknown weight, "I didn't want to get into this, especially not like *this*, but it just so happens that I've been wary of the boys' relationship, in particular Jonathan's influence on Alec."

"Jonathan's—"

"Yes," snapped Sheila, her eyes piercing Mrs. March's. "Jonathan has . . . *ideas*. Strange ideas which, frankly, frighten me a little. And what with Jonathan's suspension and—well." She shook her head, still looking at Mrs. March, her voice almost a whisper: "I heard what Jonathan did to that little girl."

Mrs. March leaned forward abruptly and was pleased to see Sheila flinch. "You think you know, but you don't know *anything*," she seethed, spittle flying, her twisted lips twitching. Hearing the creak of a door behind her, she flung her head around, where half a dozen curious neighbors were peering out of their apartments. Stumbling on Sheila's welcome mat as she dragged Jonathan to the elevator, she cried, "None of you know!"

◆

MRS. MARCH had not seen any cockroaches for weeks, but that night she opened her eyes to something worse—bedbugs. Scores of them all over her body, lodged between her breasts and between her toes, crawling over her knuckles and into her belly button. Round, brick red, and prickle-legged, fat with her blood, squeezing out of crevices in the walls and from the seams in the mattress for their nightly feed.

With a howl Mrs. March slapped the light switch on the

wall by her bed. The bedbugs were gone, replaced by *them*, kneeling on the floor around the bed—Sheila George the gossipy neighbor from the supermarket Gabriella Edgar the investment banker from the party Jonathan the day doorman Paula and even old Marjorie Melrose. All of them. Staring at her, mouths agape, drooling.

Mrs. March woke up, choking, and bolted upright in bed. She turned her head to see, for once, George beside her. She counted down from fifty, letting her heart settle, then slipped her hand under her pillow, feeling for the handle of the butcher knife. Once her fingers found the wooden grip—cracked from one too many trips to the dishwasher—she relaxed, easing onto her back.

The next morning, over breakfast, George asked her whether she'd had a nightmare. "I was in and out of sleep and I wasn't sure if I was dreaming it," he said.

"No," she said carefully, "no nightmares. My tooth was hurting, that's all." Which wasn't a lie, for the ache had indeed worsened lately, her gums now ablaze with a deep, sharp pain that seemed to seize her from out of the blue, reminding her, with its searing, building spasms, of the contractions she'd had in the hours before birthing Jonathan.

"You have to get that taken care of," said George with an expression of concern that almost, for a second, softened her.

"Yes," she said.

"I'm going to ask Zelda to get you an appointment with her dentist. He's the best. He has a waiting list, but I'm sure Zelda can get you in by tomorrow afternoon."

"It's really no bother."

"You have to go, honey." He smiled at her. "It'll only get worse." And with this chilling threat, he was off to his study to dial Zelda.

◆

AT DINNER the following day, Mrs. March regarded Jonathan grimly. She was repulsed by the lilac shadows under his eyes, by his thick, effeminate lashes. He'd become chubby: his navy school sweater stretched around his belly, the trousers tight around his thighs and riding up his legs when he sat. The skin on his plump calves was bruised, with a smattering of black down.

Mrs. March resolved to send him away for the weekend. She would be protecting Jonathan, she told herself, from George. She'd be protecting her investigation. She packed his bag—stuffing it with socks and underwear, as if hoping he might not come back—and saw him off to school on Friday morning. She had arranged for George's mother to pick Jonathan up that afternoon.

"Oh, I'd be just thrilled to have Jonathan to myself one whole weekend!" Barbara March exclaimed over the phone. "You two have big plans?"

"Nothing special," said the younger Mrs. March, neglecting to tell the elder about the party she'd be hosting on Saturday to celebrate George's birthday. She didn't think it would be suitable for plain, portly Barb to attend. Barb with her cheap, frilly shirts and billowing slacks.

She pinched Jonathan's shoulder as she ushered him out of the apartment that morning, his weekend bag thumping against his leg. *Thump, thump*, in the elevator. *Thump* in the lobby, drowning out the doorman's greetings; *thump, thump, thump*, in the street, all the way to the cab. They rode to school in silence, the occasional sniff or cough from Jonathan making her skin tingle.

She did not get out of the cab when they arrived, but instead looked on from the back seat as he hobbled away, her lips pinched and her eyebrows so raised she felt her temples tighten. Once Jonathan disappeared into the mass of rambling children in the school courtyard, she gagged, wiping the fingers she had touched Jonathan with on her coat.

◆

WHEN SHE returned to the apartment, she found Martha standing in the hallway with her little olive purse hanging from her wrist.

"I have to give you my notice, Mrs. March," said Martha in an uncharacteristic monotone. "I'm so sorry."

"What? You're leaving us?" said Mrs. March, thinking of the party that was to come, of the state of the apartment. "When?"

"I'm afraid today is my last day."

"But that's not possible. You have to give us two weeks' notice."

"Two weeks' notice is courtesy but not legally required. I asked my lawyer," said Martha. She seemed to be taking great pains to look Mrs. March in the eye.

"I don't understand," said Mrs. March. "Have we done anything wrong? Anything to *offend* you?" she said (the last bit almost *seeking* to offend).

"No, no, Mrs. March, I—" Martha lowered her eyes to her creased, pink hands squeezed together in front of her, and said very quietly, "I think you should get some help."

At these words Mrs. March went cold. Martha wasn't embarrassed, but rather appeared almost *afraid* of her. All these years Mrs. March had feared Martha, feared her disdain, her judgment. Had it actually been the other way around?

"Well, yes, I'll have to, obviously. I can't be expected to run this household without any help. The apartment is much too large." Mrs. March said this matter-of-factly, her arms crossed as she stared at Martha, who opened her mouth to answer but seemed to think better of it.

"Very well," said Mrs. March. "I must ask you to leave now."

"Thank you for understanding, Mrs. March. Please give Mr. March and Jonathan my best. I'll leave the key on the table."

"Don't forget the mailbox key," said Mrs. March. If Martha was upset by the suggestion, however slight, that she was the kind of person to steal someone's mail, she did not let on. "Thank you," she said, and pulled the door closed behind her as she stepped out into the hallway.

Mrs. March went straight to her medicine chest to fetch one of the herbal pills to calm her nerves, and, pacing in the foyer, fearing it was not working at all, took an entire chalky fistful before leaving for the dentist.

XXXVIII

"Hello, I have an appointment, under 'March.'"

Mrs. March swayed slightly as she clutched the reception desk with her fingernails, her coat unbuttoned, her shirt untucked.

"Oh yes! You're George March's wife," said the blond receptionist brightly. "We do love your George. He's a charmer, that one. I've always told him he could get away with murder!" She grinned, revealing a blindingly white set of veneers.

Mrs. March cleared her throat. "May I see the dentist now?"

The receptionist's face fell. "Please have a seat in the waiting room. He'll be with you shortly."

Mrs. March slumped into one of the chairs, and her fellow patients' faces flashed her grim salutes. She waited and waited, looking up at the ceiling, then down at her shoes, then at other women's shoes. A woman sitting in front of her smeared lipstick onto her lips while peering into her compact: such an intimate act that Mrs. March looked away.

She checked her wristwatch and was disappointed to see that only eight minutes had passed since she'd sat down. She sighed and leaned over the glossy magazines fanned out on the table. She picked one at random and flipped through it halfheartedly until she came across George, staring at her from the lacquered pages. The headline read AN ODE TO UGLINESS, OR HOW GEORGE MARCH MADE UGLINESS BEAUTIFUL. A fawning article followed,

extolling the refreshing complexity of the novel's main character Johanna, "not intelligent enough to be evil, not chic enough
to distract from her many physical flaws, but deliciously abhor-
rent in a hundred nasty little ways." Upon reading "the reader
is drawn in immediately, a gleeful, almost active participant
in her downfall," Mrs. March snapped the magazine shut and
threw it back on the table, then hid it under the other publica-
tions. Closing the neck of her shirt as if she had been ogled by
a stranger, she stood up and approached the receptionist's desk.

"Excuse me. Will it take long? I'm very nervous." Her words
came out a little slurred, but the receptionist didn't seem to notice.

"I'm going to tell him you're having a hard time, see if we
can get you in a little earlier," the receptionist said, and Mrs.
March felt ever so sorry for herself, a hard lump like a moist
teabag forming in her throat, tears prickling her eyes.

"Would you care for some water, Mrs. March?"

Seconds later Mrs. March returned to her seat holding a
plastic cup of water. She looked into the cup to see her own
eye reflected back at her. When she sighed, it came out in a
distorted tremor, like a mirage invoked by a heat haze. She
took out another pill from her pocket and gulped it down
with the water.

When her name was finally called, she was ushered out of
the waiting room through a pair of swinging doors and into
the room with the dental chair where she was to sit. Here
everything was white—white walls, white machinery, and
white leather dental chair. In a place that saw so much spit
and blood and yellowed enamel, it was suspicious, almost, how
white everything was.

The dentist appeared—overly tan, with grayish blond
hair and immaculate fingernails—and asked her to open her

mouth. She did so obediently and he peered into it, holding her chin to steer her face with authority.

"Now, Mrs. March, we've ignored this problem for too long, haven't we."

"Yes," said Mrs. March as best she could through an open mouth. The dentist let go of her chin and she added, "I'm sorry, Doctor. I should have had it looked at sooner, but dentist visits make me quite nervous."

"I heard all about your nerves today," he replied, getting up and reaching for his rubber gloves, "but don't you worry. This won't hurt a bit. It *could* hurt, mind you, but we won't let it. There's absolutely no reason for you to suffer if we can avoid it. That's what medicine is for. We're here to help you, Mrs. March, not hurt you. Nurse. Root canal."

Mrs. March began to cry quietly as the nurse tied a paper apron around her neck and the dentist readied his tools. "This won't hurt a bit," he repeated, and the nurse pulled the rubber mask onto her face, and for a wild second she thought this was all a trap, that George had set it up to make her death look like an accident. This was her last thought before she lost consciousness—Ariadne losing her ball of thread, and herself.

◆

THE PILLS she had taken must have reacted with whatever the dentist had given her, for she was terribly dizzy and disoriented on her way out of the white room, and even more so when she stepped outside into the cold, veering senselessly across the curb. Her head felt full, as if the dentist had drilled a hole in it and then filled it up with cotton. The freezing wind whipped at her face and hair. Spring hadn't arrived after all; it had lied to her, to them all.

She was clutching her coat closed with one hand and her hair with the other, weaving down the side of the street in search of a cab amidst the oncoming traffic, when she heard a man say, in a cool dispassionate voice, and as clear as if he were right next to her: "She walked down the street."

She spun around, almost losing her balance, but she could not locate the source of the voice. He spoke again, in a plummy English accent: "She walked further down the street." Then, as she turned around, "She turned around." She tottered in another attempt to look around her, her loafered feet stepping over themselves.

She hailed a cab as the mysterious narrator described her very action, and—with the slam of the car door—found immediate solace in the silence of the backseat. She looked out the window at the pedestrians, searching for a clue—any-thing—about what was happening. Her eyeballs vibrated as the cab sped past blurs that were people—or were they people that were blurs? She touched her swollen cheek with a cold hand, which soothed her. From the backseat she glanced at herself in the rearview mirror to see someone else—another woman sitting in the back of the cab—and she thought there'd been a terrible mistake, for if another woman was in *her* cab, it stood to reason *she* must be in the other woman's. Upon further inspection, however, she realized that the woman was indeed Mrs. March, only she was smiling quite aggressively, and when Mrs. March clamped her lips shut, her reflection did not follow suit. She looked out of the passenger window for the remainder of the trip home.

Once she paid the driver, she stood on the sidewalk, look-ing up at not one, but two apartment buildings in front of her, wondering which one she lived in. When she finally made up her mind, it was with the buoyancy that often comes with clarity, and she skipped into the building on the left, cheerfully greeting the uniformed doorman.

In the mirrored elevator, her multiple reflections refused to meet her eye, turning their faces away at her every attempt.

The elevator doors opened onto the sixth floor, but it took her some time to exit, for she wanted to determine which of the women in the mirrors was her; when she lifted a hand to her face in an attempt to find herself, all the other women thwarted her by following suit.

In the hallway she turned right, checked the numbers on the doors, but the numerals were absurd, as if they had been made up by children. She stood facing what she hoped was 606 and turned the doorknob.

The apartment on the other side of the door throbbed in time with the pulse behind her eyes. As she rubbed her knuckles into the sockets, she heard the sounds of labored breathing, as if someone were in pain. She followed the groans to their source in the living room, shuffling unsteadily. She attempted to brace her hand along the wall for support, but every time she did so it moved further away from her.

When she reached the living room, the daylight blinded her despite the half-drawn curtains. The sound was louder, more urgent. Once her eyes adjusted, she saw George on top of Sylvia, his hands on her neck, on her naked body. Mrs. March screamed and George and Sylvia both turned to her. Sylvia gasped, gulping for air, and George gasped in turn, then said, "Oh damn it, honey, you weren't supposed to see this."

Before Mrs. March could respond, she felt herself falling from a great height. Her landing was surprisingly soft, and she looked up at the ceiling and wondered how she could replicate Sheila's modern cove lighting, although really, what was wrong with lamps, she thought. "Really, what's wrong with lamps?" she asked George, who was yanking up his pleated trousers as Sylvia lay there, unmoving, her dark hair spilling over her breasts.

Oh damn it indeed.

In this strange Labyrinth how shall I turne?
Wayes are on all sids while the way I misse

—Mary Wroth,
"A Crown of Sonnets Dedicated to Love"

XXXIX

Mrs. March awoke in her bedroom. Though the heavy curtains were drawn, she sensed it was now evening. George sat on his edge of the bed, holding his head in his hands. The room was dimly lit and he sat in shadow, and she doubted, at first, that he was there at all. She slowly lifted the bedsheets and found that she was still in her day clothes. The rips in her flesh-colored pantyhose looked like scarred lacerations across her legs.

Her movements alerted George, who turned his head. When he saw that she was awake, he stood up and walked to her side of the bed, as she pushed herself up to lean against the headboard.

"How are you feeling?" he asked.

A sudden anger at George flared within her, but she wasn't sure why. She untangled herself from the bedsheets and stood up, teetering a little.

"Honey?" said George.

She walked to the bathroom and turned on the light. In the mirror she could see that her jaw was only slightly puffy. Nothing that a bit of ice couldn't help, she told herself, and just in time for the party tomorrow. The rest of her face, however, was a blow: the skin on her chin was flaking off; her powder had faded, revealing several blemishes; rivers of black mascara streaked her cheeks.

"Honey?" George called from the bedroom. She peered out at him through the doorway. He stood at the foot of the bed, hands in his pockets. "I think we need to talk. About what happened today. About what you saw. About everything, really."

She already had begun to retouch her face, wiping at the mascara with a moist cotton ball, then covering a pimple scar with an ample slathering of foundation.

"Listen," George insisted, "you were completely out of it when you got home, so I'm not sure what you saw, or what you think you saw, but the truth is, I've been having an affair."

She stopped in mid-dab, powder puff halfway to her face. As if in solidarity, her heart, too, felt like it had stopped beating to listen to George's words. She felt George's gaze on her, but she did not turn her head to look at him.

"I've been seeing someone for a while now," George said. "And you caught me—us, I mean—this afternoon, and I'm terribly sorry that you had to find out this way. I thought you'd be back later, I . . ." He shook his head. "Or, I don't know, maybe I wanted you to find out. The subconscious mind is a funny thing, isn't it?"

Mrs. March lowered the powder puff to the sink.

"I'm so sorry, honey. I really am. At first I brushed the whole thing off as a fling, a physical thing, a midlife crisis if you will. But I'm afraid I . . . I have developed real feelings for this woman."

"Gabriella?" she said, tentatively. Her voice came out low, gravelly, so different from its soft timbre that she glanced at the mirror to check that it was really her.

"No, it's not Gabriella," said George. "She's a woman who works for Zelda at the agency. She's been interning for a while—"

"A *temp*?" Mrs. March said, in more of a screech this time, throwing her compact to the floor and stepping into the bedroom. "You mean to tell me that you're having an affair with a *temp*?"

At her exaggerated pronunciation of the word, a fleck of spittle landed on George's face. The fact that he seemed almost *relieved* by her visceral reaction angered her even more. She wished she could return to her elegant apathy, to retouching her makeup without an ounce of feeling, without an ounce of weakness, emulating her mother's graceful insouciance, which she had never seen break. But she couldn't rebuild the wall, which only enraged her further.

"I'm sorry," said George. "I really am. I've been so unfair to you. But . . ." he said, pinching the bridge of his nose, "we're in love."

Mrs. March pressed her hands, curled into fists, to her temples, and squatted, fearing that she was going to be sick. What came out of her instead was a rumbling, guttural moaning. "No, no, no, no, no . . . you SWINE!" she said. Then, worried the neighbors could hear, she said, more quietly, "You swine."

"I know, I know, it's unjustifiable, so I'm not going to even try to justify it, but I *am* going to say that in the last few years you have been distant and I have *tried*—"

Here she stopped listening, while her mind revised all the instances where George might have been cheating, rather than killing women. Was it possible? Could it be? Surely this was just an excuse—a perfectly plausible one—to cover up what he had done.

"Those times I told you I was with Edgar at his cabin and instead I was—"

"What?" she hissed, her sore gums throbbing. "Like when?"

"A few times. Like before Christmas, when I came back empty-handed . . . the truth is I was right here in New York, at the Plaza—with Jennifer." Mrs. March shuddered at the name. "I'm not proud of it, you know, wasn't proud of it then, either. That's why I came back early. I wanted to tell you then. I almost did."

It was all beginning to make terrible, screaming sense. George's stained shirt—lipstick, not blood. George's odd looks—conflicted, not threatening.

"But you said," said Mrs. March, pointing her finger at his stupid face, his stupid tortoiseshell glasses, "you said the police asked you about that girl who'd disappeared. You said there were flyers all over the place. You said the police were there and asked you about her. About *Sylvia*."

George shook his head, his eyes moist. "I don't even know what I said. I wanted to admit it all, right there in the hallway. But I didn't because, well . . . because the funny thing is, you seemed to *know* I was lying, and it got to the point where I almost felt like you would rather I lie to you than go through a scandal. I know how important appearances are to you. But I'm tired of pretending. Aren't you?"

She gasped at this, her heart hammering so hard that she pressed a hand against her chest for fear it would burst through her ribs.

"I didn't know what we were playing at anymore. It didn't seem honest," he continued.

"But, but . . ." Mrs. March pulled at her hair with both hands, squeezed her skull in her fists. "What about the newspaper clipping?" she said. "You had an article . . . in your study. About Sylvia Gibbler."

"That was research for my next book," said George. Then,

as if remembering something, he asked, "Did you take that from my study?"

"Oh, stop pretending, George. Stop pretending." She laughed. "You *knew* Sylvia. You signed her books for her. She had signed copies of your books, George!"

"What? But how would you . . . ?" His frown faded. "What did you do?"

Mrs. March thought fleetingly of the night-shift doorman and how kind he'd been to her, and how he had to have known about George's mistress, had witnessed George kissing her as the elevator doors closed or placing his hand up her skirt as she climbed into a cab. How he must pity her! She paced in circles, distracted by this acute embarrassment. What would become of her now? Mrs. March pictured herself coming home to an empty apartment. Would she manage to keep this one? Or would she have to move? Would she have to raise Jonathan alone? Though he'd surely choose his father, as would their entire circle, most of whom were George's friends to begin with. She could see herself at the supermarket, avoiding every-one—or everyone avoiding *her*—and she almost split open right there and then on her bedroom floor.

But there was still a chance, she told herself, that he was guilty of the greater crime. He had hidden the newspaper clip-ping in his notebook—Jonathan could attest to that—and the signed books were on display in Sylvia's room—Amy Bryant could confirm. Then there was the proximity of Edgar's cabin to the body. It was all too much of a coincidence not to be inves-tigated. She could take this information to the police. She could destroy him, even if he wasn't convicted. "I know you killed that girl, George!" she growled, shaking a finger in his face.

George raised his eyebrows in surprise. "What the hell

are you talking about?" he said, his lowered voice trembling slightly. "You're scaring me."

"You killed that poor defenseless—"

"Listen, I know I've hurt you, but I want to help you. For your own sake, for Jonathan's sake—"

He raised a hand to touch her, but she leaned back out of reach. "You are not going to end me," she spat, her jaw jutting forward, her lower teeth bared. She pushed him and ran to her side of the bed, contemplating throwing herself through the window. George put his hand on her shoulder. She screamed. He tried to reason with her. She pushed him again, looking for an exit—any exit—as she tugged at the curtains, considering strangling herself with them.

"This doesn't have to be the end of the world," George said, over the keening moan pouring from her throat. "It can be a new beginning. We weren't happy. We deserve to be happy. We can have it all. Just not with each other."

She shoved and shoved him, clawing at his face, swatting off his glasses. When he bent down to retrieve them, she pushed him again. He fell to the floor. She slapped at the walls, wailing, and as he picked himself up and made his way to her, arms outstretched, cheeks bleeding, her ears began to ring. George started talking but he was on mute now—all she could hear was her own paused breathing, loud and enveloping.

She glanced over to a corner of the bedroom, where she met her own eye. Another Mrs. March was standing there, in her fur coat, pantyhose, and loafers, arms hanging limply. Next to her stood the naked Mrs. March from the bathtub, breasts sagging, dripping onto the carpet. Followed by Mrs. March in her nightgown, beaked Venetian mask clamped tightly over her face, her eyes blinking through the cutout holes. And then, the blood-drenched Mrs. March she'd spied on through the window, her mouth slightly agape, her eyebrows buried under the blood. A Greek chorus of Mrs. Marches, all standing before her in a neat row in her bedroom. Silently, simultaneously, they pointed at George. Mrs. March looked over at him. He was gesticulating as he spoke, glancing at the floor, adjusting his glasses.

She looked back at the Mrs. Marches. In unison, they raised their right hands to their faces, covering their eyes. Mrs. March smiled, enjoying the game, as she followed their lead and she, too, lifted her right hand, and cupped it over her eyes.

XL

When she lowered her hand, the morning sun was glaring through her bedside window. Her head ached, and her body—apart from the dull pain of dental surgery—was sore in the oddest places: her neck, her upper arms, her fingers. She silently cursed the dentist and his anesthesia.

"George?" she called out.

She started to pull on a robe, then remembered that Martha was not expected, nor would she ever be expected again. She could roam the apartment uncovered, free of judgment.

She ate her breakfast in the dining room—cold cereal and stale croissants—without bothering to comb her hair or wash her face. She had expected an apologetic George to walk in with some flowers, for she faintly remembered some kind of awful quarrel they'd had the night before.

The silence in the apartment was interrupted by a sharp buzzing. She looked down. A fly was stuck to a croissant. Legs spinning, one wing torn off. Was this the same fly she had heard, and failed to find, during the snowstorm? It couldn't possibly be, she reasoned. Ordinary houseflies didn't live that long.

There was no sign of George throughout the entire morning. He must have stepped out, but he needed to be back soon. They would be celebrating his birthday tonight. Fifty-three, the age at which George would surpass his father. There was no way he would miss it because of some silly words uttered in the heat of the moment.

Feeling a little more optimistic, Mrs. March made an appointment at the hairdresser's for one o'clock. She watered the ficus in the living room until she realized it was artificial. She chewed on cold sticks of butter, something she never would have done when Martha was around to see the bite marks.

She attempted to make herself an early lunch, taking a piece of meat from the fridge, but it had gone bad. She washed her hands thoroughly, but the putrid smell lingered on her fingers for hours, settling in the air, on the upholstery.

She set out under the vaguely comforting impression that things would somehow resolve themselves before she returned.

◆

THE HAIR SALON was busy, the air humming beehive-like with chatter and the piercing whines of the hair dryers.

Mrs. March was greeted warmly (but not warmly enough, she thought) by the receptionist. Once seated, she asked for a fancy updo and, in an uncharacteristic fit of whimsy, highlights.

She had never summoned the courage to get much more than a basic trim done. She did ask for an elaborate style, once, inspired by a patron who was leaving as Mrs. March was entering the salon, but the intricate curls framed her face unflatteringly, like a cheap clown wig. She had feigned approval only to leave and unmake the hairdo at home, plunging her head under the bathtub faucet. Today, however, as she sat in a plain white smock, she felt hopeful.

The task of washing her hair was assigned to the only male hairdresser. He was polite but tentative, signaling that he was new to the job. It riled Mrs. March, to be cast off to the new hire. The young man rubbed her scalp clumsily, as if he were petting a dog. He used far too much soap and water that was too cold, but Mrs. March said nothing to express her discomfort and instead chewed the inside of her mouth until it bled.

Hair washed, cold water dripping under her smock and down her back, she was led by a stylist to a chair, and on their way, Mrs. March spotted a woman under a hair dryer reading George's book, holding it with both hands as the dryer sucked on the top of her head. As Mrs. March looked to either side of the woman, a complete row of dryer-hatted ladies came into focus. They sat, legs crossed, eyes down, all clasping a copy of George's book in their manicured hands.

"You know her husband wrote that book," said the hairdresser as she settled Mrs. March into a chair facing a lighted mirror.

The ladies under the dryers turned their heads in unison toward Mrs. March.

"You must be so proud," said one.

"I've almost finished. Please don't spoil it!" another pleaded.

"He certainly has a dark imagination," said the one nearest to Mrs. March.

"Oh, you have no idea," said Mrs. March, turning to face herself in the mirror.

◆

EVEN THOUGH her highlights streaked her mane in questionable, skunk-like stripes, she accepted the hairdressers' compliments gracefully and, inspired, picked out a lovely peach lipstick from the shelf behind the counter.

"Would you like to get your makeup done professionally by one of our resident artists?" asked the woman at the register. Mrs. March checked the time on the clock on the wall above the counter. Why not? A party was an occasion, she told herself. "Yes, I think I would," she said, and she was led, once again, to a chair facing a mirror.

◆

AND SO it was that Mrs. March came to find herself, hours later, sitting in her dining room, her face creamy and pastel-colored like a cake. The table stretched out in front of her as the grandfather clock ticked away the seconds.

She had arrived to an empty apartment, somewhat surprised that her problems hadn't disappeared in her absence. She couldn't believe she was to throw an entire party on her own. The shelves were undusted, the bed unmade. The living room had to be spotless. The food and wine delectable. She had called Tartt's to order the meal, which had been promptly delivered by a rather pricey express delivery service (she rattled off George's credit card information over the phone). The waiters were to arrive at five-thirty sharp. She had bought the latest issues of their favorite magazines—or rather, the magazines she wanted everyone to believe were their favorites—and filled the magazine rack next to the fireplace. She had wheeled the television out of the living room and into the bedroom. She turned it on to keep her company as she tidied. The photograph of Paula had been exiled again to the highest shelf, facedown.

The grandfather clock struck five. The waiters would be arriving soon. She looked down at her abandoned game of solitaire upon the cedar dining table. A fly sat fatly upon the queen of spades. She considered swatting it, but instead let it walk onto her freshly manicured thumb.

She stood up—the fly flew off—and tried reaching George. She had called his mother—under the pretense of asking after

Jonathan—his barbershop, where he often trimmed his beard, and even Edgar—under the ruse of confirming his attendance. She dialed the private men's club he sometimes frequented, copying the number from a business card she had found in George's desk.

A flat male voice answered.

"Yes, hello—this is Mrs. March. I'm phoning to see whether my husband is at the club. George March? I—he said he might be there this afternoon."

"Certainly, madam, let me see if he's here," said the man, his tone betraying an almost intrinsic boredom. Mrs. March suspected he must be quite used to jealous wives calling to ask after their husbands. He might even be trained to return with a rehearsed excuse on behalf of the club's members. She pictured George drinking a whisky, his face flushed and moist, his eyes glassy in the manner they always got when he was tipsy. The bored man saying, "Your wife is on the phone, sir. What should I tell her?" And George pausing, contemplating their argument, deciding to punish her a bit longer: "Tell her I just left. No, better yet—tell her I haven't been here at all today."

"He hasn't been here at all today, madam."

There was a pause on the line as Mrs. March took in this information. "Ah," she said. "All right then. Thank you." She hung up.

Mrs. March wrung her hands, and, for reasons she couldn't quite explain, she made her way toward her bedroom, toward the sound of the television.

The room smelled stale, like bad breath. She opened the windows to let in fresh air, as Martha would have done, then stood, regarding the tousled mass of sheets on the bed. She had never liked the sight of an unmade bed, but something about this scene nagged at her. She had avoided the rumpled bedclothes all day, not giving them a second glance, but all the while, they had been buzzing in her deepest thoughts, like the fly. She put one tremulous hand to the bedsheets and pulled them back. They seemed to be stuck to the mattress. She tugged harder until they peeled away.

Dead for less than twenty-four hours, the body already sported a subtle, greenish sheen, and the skin appeared to have loosened, like an ill-fitting ironing board cover.

She had stabbed him. She remembered it now. She had stabbed him. Almost tenderly at first, then more forcefully, faster, the wooden grip of the butcher knife chafing the skin of her hand. She had blisters on her palm; the manicurist at the salon had commented on them.

A warbling scream bubbled out of her, and she slapped her hands against her mouth.

George remained still. His head, George's head—cross-eyed and hollow-looking, like the head of the suckling pig they had once been served in a restaurant in Madrid that specialized in offal and giblets. She remembered the taste and texture of the braised gizzards and tongue and ears, the cartilage crunchy in her mouth. And the pig's head, cooked in its own fat, so much like George's, the teeth protruding awkwardly from the gaping mouth, the vacant stare. Its face had given way as they had stabbed their forks into its surprisingly soft flesh, which seemed to melt right off its skull.

She ran into the hallway and threw up, leaving a trail of vomit on her way to the guest bathroom. The painting over the toilet now featured the bathing women with rotted, sagging breasts, their mouths contorted, eyes bleeding. She could hear them screaming.

Mrs. March heaved one last time, spewing out bile that was black and thick and gleaming, like tar. She felt something dislodge from her body like a loose stone as she panted, grasping the edge of the toilet seat, her wedding band clinking on the porcelain.

Hearing the neighbors' movements through the wall, she clasped a hand over her mouth to mute her ragged breathing. She flushed, twice, and stumbled into the hallway.

There was a knock at the door. Mrs. March swung the front door open and was surprised to see a group of uniformed waiters, who all filed past her, ignoring her as they settled into the kitchen and began unwrapping the prepared food.

She looked over to the grandfather clock, ticking brazenly, like a wooden telltale heart. Its smiling moon face winked at her. "What?" she asked it. At this, the television in the bedroom erupted into joyous peals of laughter. She followed the sound, with some trepidation, into her bedroom. On the screen was *The Lawrence Welk Show*, where a choir clad in canary yellow—taffeta gowns for the women, polyester suits for the men—swayed from side to side, smiling, as they sang *"Although it's always sweet sorrow to part . . . you know you'll always remain in my heart . . ."*

The voile curtains undulated, ethereal, in the breeze through the open window. Mrs. March sat at the foot of the bed, George somewhere behind her, his swollen, detaching flesh hidden among the stained pearly sheets.

She checked her watch. The guests would be arriving at any moment. All right, she thought, all right. I can do this. I can handle this. Like Jackie Kennedy, graceful and dignified in her mourning, witnessing Johnson take the oath of office on Air Force One, her husband's blood speckling her skirt.

She slouched—her knees together, her feet pointing in opposite directions, as if in a half-formed ballet position—and as she waited for the first guests to knock, the TV choir smiled at her and, accompanied by a playful flute, bade her good night, and farewell.

The sound of knuckles on the front door punctuated the end of the song. The party was about to begin.

What have you done, she asked herself. Agatha March, what have you done?

Acknowledgments

MY FIRST BOOK IS DEDICATED TO MY FATHER, WHO WAS my first storyteller, and to my mother, who was my first reader. Thank you both for supporting me, in all senses of the word, since birth. Please stop paying my phone bill.

Thanks to my wonderful, obsessive brothers. To Dani, who put up with many prolonged, shaky-voiced phone calls. To Oscar, who taught us to follow our dreams (albeit a little grumpily).

To Kent D. Wolf, whose commitment to this book (and to its author) is so unwavering it's frankly alarming. *Mrs. March* would only exist in a drawer if it weren't for sharp, hilarious, incredible Kent, who, incidentally, can also pull off a zebra print.

To my delightful editors: Gina Iaquinta, who soothingly coaxed the best out of me, and Helen Garnons-Williams, who always encouraged the maggots. Our three-way conversations in the margins are some of the most fun I've had with this book.

To the rascally bunch at Liveright/W. W. Norton, who fought for me from day one; I felt immediately comfortable in your midst. To the star that is Cordelia Calvert. To Anna Kelly and 4th Estate. To María Fasce at Lumen for her passion, kindness, and enthusiasm. To Teresa, who touchingly always laughs at my jokes. To Lizzie and Lindsey for championing *Mrs. March* and for giving me the chance to envision this story from a different angle. To Mr. McNally, reader and critic since

I was fifteen, who "graded" the very first draft. To Charles Cumming, the most supportive of mentors.

To Moni, who sent the flowers, and Pacheco, who opened the champagne.

Por encima de todo gracias, Lucas. Todo es por y para ti.

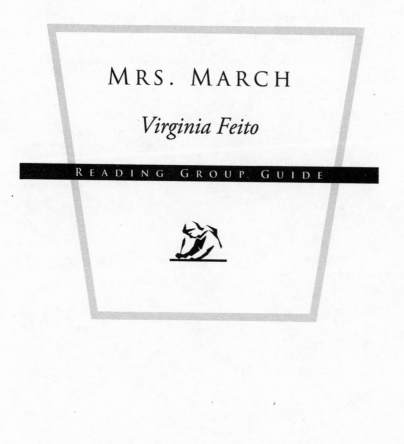

MRS. MARCH

Virginia Feito

READING GROUP GUIDE

MRS. MARCH

Virginia Feito

DISCUSSION QUESTIONS

1. What are your initial impressions of Mrs. March? What are your initial impressions of George March?

2. Mrs. March's mother tells her "numerous times, that a healthy marriage is built from the outside in, not the other way around" (p. 19). Why do you think Mrs. March married George? Do you find their relationship "healthy"?

3. Consider Mrs. March's predicament: her husband may have written a detestable character based on her. How would you react if you were in her place?

4. Throughout the course of the book, the narrator never refers to Mrs. March by her first name—even in flashbacks to her childhood. What do you make of this?

5. How does author Virginia Feito establish Mrs. March as an unreliable character? While reading, did you see deviations from objective truth or reality?

6. What is the significance of Mrs. March's mint green gloves? What do you make of the book's cover?

7. Consider Mrs. March's relationship to her son, Jonathan. How might her own childhood affect the way she treats, views, and feels about Jonathan?

8. As Mrs. March's paranoia ramps up, readers are met with an array of horrific images and scenes. How did these moments affect you? Would you categorize the novel as a thriller, horror, or something else?

9. In chapter 12, Mrs. March recalls a professor saying, "Art is intention. . . . Art has to move you. In any way—positive or negative. Appreciating art is really just about understanding what the piece set out to do. You don't necessarily want to hang it in your living room" (p. 73). Mrs. March doesn't know how to interpret these words. How do you interpret them? Do you agree with the professor? Why or why not?

10. One review of George's book says that "the reader is drawn in immediately, a gleeful, almost active participant in [Johanna's] downfall" (p. 264). Are there any parallels or similarities between *Mrs. March* and what we know of George's book? Between Mrs. March and Johanna?

11. Mrs. March begins to see her "friend," Kiki, as the story unfolds. What do you make of Kiki? Why does Mrs. March start to see her again?

12. Is the final scene in the novel fated or inevitable? Could something have been done to prevent Mrs. March's actions?

13. What do you think will happen to Mrs. March after the final pages? What do you want to happen to her?

Diana Abu-Jaber	*Life Without a Recipe*
Diane Ackerman	*The Zookeeper's Wife*
Michelle Adelman	*Piece of Mind*
Molly Antopol	*The UnAmericans*
Andrea Barrett	*Archangel*
Rowan Hisayo Buchanan	*Harmless Like You*
Ada Calhoun	*Wedding Toasts I'll Never Give*
Bonnie Jo Campbell	*Mothers, Tell Your Daughters*
	Once Upon a River
Lan Samantha Chang	*Inheritance*
Ann Cherian	*A Good Indian Wife*
Evgenia Citkowitz	*The Shades*
Amanda Coe	*The Love She Left Behind*
Michael Cox	*The Meaning of Night*
Jeremy Dauber	*Jewish Comedy*
Jared Diamond	*Guns, Germs, and Steel*
Caitlin Doughty	*From Here to Eternity*
Andre Dubus III	*House of Sand and Fog*
	Townie: A Memoir
Anne Enright	*The Forgotten Waltz*
	The Green Road
Amanda Filipacchi	*The Unfortunate Importance of Beauty*
Beth Ann Fennelly	*Heating & Cooling*
Betty Friedan	*The Feminine Mystique*
Maureen Gibbon	*Paris Red*
Stephen Greenblatt	*The Swerve*
Lawrence Hill	*The Illegal*
	Someone Knows My Name
Ann Hood	*The Book That Matters Most*
	The Obituary Writer
Dara Horn	*A Guide for the Perplexed*
Blair Hurley	*The Devoted*

Meghan Kenny	*The Driest Season*
Nicole Krauss	*The History of Love*
Don Lee	*The Collective*
Amy Liptrot	*The Outrun: A Memoir*
Donna M. Lucey	*Sargent's Women*
Bernard MacLaverty	*Midwinter Break*
Maaza Mengiste	*Beneath the Lion's Gaze*
Claire Messud	*The Burning Girl*
	When the World Was Steady
Liz Moore	*Heft*
	The Unseen World
Neel Mukherjee	*The Lives of Others*
	A State of Freedom
Janice P. Nimura	*Daughters of the Samurai*
Rachel Pearson	*No Apparent Distress*
Richard Powers	*Orfeo*
Kirstin Valdez Quade	*Night at the Fiestas*
Jean Rhys	*Wide Sargasso Sea*
Mary Roach	*Packing for Mars*
Somini Sengupta	*The End of Karma*
Akhil Sharma	*Family Life*
	A Life of Adventure and Delight
Joan Silber	*Fools*
Johanna Skibsrud	*Quartet for the End of Time*
Mark Slouka	*Brewster*
Kate Southwood	*Evensong*
Manil Suri	*The City of Devi*
	The Age of Shiva
Madeleine Thien	*Do Not Say We Have Nothing*
	Dogs at the Perimeter
Vu Tran	*Dragonfish*
Rose Tremain	*The American Lover*
	The Gustav Sonata
Brady Udall	*The Lonely Polygamist*
Brad Watson	*Miss Jane*
Constance Fenimore Woolson	*Miss Grief and Other Stories*